AUTHOR	CLASS	F
REYNOLDS, A.		

TITLE
Insanity

INSANITY

Anna Reynolds was born in 1968. She is author of *Tightrope* (1991), three stage dramas, including *Jordan*, Best Play of 1992 at the Writers Guild Awards, co-author of *The Winding Sheet*, a film which won a Silver Hugo at the Chicago Film Festival, and a BBC2 drama in 1994. *Insanity* is her first novel.

INSANITY

Anna Reynolds

FOURTH ESTATE · London

First published in Great Britain in 1996 by
Fourth Estate Limited
6 Salem Road
London W2 4BU

Copyright © 1996 by Anna Reynolds

2 4 6 8 10 9 7 5 3 1

The right of Anna Reynolds to be identified as the author
of this work has been asserted by her in accordance with
the Copyright, Designs and Patents Act 1988.

A catalogue record for this book is available from the British
Library.

ISBN 1–85702–319–6

Typeset by CentraCet Limited, Cambridge
Printed in Great Britain by Clays Ltd, Bungay, Suffolk

For Elizabeth and Alex

Pick me up

Won't you

Just pick me

I dream in numbers

I dream three

But when I wake there's

Only

Me

Prologue

Mary sits by the side of her child, its fingers grasping feebly at the air. An old man sits by the fireside, waiting. Mary has not slept for three nights and three days because she knows that Death is waiting to take her ailing child from her. Waiting for her moment of weakness. Waiting to snatch her child, her red child. Her child.

'You think I shall keep her, don't you?' she asks the old man. 'He won't take her from me even though she is born of sin.' But the old man only moves his head and she cannot tell if it is yes or no. Just for a second, Mary closes her eyes in weariness. Just for a second, that is all.

When she opens them the cradle is empty and the door is open. The old man is gone.

Mary hurries outside, into the biting wind. Seeing a woman in black cloaks, she pulls at her sleeve. The woman's face is deathly white and mournful. 'You must help me,' cries Mary. 'Which way has Death gone?'

'I have not slept for a thousand years,' says the woman, who is Night. 'Sing me the lullabies I have heard you sing so tenderly and I will tell you which direction to take.' Mary pleads with Night but Night is silent and still. So Mary sings desperately until, sighing, Night points her finger to a dark wood.

At last, terrified and chilled, she comes to a curious house by a crossroads. An old woman's face peers through the window at Mary. 'What do you want?' she asks crossly.

'Death has taken my child,' says Mary. 'Help me.'

The woman, who is Age, deliberates, but not for long, because she desires Youth. 'Give me your long black hair,' she says. 'I will give you my white hair and that will always be something.'

'I will give it to you gladly!' cries Mary, and she tears out her beautiful hair with a terrible ripping and rending. The old woman shows her where Death's journey must take her.

Mary comes now to a great lake, upon which there are no ships or boats. No frozen ice to walk across but somehow she must get over it to find her child. She kneels, sobbing, by the water's edge and tries to drink the water all up. She is sick instantly.

'Now this will never do!' says the Lake. 'Your eyes are the brightest I have ever seen. If you will cry them out for me I will carry you over to the Garden of Eden where you may find your child. Every plant and flower is a human life.'

And Mary weeps more than ever until her eyes drop down to the depths of the Lake like two precious pearls. The Lake lifts her across and she stands in the garden scenting the lives newly taken.

Mary can no longer see but she bends over the tiniest plants and listens for her child's heartbeat. Amongst a million she knows her child's at once.

And then an icy wind comes through the place where she kneels and she knows that Death has returned. 'How did you find your way?' he demands. 'Nobody can arrive here before me.'

'I am a mother,' she says.

Then Death stretches his hand out towards the little flower Mary bends over. She clasps her hands in terror round his but his hands freeze hers and she falls away. Her wrists are blue and red. She seizes two flowers that grow nearby.

'Give me back my child!' she sobs. 'I will pull up these flowers else, I am in such despair.'

Death sighs. He takes two pearls out of his pocket. 'Here are your eyes back again,' he says. 'I dived into the Lake for them; they shone so brightly. Take them back. They are brighter than ever ... Look now down into the Lake at the lives you were about to destroy.'

And Mary looks down, deep down, into the Lake. A joy, such joy! To see how one life became a blessing to the world, surrounded by happiness and light and love. Then she sees the life of the other; and that life was all sorrow and need, sin and misery.

'I may not tell you which is Misery and which is Joy,' says Death, sadly, 'but I may tell you that one of the flowers is your own child's; it is your own child's fate that you see.'

'But which one?' asks Mary.

I look in the mirror. When I grow up I want to be happy. When I grow up I want to be older. When I grow up I want to be *someone else*.

Look at me. I am sixteen and I have spots. It doesn't stop me being pretty but it stops me being able to look anyone in the eye. My mother says that I'll grow out of it, it happens to everyone, although it never happened to her, but that if I don't eat so many chips and wash more they'll go away.

That's how I met Danny, see. The doctor gave me this white stuff to paint onto the spots and I painted religiously. My face glowed, in patches. And Danny, he walks up our street every night, wondering where I live. He'd seen me in town and wondered. I never saw him but then I wouldn't, would I? I never see anybody. I don't look up, I look down, so very small people maybe, but he was tall. Really tall. And so every night he walks up and down, up and down, and one night I stand in the window. Light off, clothes on. And he sees these white spots glowing out at him and he knows.

My mother glowers. He's twenty, left school behind long ago. I am sixteen but I hardly ever go to school. I can't, it upsets me. I can't tell you why. I can't even tell the school counsellor why and he's paid to listen. He has a beard and a nurse. We don't pay him, the State does. Like the State says I must go to school and the State makes you pay taxes and, oh, all sorts of things.

Some people, they have a dog and the dog gets sick and they take it to a vet, and other people, why, they have a kid and when the kid gets sick they take it to a shrink. Only nobody took me, see. The school says that if I don't go to school there must be A Reason Why. My mother is more embarrassed than I am even.

'What does he say?' she asks.

'He tells me to talk,' I reply gloomily.

Silence, then, 'What about?', puzzled.

We don't really talk much, see, so it's a bit difficult. Like going to Confession when you don't really have anything to confess, so you make a list. 'Well, I could always say I told a lie, was neglectful, took the Lord's name in vain . . .' Now I have to make up lists for the counsellor, my mother and God. Two of things I have wrong with me, one of things I'm getting better at. It confuses me.

Danny toots the horn. He sits outside, nervous in his Capri. My mother sniffs as I come down the stairs.

'Just going to say goodbye,' I say airily.

My mother smoothes the front of her jumper thoughtfully. 'Not outside the graveyard?' she pleads.

'No,' I lie, crossing my fingers behind my back.

The hall smells of Pledge and air freshener and Poison. Mine. Danny brought some back from a holiday in Fuengirola and we both loathe it, my mother and I, but it's so strong that you don't have to wash first.

One of the neighbours waves at me. My hair is pink. Danny stares as I climb in the car.

'Pink,' he says, staring.

'God you're quick,' I say, making big astonished eyes at him. Danny doesn't like sarcasm but I have just learned it so I practise, on him. My grandmother would kill him with her bare hands if she heard him, for his stupidity. This is why I have not really introduced him to my family. I mean, *I* haven't really been introduced to my family yet. It takes about four generations, we're slow learners.

Danny drives me, pink hair and all, to a pub, in silence. He is smarting, I suppose. I squeeze his thigh, it's all I can manage. I don't really like him all that much, but when he says he loves me I believe him. When he says, 'I love you, let's do it now, Mum's watching *Coronation Street*.' The commercial breaks come on and we have to get dressed, then the *Corrie* music comes on and we start all over again. He doesn't hurt me, because I don't feel anything. Can only hurt when you're alive, can't it? I'm just a body. A blow-up doll. I make myself dead and then afterwards in the wetness I come back to life like Christ.

In the pub we sit watching older people. 'I'll never be like that,' says Danny suddenly. I am surprised. 'Never wear a sweater like that. Sweaters!' And he snorts. I go to the loo and stare at my face, wondering what I am doing here.

'Terrible hard paper,' says a lady behind me, emerging from the disinfected cubicle.

You see, tomorrow I'm leaving. Going. Getting out. I've lived all my life here. This town, with one street and lots of little capillaries leading off into nothing. Fields. There's no train station, no buses after seven at night. We're near a big city, but taught to be properly afraid of it. No cinema, but a Catholic youth club where discos are held weekly, under depressed lights. The priest spins the records and even the lemonade is watered down. If I were a parent I'd want to bring a kid up here and it would hate me for it, I guess.

It doesn't matter to Danny, not really. 'I'll write to you,' he promises. When I ask him exactly where I'll be, he closes his eyes and then, after a pause, says, 'You'll be in Norfolk.' I shake my head. 'Suffolk?' he offers. 'Same, innit?' I nod and smile like a toy dog. 'Have I got it right?' he says, worried.

'Just copy the address down from this piece of paper,' I tell him. His face darkens and he leans across the wheel and unsnaps my seatbelt. Yes, we are outside the graveyard. A lot of my family are buried here but nobody disturbs us. I wish they would.

I'm not taking much. What's to take? No photos, no memories, just a rucksack crammed with words and hopes. Some cochineal for my hair and a lipstick. Travelling light.

★

The next morning, everything seems different. My mother smiles at the removal men and doesn't scream when they handle her dark, ancient furniture carelessly. The rain falls lightly. We both like rain. Sun seems inappropriate for us. The house is bare and shorn of us, but we never really marked it. There are no signs of our life here now and we haven't even left yet. We can't wait to be gone. The men sit on the doorstep and suggest tea. My mother is not inhospitable but we cannot wait. The men sigh and climb into the lorry. Our belongings disappear.

Everything is small now. I watch my mother walk around the empty shell, the house so lightly marked. She touches nothing. She looks out of the window to the long, thin garden, my childhood swing moving in the breeze, spotted with rust. 'Oh . . .' I hear her say, ending in a sigh, maybe a sob. I stand behind her, nearly touching her. 'We had such plans,' she says, not turning, 'such plans.' My dad left. That's all anyone needs to know, isn't it? He left without many words, and she did not. She managed. We never mention him now, and on reflection I think that's best, don't you? It hurts her.

'I wanted to make things,' she says.

'You made me,' I offer.

Her eyes dart towards me then, but she has forgotten who I am, for a second. She is thinking backwards, of him, of then, and I am moved to silence.

'And I made vegetables grow, didn't I?' she says anxiously, as we move through the hall to the front door, no longer ours. As we stand inside the door, reluctant to open it one last time, to make this gesture, the sun comes out. Suddenly, I want to stay. I am filled with love for this place, filled with fear, filled with the need to stay here. My mother is not sentimental on the outside. She whips her headscarf on and we stand poised on the brink. She is leaving her life, her memories, her family. Me? I'm leaving my childhood, that's all.

'You were never happy here,' says my mother, her voice quiet and sure. Her hands shake as she lifts her coat.

'I was,' I protest. 'Some nice things happened, didn't they? Didn't they?'

'But you were never happy.'

My mother smiles, again. At me, into my face. I feel it, feel the sudden unexpected heat of it. 'Neither was I,' she says finally. And then she pulls her head back and looks me right in the eye and says, 'Come on. Let's go.'

And I could swear that I hear a catch in her voice.

'Let's go,' she says again, with finality.

And we do. *We do.*

CHAPTER 2

Days later I sit at home. Our new home. A smallish Twenties house, in a road full of similar buildings. It has a small ready-made garden with a high fence, not to keep out burglars but to keep our life in. Double-glazed sliding doors lead to it but we never sit out there. We have now acquired a dog and the dog races around frustrated in the tiny space. Because he is so small, so very small, he has a pen to keep him from getting out and being run over. A prison within a prison, for him.

We chose this place because it was reasonable. At least, my mother chose it. She had the whole country to choose from but settled, exhausted, for this particular small town. However, we are here now and 'making the most of it'. There is a bank and a row of tired dusty shops and a Catholic church. We are not middle-class despite my mother's best efforts and so we are not quite, which suits fine. This is a not-quite town. We have found our natural home, even though within hours we look at each other briefly and know that we have made a mistake. 'Offer it up,' my mother says finally, and our eyes meet. We share a small, barely heard laugh of slight despair.

My first week here, I wanted to explore. You do, don't you? I found a boutique called Buttons and Sews, a cafe called Lately's, and a tiny office that housed the local newspaper. A pub, with men in corners lining up their pints, windows darkened by their nicotine.

You must understand that I had nothing else. Except –

Life in this place went on uninterrupted by our arrival. Every morning my mother and I heaved ourselves up the hill to the shops, the old town. A sixteenth-century coaching inn, a new and daring rival cafe which sold cappuccino. The locals stayed away. We drank Rombouts coffee before attempting anything more adventurous and sat until they closed. I still couldn't say, now, what we talked about.

I wish that I could –

The week that I started at college I bought new clothes. You know: black, black and more black. The first day, everyone else wore this . . . *uniform* that nobody had told me about. A uniformity of dullness but, of course, that was okay. I was trying, okay? Nobody spoke to me, though. At home, later, I spoke to my mother through the veil of the kitchen. 'I'm making rice,' she said. We had just discovered rice.

'No one spoke to me,' I said.

'Well,' she said, through the veil of rice and carrot steam, 'they'll get used to us in time.' And she dished up, her lips tight against the tide of local disapproval.

This became a well-worn chorus. They'll get used to us in time. They'll get to us in time. A town built in 1652 with houses still occupied by the surviving relatives of those who had chosen to settle here. They wore anoraks of sludge green against the wind and faces of granite set in the tide of disapproval. No, mother, they'll never get used to us.

Funny thing is, they tried. Yes . . . There were discos, in the common room. Nobody really went in there. Just Sandy and Vi who were as sad as me, as eager to please. Notices in the common room. 'Disco tonite everybody invited!' And no reason for the exclamation mark.

Flowers in the church. 'We could fit you in on a Saturday. Mrs Brook could do with some help.' But my mother didn't want to be *a help*. She wanted to be *something*, but she never knew quite what. Church on Sunday and she saw that the flowers were wilting. So were the congregation, but after all we were Catholics, what do you expect?

In the mornings we make the long trek up the hill in fake fur and denim. Clothes mattered to her, you see. That was all. Some old but good tweed skirts and jackets with shoulders made to withstand the war with style. It mattered then and it mattered now but the in-between years were the problem. And me? I strode up the hill surly in shredded jeans and an attitude. Past the new red houses and the abattoir that stank, day and night; past the hated college with its smug country girls and dead minds; past the tiny, hopeless market selling cheeses already shrunk in the air and cheap bright knickers.

We would sit in the Three Horseshoes Hotel and drink stale coffee in the yellow-stained snug. The Three Horseshoes had a reputation in a town without one of its own. American soldiers from the nearby airbase stayed there and *ordered room service*. They smiled at the waitresses and called them Ma'am. One tried to pay in dollars . . . It's easy to poke fun at small towns, isn't it? But it's not easy to laugh. No.

'I never wanted to live here!' I wanted to shout out sometimes. 'Take me back!' But there was nowhere to go back to. Back to the other small town, ninety miles away, with failure of a small kind written on our luggage? I don't think so. That was when, in our mutual and silent unhappiness, we started making trips to the nearest big city.

In department stores we bought clothes by the mile. Nothing glamorous. No silk, no glitter. Sensible, well-cut skirts, demure blouses, shoes for walking in. Walking up hills and down again with barely a pause in between. I don't know why. It made her feel that something had been accomplished, these bags of goods purchased expensively and well. Bags piled beside a chair in another musty hotel dining room, the smell of dinner.

'I think I'll have the roast,' my mother would say after rumination. 'Shall we have a drink?' Because the most astonishing thing was that my mother had learned to drink. After forty years of saying No I don't think I will, isn't it a little early isn't it a little late is it the right time of day for she had discovered not the pleasures of alcohol but the release of it.

At college, the teachers are absent more often than the students. They are as depressed as we are by the air of lethargy that palls the place. A careers adviser comes and, like a palmist, divines our innermost thoughts, but wrongly.

'You're going to be a marine biologist,' he tells me. His left eye is uncontrollable; it moves off of its own accord. I wonder if anyone ever told him he'd be a careers adviser. 'But I have never passed a biology test and in fact failed my O Level very badly,' I point out. 'No. The computer is rarely wrong,' he says, firmly. Well, it is now, sweetie.

I leave his office worried. How many vacancies for jobs involving large mammals will there be in my life? I go straight to the shops to buy a large amount of sweet things as distraction. There is a sign in the pub window . . . .

Of course I get the job. People don't beat down the doors to work in the Stag and Crown, believe me. With enough eye make-up I look old enough to pass the Police Raid test and, anyway, they really don't seem to care. Carefully I tell my mother they have a restaurant in the back and that I am a trainee waitress.

'That's nice. I'll have to come and eat one night,' she says.

'No, you mustn't,' I say, horrified. 'They make me recycle the leftovers off other people's plates. They're terrible, it's awful, you'll get food poisoning and it will all be my fault.' Startled, she agrees, deflated.

My first night, I am delighted. Although I get a lot of things wrong, everyone buys me a drink because I am new. And even though I add up all the rounds wrongly and overcharge a lot of people, strangely they don't seem to mind. By ten I have passed out in the cellar over a barrel. Somebody scrapes me off the floor and sets me on my bicycle to go home. When I sober up I realise that I will have lost my job. My grotty, hopeless job.

'Well, what d'you expect?' says Ron the landlord. 'Eleven snakebites and a packet of dry roasted, no wonder. Have a bit of class, learn to drink shorts.' He says I must learn the job properly, understand the punters. Most of the old men who hog the bar stools have their own silver tankard and each has a different kind of beer. 'This one, he likes it poured without any head. That one, lots of froth. Him over there – never ever fill it to the top. Drives you mad, it does.'

They also employ a pot man. Albert is seventy and a bit

odd. He doesn't wash but everyone likes him because he smiles all the time. I can feel him hovering behind me and he moves quietly, stealthily, like death. They trap me in the cellar with him for thirty minutes one night. Supposed to be a joke, isn't it? Neither of us laughs about it, though. His smile fades after a while and his mouth falls slack, unsure. They tell me later that it is some sort of test and, strangely, I have passed. That's a first, then.

I am starting to get used to it after a week though. My mother picks up my drink-sodden clothes with sugar tongs and sniffs, but doesn't comment. She is needed in the church this week; the Bishop is to visit and she has given in to their demands for help, in the hope of some sort of acceptance. Another initiation test. I trot along with her on a Sunday and daydream while the sermon drones. Before Mass I can see the priest waiting for his cue to go on, smoking a cigarette, jeans beneath his frock. After Mass he pats the ladies absently and thanks them for the flowers. Passing the abattoir, my mother says, 'I think he drinks at the Stag and Crown.' I try not to breathe the dead scent of burnt flesh. 'Hear me?' I don't look at her. 'When I brought you here it wasn't to make a fool out of me in a – a pub.' Back home, we lay the table in dead silence and talk to the dog. The dog is confused at all the sudden attention.

'You'll give in your notice, of course.' I put down my fork and notice that her eyes are watering. 'You're going to be something, not – not a barmaid . . .'

'I won't give in my notice,' I say. I say it very quietly because it is unusual for me to challenge, and this is how we exist, without challenge.

'Then I'll go in tomorrow and do it for you. We won't discuss it any further. Bring the rice pudding in,' she says, and I can see that she has already forgotten all about it. Her eyes are on the past, on the dull rural landscape, on the plates laden with dead bones picked clean by our teeth.

It's a dead night in a pub, Sunday, rain pattering the windows, and I'm trying to work out exactly how awful my life is going to be if I stay in my job. In this place we are condemned to live in life stretches ahead dreadfully. Danny is far away in another pub, another town. I briefly consider marrying him but the thought is blank. There's nothing there either, just a space. Ron jolts my hip and I look up and serve. More Americans, a group of men in newly pressed jeans and baseball caps. The town is not sure about baseball caps but they spend a lot of their useless money so that makes it easier to swallow.

'. . . and one for yourself. Is that right?' A soft voice, surprisingly. I know by now to take the money and run from the vodka. 'You won't let me buy you a drink?' he says, a line appearing between his eyes.

'I don't drink,' I lie, and turn away to the till.

And under the bed I have a growing collection of cans of lager that I flirt with nightly. Shall I have three? Four? Six, eight, shall I, shan't I be sick? –

As we fling the cloths over the pumps and clean the ashtrays, he's still there, with his mates. And when I unchain my bike and prepare to climb on it, weary and dreading opening the front door, he's waiting, leaning against the wall. 'You can't be serious!' he exclaims. He begins to laugh, as I stand with the bike, feeling stupid. 'You don't need that,' he says, seeing my face. 'I'll see you home. You'll be safe with me.'

He takes my free hand in the alley-way; in the graveyard he stops me and lets the bike rest on a fence. I let him take me in his arms without protest but he just holds me. Doesn't try to kiss me. Why? I don't understand. I suddenly start to cry but it doesn't matter because he doesn't even notice. His mind is on other things. I cling to him like life cling to him cling and then he steps back in surprise and a little alarm, maybe. He laughs softly, in his throat, eyes glittering.

'Baby, baby, there's no hurry,' he says. He slips his hand inside my jacket. 'My, you're ready,' he whispers, his face looming larger. 'Boy, you're ready, aren't you?' His hand stays where it is, sure of itself. I try not to breathe; the graveyard is covered in mist and I am cold. His skin is warm and fleshy and he would lie down and cover me if I were willing.

I leap onto the bike and pedal away, crying soundlessly all the way home. I can't say why.

The next night, Janey and Maria from the late-night shop next door pour in. There's not much to do here so it's a bit of fun for them, half a night out. Janey is small and pretty in a tiny sort of way with short blonde hair and enormous breasts. She does not try to hide them. Good for her. Maria is tall and whippet-thin, and dark, and she hides her face in shy pleasure when a man glances at her in the bar. She is shockable and she gives me a lift home.

'Maria from work,' says my mother flatly when I finally return home, having sat outside the bungalow in her car for – hours. 'Don't give me that. You should tell Danny.' But it is the truth, for once. Having spent the evening being pleasant to nasty old men with their tankards, I am happier than I have been in a long time to sit in Maria's battered Cortina outside the house and talk. I couldn't tell you what we said for those hours, because I don't think it mattered. I was so lonely that there's no knowing what I said, exactly. There's no knowing.

'Do you like him, this American?' she asks gently.

'I don't know,' I say thoughtfully. 'I don't know him, do I?'

Maria yawns carefully, almost hiding it. 'You could do worse,' she says, 'than America.'

'America,' I repeat.

The word hangs between us like a charm. Like a pathway in the water.

The next day at college, I sit in a dream, waiting for my name to be spoken by the wistful English lecturer. I am not a bad student, you see. I read the books and the poems and they mean more to me than life but I am alone in this. Natalie is a good student. Look, here is Natalie, she has a suit on and very high heels that make a sound like pain on the floors and a *hairdo*. Natalie is seventeen and very old. We are all misfits here in this dead or dying place. Natalie writes down everything that the teacher Mr Peters says. 'Good morning, class, how are we all today?' he says, and Natalie has to stop herself from making notes.

Natalie is having an affair with a lorry driver. *A married lorry driver.* We all know this and to me it seems simply a bit sad, but to the others, the Girls, it is a matter for the Old Bailey. Like eating garlic before a date or talking about periods, it is Not Done Here, thankyouverymuch. I think of announcing the American to the girls. I ask Mr Peters about American literature. He pauses. 'America,' he says, with pursed lips. 'Yes. America is a new country. Let us turn to Chaucer, please.' And Natalie is confused already.

I walk her to the main road, where she waits for Him . . . 'Lorries are great, you know,' she says, turning her huge blue-rimmed eyes on me. 'He says that lorries are the business. I ride everywhere for free.' And she climbs aboard. Not for free, I think, as I see his sweaty moustache and snake eyes. Not for free, love.

That night, the American sits at the bar until I raise my eyes to his. His face is fleshy and open. He is toothsome and from the South and he misses home. 'Girl, you gotta see the Bayou. The swamps, why – '

I believe that I can live without this. All the same I apply more lipstick.

Ron tells me to go home early because it is quiet tonight and his wife, who has frightening hair, will look after the bar. He winks. 'Yee-ha,' he says. He is shorter than me. Albert watches me go anxiously. Albert thinks I am in danger with foreigners, thus including any drinkers from the next village.

I walk tonight. I don't know why. There is no rain and the street is empty. I walk slowly, breathing in the time. The car that has trailed me from the pub slows to a gentle, discreet halt. I stop. There is a park to my left and I have never been in it. Shadowy figures younger than me slope drunkenly on its grass. The car door opens and not a word has been spoken. I get in.

Later, I realised that I should have known what it was all about. Not that it would have mattered. He took me to his home, a small new house on the outskirts of town, and we fucked. I pretended for at least, oh, ten minutes, that we were there for a drink and then we fucked all night. And then I discovered that it wasn't his house but a friend's – he had forgotten to tell me. He also forgot to tell me that he was married. And had a child of nearly one.

'I gotta go,' he said, towards morning. His belly was soft and white but his face still sweet.

'Why?' I said.

'Got to get back to the base.' He was grinning all across his face. His large hands still splayed across my stomach.

'Don't tell anybody, will you?' I asked pitifully.

'Baby – ' he said, and kissed me. 'Know where the john is?'

But he had held me, and he had smothered my mouth when I made small squeaks of surprise, and he had stroked my hair and wiped the sweat from my face and that was something. And I had not felt a thing.

I hardly knew it was happening. Like he said to me, I was dying for it.

At six I walked into the house, knowing there was no use in tiptoeing. She was sitting in the chair opposite the garden and never looked at me. She looked at the sky, drawing towards morning.

'I don't know what to do any more,' she said, and it was true. 'You are beyond salvation,' and that was also a truth.

My teachers heard the click of my heels late in a lesson.

My mother heard the clink of the cans as I put the rubbish out.

Me? I never heard a thing.

And Danny? He hears me now, believe it.

'Do I have to see him?' asks my mother. She doesn't disapprove of him on moral grounds, especially since we have put more distance between ourselves and him. 'He has such enormous feet. Put the mat down on the hall floor and keep him in the living room.' He is large and, being a builder, you might think this means muscles but since the last time I saw him his belly has increased with white bread and jam and chips, and his feet step carelessly onto the dog, which we treasure. We cannot speak of love between us but the dog is called Lucky. Last week the dog got out of the small enclosure in which he roams and we caught our breath, united in fear, until he was returned to us by a neighbour. He had sat, disappointed, at a crossroads, not knowing how to make the next move.

Danny rings the chiming doorbell on time. He is always on time. It irritates me. His hands are thick like chipolatas and slip with sweat when they clutch mine. Maybe it's my hands that slip. I wear a white shirt and white leggings and I look like a pear that has been grown in the dark of a very small room without windows. Beads and earrings are everywhere about me, for the purposes of distraction.

'You're jangling,' says my mother. 'Don't worry so much.' She is in the process of rearranging her face into a smile. 'Danny, how nice to see you. Again . . . Now do sit there.' He is given a drink and told not to rise, how thoughtful. The dog sobs from the garden and Danny opens his mouth to enquire. All his movements are slow. In tandem we explain that the dog, the beloved, has eczema. So.

Several months ago Danny, his father, mother and sister and I went for a holiday in Scarborough. Bloody camping . . . It rained. It seems unimportant now, in the great scheme of things. There was a market town, not unlike this one, with Yorkshire accents, where a man suggested that Danny could sell me if he so desired because of my enormous breasts, and a beach with not pebbles but rocks and a hotel bar where I drank inordinate amounts of Malibu. And a field, in the darkness, where we parked Danny's car and I pretended that I had finally reached some kind of heaven . . .

Months later, my mother now sniffs Danny's discomfort. 'How was your holiday?' she asks. 'It rained, I believe, and how then did you occupy the time?'

'Ah. We. Shopped?' Danny offers. He does not dare glance at me.

'Beads,' I suggest. I shimmy mine, to remind her. She breathes loudly. It is not a sigh.

'How is your leg?' she asks. Danny fell off a building.

'Mother,' I say, knowing her fondness for blunt speaking.

Danny pats his hip lamely. 'It's better, but I find any sudden movement difficult,' he says, with a terrible shake of his head. 'I've given up exercise, just in case.'

'Men take illness too hard,' says my mother. 'You're a young man, look at you. Get yourself a bike, that's what you want to do.' The picture of Danny, fat shaking with exertion, causing hazardous spills on the highway occurs to both of us at the same time and a slight tremor passes through the house which might be laughter but might not.

I shepherd Danny through the house and we leave. The dog moans pitifully from the garden. It upsets me. 'Catching, the eczema, is it?' asks Danny fearfully.

We are in the shopping mall of the nearest town, at eight o'clock. The girls in their short skirts are skittering on their heels, pulling down shutters, skidding down the slimy nylon floor as we walk through. Outside Miss Selfridge I stop and stare at the skinny mannequins, wanting to reach in and lift the clothes from their plastic flesh. Danny raises his white eyebrows and snakes his arm awkwardly along my back. In the mirrored wall, with my white outfit and his colouring, we are the Snow Couple. Mirrored a thousand times down the halls of the dead echoing mall, we are pale and pudgy, stretched sideways by the cruel reflection.

'I'm pregnant,' I say suddenly.

One month later I am in the college common room, that despised place. I have had no strange cravings, no sickness, no tightening of the waistband on my jeans, and so therefore I am not pregnant. Everything is alright, I tell Lorraine, who is, if not a friend, an acquaintance. Like me, she does not quite fit in here, although there is no reason for it that we can see.

Everything is alright.

'I'm pregnant,' I had told Danny. 'But it's not your problem. Don't worry.' And he did not. He gulped like a fish for a short time, he swallowed hard and held out his hands, then shook my knee and smiled at me bravely. When we parted he hugged me, as you might a blood relative, I suppose. I wouldn't know, I never wanted to hug mine. I patted his shoulder and got out of the car. My mother awaited. She knows nothing and now there is nothing to know, I am sure, so that is a good thing.

I made a mistake, that's all. But the next day I am sick instantly when I wake. I swallow it with hate and ring the doctor for an appointment. In our white bathroom my face seems to have grown and widened like the moon.

'Four gins and the best part of a bottle of wine,' says Dr Hands. 'A hangover is not a medical condition.' I am silent. The possibilities are too terrifying. 'How often has it happened?'

He tests my urine. I wait behind the plastic curtain. He examines me as I lie on my back, legs spread in a grim rictus of love. His cold gloved finger presses deeper ... *Does that hurt? Is it hurting you is it is it?* Don't stop –

I don't care if it hurts o i dont care! I just want to be sure –

Yes. 'Yes. Ten weeks, I would say. You'll need to have a scan, but I would suggest . . . Ms Raine?'

I walk out of the pale walls and into the street. Outside, women carry their shopping bags and children as before only now I am seeing double. That's all.

CHAPTER **3**

Dear Rosa,

Am missing you a lot alright? It's nice to think about you just at home, sitting around. Glad you're not expecting anything, thanks for telling me, I was a bit worried. Me mum wouldn't have been too pleased. I mean, probably we'll get married someday, won't we, anyway, but no kids just yet, alright? Hahaha. Good. You had me worried because we always used rubbers anyway. Did one break? Better be more careful in future, eh?

Love Danny xxxxx

The paper is thin and yellow as always, like old skin in winter. I crush it into a tiny ball and throw it into the gutter. This city, the nearest and only place of size and relative excitement is cold and posh, shops with carpet like a painting and dummies in the window with eyes that see far beyond me. There is a notice in the window: *Sales Consultant required, good grasp of latest fashions essential. Apply Within.* I move on, sunk deep into my coat.

Now here I am, worth sixteen years of life, in stirrups, with a consultant gynaecologist deep inside me. 'Try to relax. Not hurting you, am I?' A deep-sea diver with no permit for these waters and I shake my head. 'Good. I'll go deeper then.' I've had worse and at least you've got a licence for it. He withdraws sharply. 'Eight weeks, no more. See the lady downstairs, thank you.'

Downstairs the lady from Pregnancy Counselling Choices Ltd talks at me for twenty-three minutes. I time her because I have to catch the bus back to Hell. I have time to spare. On the way I pop into Miss Selfridge and apply for the job. They give me a form: Name. Address. Marital status. No. of Children. Position. I resist the temptation, fill it in and hand it back to the sullen sixteen-year-old at the cash till.

The bus roars stinking into the coach station and although I need to get on it, I let it go, without any sense of time. I have no sense, any more, of anything. The consultant has seen to that. I stand not wanting to go home. It is approaching evening and I would like to be home in time to be pissed but I remember, frighteningly late, that I have nowhere to go.

At the leisure centre I stand like an idiot in the middle of the ice-skating rink. Somebody once told me never to stand in the middle or you get your fingers cut off, but it seems a risk worth taking and so here I stand, waiting for a better idea to come to me. I wait for ten minutes and I move around in a small circle because I don't like waiting, it makes me nervous. As I move out cautiously a huge school of children swims towards me on the glassy ice and I am going the wrong way. They push forwards with force of numbers, screaming with fearful pleasure, and I am caught and drawn backwards, which is amazing because I can't even skate, let alone in reverse.

I dance with myself on ice for an hour and then I make my way to the train station. It occurs to me, once there, that there is no station where I live and, so, I must leave.

But I don't. I stare up at the departures board and wonder what it would be like to get on a plane and leave the ground, for ever, to feel the thrust and surge of the air and power. Sometimes, in dreamtime, lately, I have been in a plane, flying low between tall buildings, dipping and climbing, always just missing the point of explosion, exalting as we avoid impact. Is that what it's like, to fly?

What would happen if I were to just climb on a train and

let it pull away, pull away and out of my life. Would everything stop, like Pompeii, frozen in time?

I am six. We go on a train, me and my mum and dad. We do not speak on the long journey but we eat the egg sandwiches my mother has made for us. The smell fills the carriage and an old man leaves. My father laughs and my mother slips him a quick look like ice, but I'm too young to know what it means. I sleep in the space between them and when I wake up it has grown wider and we are here.

On the beach, the tide is out. I have never seen the sea before and am not about to, not yet. My mother is disappointed. 'It'll come back,' she tells me, and while my father struts with impatience, she leans down and points into the distance. 'Look,' she says, and I follow the line of her hand, the sweep of her finger. 'If you try hard you can see it, out there. Look!' And I look and look, but all I can see is a shining, sparkling line, a straight line, like God. Now grey, now white, now silver, shining in the distance. Just a line, that's all.

We go to the room where we will spend the week. It smells of families and food. I curl up on the small bed that is mine for now and watch with delight from the high window. There is the line, still sparkling, still waiting, growing wider and thicker, spreading in towards the sand like magic.

When we go out again, in the evening, I can hear a sound I've never heard before. When we get near the beach, I see that the water is flooding the round bay, the silver edges of the waves lit by the fading light. 'It's beautiful,' my father says, and he takes my hand briefly. His face is lit, too, by the light. 'It's dirty,' my mother says, and I can see when I look up at her that she was hoping for something else, but I don't know what. The water hisses and seethes as we walk along the beach until we are hemmed in by the tide and we have to leave.

'Can we come back?' I ask my father, but he doesn't hear me because he is arguing with my mother. 'Will we come back here again?' They hiss and seethe at each other too, and my words are swallowed by the noise.

★

When I wake I am lying on a bench in the station. It is deserted by now and all the trains have left. There is only me and it is cold. A tramp wanders over towards me, half asleep, half dreaming, twitching as he walks and settles. It is seven in the morning and there is no possible way that I can get home for at least an hour.

I phone my mother.

'Where are you?'

'Staying with Lorraine.'

'Why didn't you call me last night? I was worried.'

'It was so late . . . didn't want to . . . wake you . . .'

Silence, then, 'I called Lorraine. She said she hadn't seen you since school.'

Heat washes over me. Is it shame? Shame, I suppose. I put the greasy phone down, softly. I swear. I don't often, although you might suppose by now that I do. In the phone box I can smell myself, suddenly. Can smell sweat and trains and shame. Shame.

Inside me something starts to turn over and heave its way to my throat.

Is this it? Is it?

When I get home there is nothing but silence, no one but the dog, and he sleeps in his plastic basket, lifting his head to glance at me, disgusted. I want to sleep but know better. In my bedroom my mother sits very still. Oh. She has been spring-cleaning, although it is nearly August. Has she looked under the bed yet?

'Are you ill?' she asks, very quickly. I swallow. It scares me. Think about it.

'It's a full moon,' I offer. She sniffs. I gain hope. We might yet be on safe ground. She stands and goes to pass me. She sniffs again and this time it is a detective sniff.

'A man,' she says, after a time, 'Has been near your person.'

'Okay,' I say. Tired, my truth is bound to sound like lies. 'The truth is – '

She stands now at the door of my room. 'What does it matter?' she says, sadly. What indeed?

★

Later that morning, Lorraine touches my arm between lessons and I turn with surprise at the contact. I miss the first lesson because I am sick as a dog but I make the second. 'I bumped into your mum and she said you were sick this morning,' she whispers. 'Good on you for coming in.' I spend the next lesson frozen.

'Rosa Raine,' says Mr Peters. 'Tell us what Shakespeare meant in this speech,' and I stare at the tiny words, reduced by time to something I cannot understand.

'What he means . . .' I say. My heart pounds unevenly, a double beat.

'What he means,' Mr Peters says, his foot tapping impatiently. The class, bored, waits. Sweat runs down my back.

'He means nothing to me,' I say eventually, and it is the truth. Mr Peters rises, annoyed by wasted time, chalking words on the blackboard that I can barely see. Natalie writes furiously.

At lunchtime we spy my mother, chatting to the priest, and I know that they are arranging the trip to Purgatory for me. 'Hello Father,' I manage.

'Ah, Rosa. Your mother tells me she's concerned for you,' he says mournfully.

Lorraine slides away to the bakery. 'Nothing for me,' I tell her.

'She says you're staying out late and coming in smelling of drink.' And he has the nerve to look me straight in the eyes.

'Father, I'm fine, no use worrying about me,' I say. My stockings are falling down with shock. I see Natalie tottering across the road, away from me and my nightmare group.

'What are you going to do with yourself?' asks the priest. 'You have a lovely mother, good with flowers and a credit to the Church. She wants to see you do something with your life.'

'I'm going to be a marine biologist,' I croak. Don't blame me, that's what they told me. We are standing by the market. My mother likes to shop here. 'Can I have a yoghurt?' I ask her. She sighs.

'The joys of family life,' says the priest. He looks lonely.

'Don't you get lonely Father?' I ask. 'Without a wife?'

'I have the family of the Lord,' he tells me. He walks on, heading for the cheese stall.

'Lorraine's a nice girl,' says my mother. 'Stick with her, she won't lead you astray.'

'Is that it?' I ask. My mother buys me a yoghurt and we walk on, uneasy but together.

'Are you alright?' she says suddenly when we are outside the college. I am astonished.

'Yes. Why not?' I ask.

'You put a photograph of your father up,' she says. 'In your bedroom. Since he went there has been no photograph of your father. Why now?'

'I have to go back to college,' I say and, luckily for me, the bell rings loudly. Half its patrons do the fifty-yard dash back to the old buildings, clutching sausage rolls and pasties leaking a meaty smell through paper bags.

My mother despairs of me. My father left and now I have an appointment with a social worker instead of a lesson. She is called Janet, she tells me – 'No surnames, dearie, not if you don't want' – she is fifty if she's a day, thin and hard as a bone. We eye each other with suspicion and possibly dislike. Janet has a set of questions and a notepad. I have a lump in my throat and the onset of claustrophobia. But then Janet may hate her job, I don't know. We are here to mutually discuss my predicament. Her term. The room is small, in a building just off the High Street, opposite the college. The room is light and sunny, and filled with children's toys: bright posters, fun chairs and games on the floor. It is the same room that they use for Children At Risk interviews and How Are You And Your Child Getting On? appointments.

Unfortunately the radio they have left on to relax us plays Abba's 'S.O.S' . Help. Janet regards me kindly, with tired eyes and a chicken neck.

'You're pregnant,' she says. 'You're expecting.'

We both wait. I nod. It's obvious, isn't it? She picks up a

toy that has soft velvet on one side and a mirror on the other. She smiles. I expect that she is not trying to be cruel.

'How did it happen?' she asks. 'The usual way?'

'What's usual?' I ask. 'Which position?'

'Would you like to tell me about it?' she says. Kindly, I expect. It's difficult for me to know. 'Would you like to tell me about it?'

'No,' I say.

'Oh,' she says crisply. 'I see. And what about father?'

I stare at her. 'Well, I can't tell you!' she says, astonished.

'Did you have a boyfriend?'

'No.'

'A pretty girl like you? I don't believe you. Come now – '

'Listen,' I say, leaning forward. My teeth are clenched. My jaw aches in surprise when I open my mouth. 'Nobody must know about this. I can't tell anybody, d'you see?' She is frowning now. In the hard light her face looks a million years old, dead already.

'All I need to know,' she says, pen poised over her bloody form, 'is who the father is.'

After three minutes she says, 'Are you a Catholic? Is that it?'

After five. 'Look. It's not my business – '

'No,' I say, but it is her business. I've made it so. I keep my eyes on my grimy nails. They are clutching the arms of the chair. I hate this. I hate this with such a hatred it makes me feel faint. Panic rises like saliva in my brain and I swim away from it, very fast. I get up.

'Where are you going?' she asks with faint surprise as I reach the door. 'There's nowhere to go, dear. There's nowhere for girls like you to go, you see.' She smiles, showing me all her teeth, pats the chair and says, 'Now sit down and be truthful with me.'

And so I tell her. I tell her what she wants to hear so that she can make her notes. She writes fast and furious for her files, and I hear the sound of my voice, tinny and thin in the sunny room. When I am finished I hear her lay down her pen and she smiles at me, a smile of relief. 'Thank you, dear,' she says, and I arrange my frozen face into an answering smile.

But I have told her exactly nothing.

The weeks eat themselves away when you are pregnant. I've heard women say that time goes so slowly when you're just waiting, but every day disappears before I have time to come to and open to the morning. I live in a state of numbness. Nothing seems to wake me and yet sleep is a stranger. How can this be? 'You're putting on weight,' says Lorraine, correctly. 'Shall we go on a diet together?' I will grow big as you grow small and disappear from my view.

'No,' I tell Lorraine, and the next day I bind my waist and belly with bands of material, swaddling myself up so that my body is stiff and flat like a board. I eat almost nothing and what I do eat I throw up, neatly like a cat, in toilets all over the town. I keep it away from home, you see. At night, often drunk, I lie very still and listen to my shiny hard belly burble with life. It terrifies me. Not knowing what else to do, I start to make plans.

'Forty a week,' says the landlord. He sniffs with laughter when I weakly try to bargain. 'It has a view,' he gestures vaguely. The room is tiny and high and overlooks a canal, littered with rubbish discarded by the dank waterside. The sour smell rises through the window. 'I'll only want it for a while,' I say. 'Maybe a month.' He doesn't care, his eyes have already moved past me. This town is bigger than mine, a city. It is eighty miles from home and it will do. I go back home, safe for now.

My nipples are growing. Truly, there is something alarming about their growth rate. Even my teacher has noticed. 'You've not been here much, lately,' he says, dragging his eyes away. 'Your attendance has been very erotic.'

'Pardon?' I say, but the class have begun to grow restless and he opens his Chaucer briskly.

I like to doze a little in the afternoon, to rest while my body races ahead, growing frantically like some kind of monster. I eat all the time now, secretly. Everything I do is secret now. When Danny rings up I whisper.

'I can't hear you,' he says, roaring like a monster.

'Shush,' I say.

My mother sits in the gloom of the house watching the neighbours climb trees. They are practising for their mountaineering holiday. The branch snaps. There are no mountains here, everything is flat. I hear my mother laugh, guiltily. I join her and we stand hidden by the curtains, watching the man retrieve himself and the woman pick leaves from his hairy jumper. We are suddenly nearly helpless. We look at each other and see our likeness reflected back at us. My mother nearly smiles. 'Will we have a sherry?' she says suddenly. I have not let my growth stop me drinking. That is how I think of it, as a hideous cancer that will soon burst out of me, an alien thing, and everything will be alright again. I told you so, didn't I?

Everything will be alright again. It has to be.

'Sherry would be nice,' I say, even though I hate the sweet sticky taste, the dead rotting sweetness of it. We silently toast the broken tree. They are arguing now. We eye each other. *We* never argue. Oh no.

The next evening Danny calls again. 'I've missed you,' he says, his voice thickening with hormones.

'Danny – '

'Danny's thought a lot about you, a lot. Is everything alright now?'

He can't count either. 'Danny – '

The clock ticks nearer to seven as he talks. 'Listen,' I tell him. 'I won't be seeing you any more.' There is an incredulous silence. 'Sorry,' I add as an afterthought.

'You're dumping me? Me?' he says, voice rising to a squeak.

'Well, yes, I suppose so,' I say.

'Right,' he says. 'Fucking – fucking right. We'll see about that. I'm on my way there now.'

And he bangs the phone down. Strangely, he never asked why.

I wind my swaddling around my swollen body and set off for work. I have given up cycling because someone stole the wheels off my bike. The walk gives me time to empty my mind and become a barmaid without a brain. It helps.

After a shift, I am weary beyond belief but my mouth carries on chattering brightly without me. Working here has given me the art of conversation. 'Pulls a lovely pint, don't she?' 'Oh, go on, I bet you say that to all the barmaids.' 'No, but, she does, don't she? Big bottom, love a barmaid with a big bottom. Eh! Big Bottom, give us another – ' This from a man who asks for the monster- or spider- or fucking rat-flavoured crisps, or whatever they are, under the till so that I have to keep bending down. We exchange clichés every evening and I rip the expressions off my face before I turn to face him. All he sees is a bland smile and a barmaid with a big bottom. If he ever looked me in the eyes he might see the rest.

As I leave the warm thick smog of the pub, the air shocks me. Beyond that is Danny, a wrathful stocky chunk of rage and indignation. I am too tired to be surprised.

'Oh,' I say. 'I thought you were somewhere else.'

'I told you I was coming to see you. You forgot, didn't you?'

He takes my arm and leads me to his car and I almost get in, then I remember.

'Where you going?' he shouts after me. 'Where are you going to go? Eh? Who else'd want you?' I swallow my words because it is true, he is right, but that is not a good enough reason to get in his car, and so I walk on, trying to maintain some dignity. He follows, bellowing. 'You silly little slag!' he screams. I can hear the spit at the end of his words. 'Dirty little tart. Thought I'd marry you if you were up the stick. Christ!' and now the spit reaches me. I stop. Everything around me seems to rush past very fast. His breath is close behind me now in the air. I want to cry. 'I'd rather cut my own throat than marry you now,' he says, with the slow careful precision of pride, 'you stupid cunt.'

I walk on until the sound of his voice has died away. I walk all the way home until the dry heat reaches me and my mother's figure is still sitting in the complete darkness.

'Night,' I say, and it is all I can manage.

In the morning I tell my mother the amazing news that I have been given a job in Miss Selfridge at a branch many miles away. 'As what?' she says, wiping up dog sick. He drank too much gin last night when my mother was in the kitchen and now he is paying for it.

'Clothing consultant,' I tell her, picking up the squirming dog.

'Shop assistant,' she says flatly. 'Put the dog down, he'll sick on your shirt.' The dog eyes me with hate. I have no sympathy with him. My mother gives him an Alka Seltzer in his Chum in the hope of curing him and watches him sadly. The stench makes my stomach turn. Fighting rising sickness, I tell her that I am going to take the job and that it involves travel.

'What about university?' she asks. I have applied, it is true, half-heartedly, along with the rest of the no-hopers in the class.

'I've been turned down,' I tell her. This is no surprise for me but a bitter one for her.

'By all of them?' she asks, incredulous. Nothing that she is feeling now can possibly be as bad as the truth, however, so I plough on.

'There's promotion, and the pay's not bad. I get a dress allowance.'

That cheers her up, a little, for the moment. 'Good fabric,' she says. 'That's what you need to buy. Several good pieces, classics. None of this leggings rubbish.' I nod and we discuss the value of a well-cut jacket for at least ten minutes. The dog burps and I am released. She is cheered only a little, because the devastation of my shop-assistant, Oxbridge-less future has barely hit her yet. She stares at me as I turn to go.

'Have you been to Confession?' she says, and then, eyes narrowing as I bend, 'My God, you're putting on weight, aren't you?'

'Crisps,' I say, pulling myself even tighter. It hurts.

'It doesn't come from my side,' she says, remembering. 'No. We all had good legs. They run in the family.'

'Legs run in everybody's family,' I say.

'Where could you have got it from?' she says, frowning, ignoring me. 'Your father – '

Her hands shake suddenly with the teapot and she scalds herself. She does not make a sound. I rush towards her with the towel and try to force her hand under the tap but she is stronger than me. She does not flinch. How strong must you be if you can live without love?

Later I pack my bag. It is heavy, full of books. I am not an extraordinary child by any means but I have discovered the means to an end. Two packs of sanitary pads and a Walkman and some clothes. It doesn't matter what I wear any more, does it? Colours are flung together regardless.

As the light outside the window fades my mother comes into my room.

'Danny called again,' she says, expressionless. 'You can't put the green and the blue together – take the grey dress.' The grey dress is fitted but I take it anyway, to please her. Why not? 'He cried, also,' my mother says, as I scrumple the dress carelessly. 'I put the phone down on him in the end. I had to. His voice upset me.'

'You should be glad he's gone,' I say. 'You never liked him anyway.'

'Do you need anything?' she says, anxiously. 'Do you need money?'

I hesitate, because I do, but there are other things that I need more. But I can't tell her that and she gives me thirty pounds and I vow to myself that I will not spend it. 'Well,' she says, awkward now. 'You'll be off, then.'

Yes, I'll be off now. I'll be gone.

'We won't know you when you come back,' she says, half a smile appearing briefly.

'It's only a job,' I say quickly. I turn away and zip up the bag with a flat thwack.

We stand at the door. I cannot look at her because she does

not know. The dog, shut behind the living-room door to prevent prison escapes, barks with rage. He knows something is happening. We dance a little at the door, jostling for position, and I stand outside, clutching my nylon belongings.

'The bus,' I remind her. I have to, don't I? Don't I?

'Be punctual, be polite and be professional,' she suddenly says, madly, and I nod smartly out of surprise. Did I tell you? My mother had a life before she had me. A professional life. I won't think about that now. I nod and agree lightheadedly and she holds onto the door. Her face is white and strained. Maybe it is the light. We usually see each other indoors.

'You'll be alright, will you?' she says, as I walk toward the small dog-proof gate. 'Be alright?'

The bands around my belly tighten. I swallow.

'I'll be fine,' I say, my back to her. 'Fine. Will you?'

'Oh,' she says, making a surprised mouth, a tight mouth. 'But of course.'

And this time it's just me, walking away. Very small. You wouldn't notice it.

In the street outside nothing moves. White sky black noise inside my head and hands red from the chafing bag by the time I mount the bus. It pulls away and I don't look back.

But I can still hear the sound of her breathing.

CHAPTER 4

Here comes the winter, all of a sudden. I wind the clock up. It ticks in time to my heartbeats. There are two because I have cut myself in half like a worm and now we both grow with the cold days. Each day brings me nearer to more. Or less. When I go out, rarely, I see women's faces heavy with winter and shopping bags. Clutching hands in theirs and red bootees. I see men's faces and I wonder which one is it? It doesn't even matter any more.

Sara says the waiting is the worst time and that chocolate is bad for babies and have I thought of a name yet? Sara lives down the road from my bedsit and we sometimes meet when I slide outside, squinting into the daylight, for sugary products, my belly appearing before me. It's all I seem to need, sweetness. Sara says that she feels sorry for me, I'm so alone, and where is the father? I laughed the first time she asked this, not from cruelty but from surprise and ignorance and pain because *I don't know*.

Thought of a name for it yet? she asks. Yes. Insanity. It can sound pretty if you say it right. Sara says to call her when I go into labour and she'll take me to the hospital. I won't but it's kind of her to offer, isn't it? Don't you think so? You should. Sara knows about these things because she has a daughter. Jody. A daughter and no man.

Jody is smart. Jody is what I would want if I had a right to. Jody brings me a Mars bar for a small fee though she would do it for nothing and I cut it into tiny pieces and devour them slowly, greedily, taking my time.

I listen to Sara's wave noises on a tape recorder for relaxation. Bollocks. I swap them with Jody for Nirvana. It's better than the restless sea, noisier. Daddy will the sea come back if I make a wish? No, but you can spend the rest of your life trying, if you like. You can spend the rest of your life crying if you like.

The waves took him away on the tide. One wave and he's smaller already. Two waves and he's gone. This room is high at the top of a tower and London shrieks below. I told you it was a town bigger than mine. Three weeks and ticking. A bottle of gin and, 'You're drinking,' says Jody, all eyes. 'I'll tell me mam. She'll have you.'

Sara slaps me. A red streak across the white plane of my face and a red streak across the sky shepherd's delight. One week and Jody starts choosing names for their new puppy. Jody starts knitting, damn her. I read Dad's letters again, yellow like the sun. The print is fading by the hour and the words slip through me like the seconds. 'I must have been driving all day but I'm getting no further away, forgive me.' Yeah, right.

Take me away Daddy I don't mind where. You wouldn't recognise me in a crowd, would you? I could pluck your heart out of a million and scent your breath from a mile away but you wouldn't know me now. I could present you with a bill for the lost years but you wouldn't have the right currency to pay it and I wouldn't give you credit. Wouldn't give you the time of day but there's seven days left and where there's life there's scope for death, isn't that the case? You tell me, you chose the middle ground. I'll huff and puff and I'll blow your house down. Come out wherever you are.

In my blank grimy white bedsit I sit, whole and a half, like a corpse. My room shakes faintly whenever a bus goes past, every four minutes. I have timed it because there is nothing else to do. There is a wetness between my legs now and it irritates me slick wet slimy I start for the door for air but

the night knocks me back, cold and alive. I must get to the
end of the road must must –
o
Why won't Jody leave me alone? I raise my hand and slap her
small pinched face as a warning to *go back* but she clings to
my arms and drags me towards a car, Sara's car. No. Got to
get home first, got to explain. Got to get back to you –
but
Christ *it hurts* –
Tell me a story Daddy, send me to sleep. Tell me a story –
She told me once that you would have chosen death for me
but you were never consulted. Well
I
Choose
Life
And here it is –
O
the pain and there's a stranger's face above me, he says he's a
doctor well I've heard that one before no strangers please,
red hair and young, more scared than me he's shaking but
that's wrong, I'm not scared, no drugs I'll do it the hard way
if you don't mind. If it's no trouble to you. I deserve to feel it
all wouldn't you say?
In and out. 'She's losing blood,' I hear. Not me, I want to
shout, not me, I don't care – but my voice is ripped away by
pain that splits me apart.
'Christ, we're losing – '
o no not me not
you
not after all this I can't breathe give me something anything I
don't care just give me
not you?
it can't happen like this can it? not now it's all supposed to be
safe and there's nothing I can do for
you –

CHAPTER 5

A man runs across the street, dodging the litter left by the market, crushing the pulp of rotten fruit beneath his heels. Rain pours down and his young head is slick as a seal. His face, white under the bright light, is shiny and wet and his eyes quick, always searching, moving moving always moving in case he misses something in the split second it takes for a chance to happen. This is Soho and he is part of it. In his dark bright colours he becomes himself. He lifts his young slick head to the rain and smiles, tasting the water. Life is good to him at the moment, because it is life. He wants to grab it all, seize it all in his long thin fingers and drink it down.

When Nick was a child, he sat in a pew every Sunday until his seventeenth birthday and counted the minutes until he could breathe again. He had no voice for hymns and his belief in prayer had already slipped away, so he counted. And watched. After all, what else was there to do? Brother Daniel, picking at the spots on his neck relentlessly. Sisters Cissy and Lizzie, younger than him, apparently devout in worship, knees creased by the hard floor upon which the congregation knelt. Looking into the priest's eyes during Communion, he saw nothing, a blank, tired gleam as the wine – 'Blood of Christ, Amen' – was passed to him.

'You'll go into the priesthood, like we discussed,' said his father, a drinker, as they sat in the Catholic Club. 'Here's to you, you'll make us proud yet.' And he touched glasses with his son. The next Sunday Nick dropped a tab of acid in the Communion wine.

Amen indeed. The Bishop was seen at the door of Nick's house. His parents, prostrate with shame, were lying down when he arrived: God Surprising The Fornicators At Their Deeds. 'I'm going to art school anyway,' said Nick, unrepentant. He was a curious boy, lacking in emotion, regarding the world from behind grey spectacles with thick lenses which made his eyes appear very far away.

'Art school?' said the Bishop, rather intrigued.

'Yeah,' said Nick. He lit a cigarette, purely to annoy the Bishop. He exhaled expertly, something he was proud of. 'Don't give me a lecture.'

'I wasn't intending to,' said the Bishop. He smoothed his damp strands of hair lovingly. 'May I have a cup of tea?'

'Oh,' said Nick, looking around helplessly. 'Er . . . Cissy!' A sister, blushing slyly, could be seen round the door. 'Make some tea, will you? He'd like some.' Cissy glanced at the Bishop from beneath her eyelids and fled, sniggering.

'Nick – ' began the Bishop.

'Look, Father – ' said Nick, his lovely hands fluttering.

'Er . . .' said the Bishop. 'You know, the thing is, the priest's an epileptic.' Nick put his hand over his mouth. 'And some of the parishioners were in a terrible state. You know they've never had anything like it before. There were faintings and all sorts . . .'

Cissy entered with a tray. A lace cloth and a flower in a small vase. But Cissy wore a tiny scrap of polka-dotted material, displaying bare tanned legs and arms and a good deal of pubescent breast. The Bishop cleared his throat and thanked her. 'You're a good girl, Cissy,' he said, and Cissy winked.

'Why did you do it?' he asked Nick. The distant eyes behind the thick glass were unchanging. The hands twisted, but the eyes . . .

Nick shrugged carefully. 'Dunno. It's boring at Mass. All the time I'm there I'm dreaming of somewhere else.'

'What do you dream about?'

'I – things are always – ' Nick swallowed. He was beginning to almost like the Bishop when his father growled into the room. He had clearly just risen and was alarmed to see the Bishop.

'Oh,' he said and coughed. 'Your Worship. Telling him, are you? We can't apologise enough, he's in the doghouse alright. His mother's lying down.' And to Nick, 'Your mother's lying down, d'you hear that? Got a cigarette on you?'

He snatched the pack and sat heavily, dulled and shamed by his effete son. The Bishop gestured to Nick to leave the room and, to Nick's surprise, followed him.

On the front lawn, the Bishop tucked Nick's hand lightly in his arm. 'Art school,' he said, prompting him back to the future.

'Yes,' said Nick, farther away now. 'In London.'

'God oversees London as well,' said the Bishop. 'He has a very big parish. Be you raised high and incorruptible.' And he made the sign of the cross. Without thinking, so did Nick.

'Good boy,' said the Bishop, desperate to leave. A childish prank, he would tell his Council. A young talented boy, eager to explore the world, to escape his drunken and irresolute father. That was what he would say, and the stoned, puzzled parishioners would recover and put it all down to an act of God since, after all, it happened in a church. But the boy disturbed him.

'Go in peace to love and serve the Lord,' he said as he left.

'Jesus Christ, Amen,' said Nick. He watched the Bishop leave with glad spite.

And a year later there was our boy, installed in art school, in the very centre of London, that city of sin and corruption. He was eighteen, and he was not happy, but then he imagined that happiness was a state for housewives and children, both of whom he believed knew no better. He wanted to be alive.

'Why do you want to come to us to study?' they had asked at the interview, and he had leaned forward fiercely, his fists clenched.

'Because I can live, here,' he had answered, 'because my life has not yet begun and I will know what I am when I sit in the centre of this place with my fingers resting near colours vivid as blood and brushes light as air and shapes quick as silver.'

Of course he had not said that, but he had thought it and they saw it in his face and believed in him and he was given a place. For, after all, he was not without talent. In school he painted the other pupils while they dully and obediently painted the landscape or the clothed bored model or the apple and stick of celery or whatever was set in front of them. Nick watched their skin change colour as they recognised themselves and their fingers curl with madness they could not express. But he knew. He knew he had something. He could not find a name for it but it seethed within him.

And now he was free to stride the streets of this place, owning it, being owned by it. For it was his, wasn't it? This hard, quick, cutting place, this beautiful, terrible place, this place of rotting fruit and exquisite colours. He loved it, as much as he could love anything. As he ran up the escalators, ahead of the sluggish fearful crowds, as he snapped in and out of the paths of the pedestrians delaying the moment of arrival at their destinations, he was glory. His light feet turned neatly into the dark streets where his heart lived and the cool darkness was welcome to him.

That night he was heading west into Soho so that he could drown. His hands deep in his pockets, clenched once again, he turned at random into a side street. He did not know where he was but it did not matter. In London he was invisible and if he were dead in the street nobody would know his name. That was good, he believed, because he thought about such things, imagining himself lying in the wet dirty street with policemen puzzling over his limp body, searching fruitlessly for signs of identification. He carried none.

In the bar, his hands rested lightly on the chrome surface, wary of contact with contamination. His eyes saw everything but his head did not move. Eyes were upon him even though he was not unusual. 'Want a seat?' asked a stranger. Nick shook his head sadly at the hungry man and his eyes told a story, of regret and of a slight anger. The stranger soon left and Nick slid into the seat, watching the drinkers in the mirror behind the optics.

After half an hour his eyes narrowed and widened and narrowed and he moved, with his third drink, over to a corner occupied by several people, all isolated by leather and glass and chrome. He sat, folding himself out into a lean shape.

'Bloody hell,' he said, and he laughed, an unfamiliar sound.

I watch the rain pattern the filthy window from behind my eyes. I can feel other gazes upon me but I don't look round because I know that this is a bad move and people can be too eager to seize an opportunity that is not already there.

Sometimes men stare and that is all they want to do. Sometimes they stare and they want more and sometimes they just want. But this stare heats me and I feel the sweat run down between my breasts and I turn in anger.

'Bloody hell,' he says, and then, 'Rosa?' He laughs and I see his slick hair the colour of mud and his white long face, and he moves his hands apart in astonishment, long hands with fingers like candles.

'Yes,' I say, and he leans towards me. His eyes are luminous and the colour of toffee. I remember nothing about his eyes, but I cannot say why.

'I'll get you a drink,' he says, snatching up my glass. I nod automatically. The man at the bar who has been watching me moves off abruptly and I see him duck his head in the rain as he leaves. I am tired this evening, so tired, and not even as astonished as him by this chance meeting. Is it chance? Does it matter? He will buy me a drink and I –

'What the hell are you doing here anyway?' Nick asked as he placed the drink on the filthy surface.

'Working,' said Rosa smoothly. Her eyes were filmy and her face seemed to have absolutely no expression at all, which intrigued Nick. He was used to girls with flushing cheeks and dilated pupils fixed on him. 'Working as what?' he said.

Rosa tipped half of her drink back. 'Bloody hell, it's strong,' she said, downing the rest as an afterthought. She stood and paused over him. He could smell heat and smoke and old perfume and, he thought, sex, but wasn't sure. 'Another,' she said, and moved to the bar.

Nick followed her. 'I'm at art school,' he said, keeping the pride out of his voice.

'That's nice for you,' she said, her eyes watching him in the mirror. She smiled suddenly.

'Yeah, it is,' said Nick, goaded. 'It's fucking great actually, all those nude models and weird sexy teachers. Did you go to university?'

'No,' said Rosa, her mouth twisting a little. 'I travelled, see.'

'Right,' said Nick. He felt that she had outdone him, somehow. 'Right. Cool. Where – where d'you go?'

'Oh . . . Far.'

'Far, where?' Nick asked.

'Here and there.' She smiled at him, but her eyes held nothing that he could understand.

Nick sighed. 'You're not helping me much, are you?' he asked, his head on one side. Rosa began to laugh.

'No,' she said. 'No, I'm not.' She peered at him. 'Didn't you used to wear glasses? Big, round, thick, milk-bottle glasses?'

Nick scowled. It suited his face. 'Yeh,' he said to the mirror. 'Thanks for reminding me.'

When we are five I put a blindfold on Nick and make him find me. It is a game. 'Find Rosa' it is called. Screaming with excitement, he stumbles over the root of a tree and falls flat, playing dead. We giggle and kick at him but he is good at this, oh very good. He lies still until we get bored and run off. This game is no good.

At the hospital they rush him into surgery and barely save his left eye. His mother never forgives me but his father pats my head and says to go home and forget about it. He smells funny and his eyes are glazed. When I am allowed to see Nick he is white as paper and tubes run all over his head. I cry and am taken home on the bus with a bag of jelly babies for consolation.

Now he has borrowed height from no one in his family and he has learned to smile. Through the years, I have never seen him smile. And I have never seen his eyes before.

By the time the bar was trying to close, Nick had discovered no more about Rosa in the years since he had last seen her. They persuaded the barman to sell them a bottle of wine to take out with them and took surreptitious sips at it, giggling helplessly. The air seemed warm and red and hazy, obscuring vision beyond them.

'You were the only girl in Technical Design,' Nick said suddenly. 'You went up to the teacher one day and said, All these little straight lines and squares, I don't like them, they're boring. Can't we draw something squiggly? He was horrified.'

'He threw me out,' said Rosa, remembering. 'I only went because I fancied Johnny Kemp. He never looked at me, not once, and there was nothing else on offer.'

'Oh come on,' Nick said. 'We all fancied you.' He saw Rosa's eyes narrow in the mirror. 'Except,' he added hastily, 'me. Because we were friends.'

Rosa thought about this. 'And all the girls fancied you in Domestic Science because you could make perfect pastry,' she said.

'Except you because you always skived off,' said Nick. 'Where did you go?'

The barman placed his sharp elbows on the bar in front of them and removed their glasses.

'We haven't finished yet,' Nick said. 'Can't you see that, you miserable bastard?'

There was a broken wineglass in his hand suddenly, and he stood easily and quickly, holding it up, his hand shaking with drink and sudden bitterness that had come from nowhere. The barman moved out of his dull, tired trance and whipped it away. 'Out,' he said, but though there was no refusal in his tone his face was puzzled as he escorted them to the door.

Outside the air is cold and we sink onto the ground beneath the Opera House, dizzy with wine and confusion. The blue lights give us a cold glow and we drink the wine, moving nearer and nearer for warmth and ease.

'Home,' he says, and his face has changed. I can smell my own sweat and see his features blurring in front of me. When he looks up at me, I put my hand, hesitatingly, on the side of his wet face and discover that he is weeping. It scares me and I want to move away but I feel the cool pale skin and his glorious eyes close slowly. Pain constricts me from inside but I move through it and breathe as his face is against my neck and his fine silky hair against my hand. He sniffs tiredly and we rock gently together like children.

I have found him again. His tears stain my shoulder and he has found me, I guess. And I am held, or at least holding on. Is that really such a luxury?

At his ninth birthday party we played a game with balloons. The teatable inside groaned with good things and I was always hungry, longing for the safety of food. In the garden, dark now and smelling of cold and bonfires, spades and forks waited to trip us up as we played the game where you passed a balloon shaped like fun from between your legs to the next person. Shame came to me too early and so I shrank from it but Nick's father pushed me stumbling into the light. I wanted to say that I was only there for the food but the balloon burst with my anxiety.

Nick watched unsmiling from the sidelines, always a spectator if he could help it. His father pulled him to the centre of the small garden, an exact and furious man. I smelled his rage but nobody else seemed to.

'This is for you,' he said, and handed Nick a firework.

Later, Nick and I watched the hot squeals of fire rain white and red from inside, breath clouding the window-pane. My father had just left but we were too young to talk about such things, to find the right words. I cried quietly but Nick turned me around and wiped my face roughly with a red party napkin.

When the call came for Blind Man's Buff Nick was bandaged black and we held our breath. He was turned around too quickly but he did not fall. It must have been dark and strange and dizzy under his mask of night but I could hear his breathing, scared of getting it wrong. His father hit him when he got it wrong and we all avoided him at school, those days, because we didn't have the right words, either, in our frightened mouths.

He moved around the room like a sleepwalker and none of us spoke and I was holding my breath now. *Catch me, catch me, I'm waiting* with my uncertain smile and damp hands. I want things too badly and they say it's a sin.

I'm ready where are you? Nick says and like shadows they all move into the corners of the room. They play the game in cupboards, underneath tables, behind doors, but sometimes there's nowhere left to go and that's how he finds me.

I'm ready where are you?

I'm here.

Where are you? I'm ready.

'Where are you?' Nick called. The skyline of east London, ugly and brutal, stretched far away in the dawn, below the flat, the unearthly hours of silence broken only by police sirens wailing past at high speed and the odd scream. Nick's flat was completely silent. He moved unsteadily back from the kitchen to search for more drink, but Rosa leaned against the window, pressing her forehead on the cold glass, watching Canary Wharf blink sadly and often. Nick stood behind her now, lightly holding her shoulders.

'What do they do in there?' she asked, moving a little away from his grasp.

'They watch my flat with binoculars,' he said, seriously. 'They watch me bringing girls back here and trying to seduce them, and then they report me to the Thought Police for corrupting virgins.'

Rosa did not smile. 'I'm safe here, then,' she said.

'Yes,' said Nick. 'Quite safe. Any minute now, one will burst in here and cry "Unhand Her, Sir!" and there will be – '

'Pistols at dawn,' said Rosa, examining her nails.

'Shotguns, round here,' said Nick, who had not a clue about weaponry and had seduced many virgins, a thankless task. 'And they say "Yo, Man, Let Loose The Babe." But you *are* safe here, as it happens.' He touched her heavy knot of hair lightly. 'You always had short hair.'

'It grew,' said Rosa crisply.

'I'm just saying, you know . . . it suits you,' said Nick. 'Let me see it.' He began untying the knot while she stood stiffly, looking down the fifteen floors to the grey morning. The dark hair fell onto her neck and shoulders and he turned her to him. Her eyes were closed and he had not expected that.

'Yes,' he said, feeling his words thicken in his throat. 'Oh yes.'

He moved towards her and stood almost touching her. He could feel the heat of her skin and hear her breathing and he put his hands on either side of her face and put his mouth trembling against hers. He could taste her and he pushed her hair back and felt her respond, coolly, without opening her eyes. Her hands were spread flat on the windowsill behind her and her body was taut and unmoving but her mouth bit at his now, and he pulled her against him, drunk and excited, digging his fingers into her hair, into her back, clutching her to him.

'Wait,' she said, pulling away, distant, her eyes glittering. She gathered her hair up and left the room. Nick sighed and lit a cigarette and waited luxuriously.

I walk through the streets not knowing where I am. My mouth is bruised and tender and numb and I want to be as far away as I can right now. A lorry stops. 'Want a lift girl?' shouts the driver, and for once I am not smart and I climb up, for want of anything better, and he drives on, into the blue light. He tells me it is 3 a.m. 'Oh,' I say. 'That late.'

'Or that early, depending on how you look at it,' he says, his cheerful awake face unshaven in profile. O he does not look dangerous to me.

'How do you look at it?' I ask.

He offers me an orange. The tang fills the cab. 'Just started my shift. It's going to be a lovely day, see?' he says, discarding peel. His positive outlook is beginning to grate on me. 'I'm going to Brussels,' he says. 'Why don't you come with me? Go on, have a day out.'

I tell him I have had a night out and that is enough for me and he winks as we sit at a red light. 'Boyfriend kept you up, did he?' he says, and I think of Nick still waiting for me to emerge from the bathroom.

In my small room I pull back the yellow curtains and watch the morning appear behind the double set of bars. I am not in prison but in Hackney and I live in a room above a basement where guns and no doubt drugs are sold. It makes no matter. It is cheap. Occasionally my door handle is turned by accident and I freeze and lie silent as death until the footsteps die. Other than that, and strange noises, like sobbing, I am not bothered by them, whoever They are.

Today I am going on a journey, despite my need for sleep, which will not come. It rarely does anyway. I change in my tiny room. It is rented as furnished. I have a bed, a filing cabinet and an old desk. I place my clothes in the cabinet drawers and there is nothing to put on the desk except myself when I want to rest briefly against a hard surface. There is a chair, but why would I sit in it? I dislike this room and yet it suits me, does it not? Bare and iron hard and trapped in by bars. There is no view but then I do not want that.

I would not have you think that I complain, because I chose this place, picked it out myself amongst a host of others. Some had soft, almost plush furnishings, sharing a communal atmosphere with other young people ... 'This is Chastity, my girlfriend,' said one landlord, possibly twenty. He was clean and neat and so was Chastity, but I declined to live there. I chose this, remember. My choice.

When I step off the train at Peterborough, I am lost, again. But somebody soon directs me. And so I find where I am going easily enough. The house I find is ordinary enough, a modern semi-detached, probably three-bedroomed, with a small garden. A quiet street. I stand opposite, hidden partly by a tree. I stand there for a long time, smoking many cigarettes. At 3.30 a woman with a pushchair goes up the path to the house over the road. Her hair is damp and disarrayed and she looks like she could do with a hand to help her lift the child out.

I cross the road slowly and she is struggling, really struggling, to lift the burden and crush the pushchair into a neat shape and I watch her set the child onto the grass as she folds, watch the child stumble into a bush and sit, bemused, watch his small face, watching the world, watching his life. And then he turns and sees me, and he points vaguely in my direction and makes a noise, and the woman turns, alarmed, then thrusts her sweating hair back and smiles, helpless.

'Difficult, these things, aren't they?' she says, smiling and kicking at the pushchair. 'I've only just got the hang of it.'

I stare at her. She is forty, maybe, with a round, pleasant face, greying blonde hair in a straggly bob, a dress with flowers upon it. I am wearing black jeans and a black leather jacket but I am not sweating like this woman. The child is quiet now. He stares at me. I stare at him. He plucks fistfuls of grass as the woman finally folds the pushchair. 'Thank the Lord for that!' she says, still smiling, and she tugs at the child. 'Come on, Tom,' she says, and I am sweating now. The child is dragged backwards by her, still staring at me. 'Terrible, isn't he?' she says brightly, and I cannot fault her. 'Do you have any yourself?'

I begin to back away, slowly, watching them slide into the house at her pace, not his. 'No,' I say. 'I have none myself.'

The child starts to yell, a strangled, frustrated noise. This is my child.

This is only the second time I have seen you but I know without doubt who you are. My baby

Mine

CHAPTER 6

Nick woke with his flatmate, Patrick, standing over him.

'Unnuurrggh,' said Nick. He groaned and stretched.

'You'll miss the lecture,' said Patrick anxiously. Patrick was punctual and prudent and worried about Nick. Patrick's father was in business and had paid for the flat in which Nick had the small, single bedroom and Patrick the huge double, to which he never invited girls back. He listened, envious and sweaty, to the moans and sighs of Nick and his girls and slept little, rising early to paint.

'Fuck the lecture,' said Nick morosely. 'One got away last night.'

'Oh dear,' Patrick said, uneasy. He had heard the openings and closings of doors and, rising to a collection of bottles and glasses, had assumed the usual rapid seduction had taken place. Now, he was lost for words. 'What a shame,' he said, perplexed.

Nick stared at him, slithering from the bed and standing naked in front of Patrick. 'Do you think it's a joke?'

Patrick turned aside. A flush washed over his skin. 'I don't think anything,' he said quietly. 'We'll be late. Get dressed.' He moved towards the door.

'Patrick,' said Nick. 'You should have seen her though.' Patrick felt him close behind. 'All this hair – ' He touched Patrick's neck lightly. 'Huge eyes and a mouth that you just want wrapped around you. Know what I mean?' His hand moved down Patrick's long back. They stood frozen for moments. 'You know what?' Nick murmured.

Patrick swallowed. 'What?' he muttered.

'You should get yourself a girlfriend, you dirty bastard,' said Nick, turning lightly away.

As Patrick closed the door, Nick swept the entire contents of his floor under the bed. Candles, two. Cassette tapes, Motown and Beverley Craven. A selection of photographs of Nick with assorted attractive girls. Condoms, various flavours (rarely used, but he felt it appropriate to show willing). Somebody's knickers, a peculiar colour; Nick the artist decided they might best be described as aubergine. Old wine bottles, dripping at the mouth with dregs and wax. He stood up and displayed himself at the window thoughtlessly.

'Bitch,' he said to nobody in particular.

At work I sit in a daze, as if my head is filled with chalk. I have resisted the usual jobs open to girls like me and I sit in a small office on top of a building off Mayfair, just out of hearing of life. I temp. Of course. I have been here for a month, though, and that is longer than I would usually prefer. It smacks too much of stability. I work for a very old man who is also an academic, but only just. He runs a journal where ancient but respected academics like himself publish unreadable papers with uncertain facts and faintly puzzled, wavering conclusions. I type his spidery writing into passable letters and I answer the phone. It rings once a day on average so this is not too arduous a task. Of course I am bored, because I am not stupid, but I spend my time daydreaming. It gets so that I am not sure what is real and what is not. For instance, I am not sure that I met my old schoolfriend Nick, or that I saw a child who may be mine, or not. If it were real then it would hurt but then I am dead from the neck down, apparently, so I might not know. The phone rings. My daily call.

It is Professor Medway. He sent us a paper on how to cure homosexuality, yes. No, we have not printed it yet. We have to decipher it first.

'What what?' he shouts at me.

'Your handwriting . . . a little difficult to . . .'

'Bugger.' And he puts the phone down. I am faintly shocked, a man of his age. I go downstairs to tell my boss,

Professor Harvey. He is sitting in the boardroom, a cavernous place full of echoes and velvet and muslin. Mirrors everywhere reflect the empty space with only two old men eating liqueur chocolates furtively. I cough and the sound ripples through the space. They turn to me, affronted.

'Professor Medway phoned.'

'What did he want?'

'He told me to bugger off.' This is not quite true but they enjoy a moment's horror, at no cost to me.

Professor Harvey stands, impeccably upright and with a faintly military bearing. 'I apologise on his behalf for using such language. You may go home early. Take the afternoon off.'

It is 4.30. He signs my timesheet and I leave, winking at Gay the receptionist, who is plump and naughty and knows how to enjoy herself, even in this mausoleum. One month ago she took me to a nightclub where she shimmied and shook, the centre of attention, in gold lamé and plenty of hairspray. I choked in the dry ice and held her back but she says we'll do it again sometime. I can hardly wait.

My evening looks to be as many are; fish and chips from the greasy shop near the station and a bottle of cheap wine while I watch the evening close down slowly before me. Occasionally, like last night, I sit in a bar alone, and wait until it is the next day to go home, risking attack on the journey home. It seems a small risk to me now. I trace my footsteps like in a dream back to the bar of last night. I liked it there. The light flattered my shadowed eyes and the mirrors were kind to me. Of Nick, I cannot say. He is a man, and I have foresworn men, and what they can do for me, for now. I do not see that their sex will be any the worse for it.

Nick's lecture survived without him, and he eventually dragged himself in to the life class, where Patrick sat already, piously sketching the model, a bored woman with long thin limbs and her face turned away, even though the tutor repeatedly asked her to face the class.

'Ooh, a naughty one,' whispered Nick, sliding into his seat. 'I like these.'

'Miss,' he called, springing out of his seat again. 'Just let me see your eyes – '

The woman's face whipped towards him, angry, her eyes biting and snapping. Nick photographed her with a Polaroid camera and sat back, satisfied, as the picture developed. The woman regarded him with dislike.

'Cunt,' she said, contemptuous but calm, and turned her head again. Nick smiled. Meanwhile, Patrick had been filling out the spaces and lines of her spare flesh, oblivious to Nick's display. Two of the girls in the class glanced at Nick admiringly and he bowed gravely. They giggled. One blushed, one did not. He pocketed the exposed photo and left. Patrick began to prepare his paints. All he saw was colour and lack of it and hollows where flesh might be on a different model. One of the girls moved her easel nearer to him.

'Is he a friend of yours?' she asked, thoughtfully.

'Well, I live with him,' said Patrick, absently.

'Why don't you ask me round for a drink?' she said. Patrick put his brush down and looked at her. She had long, centre-parted hair, dyed black, and a nearly pretty face with almost colourless eyes. He had once seen a sheep with eyes like this. It had been caught in some barbed wire and was very nearly dead, but he had kept it alive, until it had been slaughtered for mutton. Nowadays nobody ate mutton and so he supposed that sheep like that were safe.

'Why not?' he said, managing not to blush.

Patrick found girls difficult, because he had come to London without experience or knowledge and lived with a boy who had plenty of both going spare. Nick's encounters rarely seemed to give him pleasure but appeared necessary, and Patrick turned away from this with something like distaste.

'I won't bite you,' said the girl, bringing her mouth near his hand and snapping inches from skin. Her teeth were white and even and they were one of her good features. 'Will your mate be there as well?' she asked casually.

'Why?' asked Patrick stupidly.

'Because I want to see him again,' she said, staring at him. She pointed at the other girl, the blusher. 'She'll come too.'

'But I thought you meant it would be a date,' Patrick said. 'You know . . .'

'Nobody goes on dates any more,' she said scornfully. 'Go on, it'll be a laugh.'

Patrick agreed gloomily. 'A laugh,' he repeated doubtfully. He turned back to his easel, wiping the last thirty seconds from his mind and concentrating on the model's chalky thighs, bleached like old bone by his paints.

In the bar I sit in the same seat as before, guarding the space around me with jacket, bag and outstretched limbs. I do not want company. You will understand this. Will you? Then what am I doing, here? A man approaches me with tired lust in his face and gestures and I lift my head from my curtain of hair to look at him. He sees my eyes and he backs away. Oh yes, he sees my eyes. I have learned to let people know what I am so that they may stay away from me. There are many things that I have ruined and I cannot go back, so I do not look down and I do not look up but straight across.

And I see him, sitting at the bar again, also as before. He sees me and he does not smile. He knows me better than that, I should think, by now. He sits on, and I sit on, separate people. I am unmoved by charm and indifferent to allure. I am buried alive by my own hand, squeaking and scratching at the coffin lid for air before it's too late. Wake me up, daddy, build a path with stepping stones in the water and make it safe and sturdy or I won't cross can't cross. I'll get my feet wet, won't I?

He's kneeling beside me now. 'Will you come home with me?' he says, and there is weariness in his voice. If I move the hair out of his eyes will that be a wicked thing? When I do, he moves his head against my careless hand like a dog seeking comfort, automatically, expecting it. The texture of him is shocking to me.

On the tube we stand in silence, pressed close by the crush and when the crush leaves at Liverpool Street we do not move apart. I leave it up to him.

In his flat, we turn into his bedroom. It is tiny, with a narrow single bed, fitting his shape, and an upturned box holding an old wine bottle with a candle dripping down its side. He lights the candle. 'Like Mass,' he says, and smiles.

'No beds in church,' I say, to turn my mind from the next few hours, from the lapse of poverty in my life.

'Unless for the purposes of procreation,' he adds. He must see my look of alarm because he shows me, discreetly, as though we have observers in the room with us, a packet of condoms. Banana-flavoured but I don't intend to taste them.

In the dim light he looks at me, head on one side, frowning. 'Ready?' he asks me, rubbing his hands over his jaw, eyes sleepy and enormous, a child up beyond bedtime. I do not move and so he comes to me and bends and puts his mouth against my skin and tastes me questioningly and sighs. I can feel his warm breath. He dips his head again, eyes catlike, sure and cool against the heat of me.

My head is filled with sugar. Help me. I'm drowning in honey.

Ready? There are pearls of tears in the corners of his eyes. I close mine to trap the heat inside me and his hands move down slowly smoothly as we stand and then stumble awkwardly to the long narrow bed.

'I always feel guilty, the first time,' he says, as he lies naked against me and nothing of him moves. The first time? There'll be more, then? How can he be so sure?

'What do you have to feel guilty about?' I say against his mouth.

'You wouldn't understand,' he says, and his eyes slide away.

Nothing of the past, now. Not now. Later maybe, but for now this must be right. It's important, do you see? I wish you could read my mind. Some things can't be said. He slides inside me, his face hiding mine, and I can barely feel him, but that is better for now. He is small but I don't mind and now he is moving like a fish. He puts his hand over my eyes and swims inside me panting and then he drowns.

I hold him, cradled in my arms. I want to make it alright, to let him grow before my eyes and restless fingers to prove to me that he is a man and I am a woman. There have been men before but I have always been a girl and never never watched one drift into sleep and heard his heart beat lightly against my skin. He stirs restlessly against my arms. He is not used to being held, I suppose, but then neither am I, and I weep for it sometimes.

In my small room the sound is carried by the wind and fury dries my face. But here his hair is silk against my neck and his mouth moves a little as he breathes. His throat is white and soft and very young; I want to bite it suddenly, to taste him, to wake him up, trap him and wind love about him and wipe everything else away.

As I slide my body from his and prepare for escape he wakes, disoriented in the dawn. We look at each other and we are both surprised. 'I'm sorry,' he says, groaning with remembrance, and folds his arms about me, and suddenly I am the one who is trapped. His lips are cool and this maddens me. I put my hand down and he gasps, drinking in air. A police siren wails past from the world. When he turns me deftly underneath him and slips into me he is small small still small. I can hardly feel him and then he begins to move against me and then I can feel nothing, nothing, nothing else at all.

God help me.

Patrick could hear nothing. The flat was absolutely silent. He padded around the kitchen, enjoying restoring order, clearing up the familiar debris of Nick's social life to make way for his own. He made coffee and set up his easel in the now bare living room. He took down the mirror that sat opposite him, disliking the constant moving reflection.

'Sorry,' said Rosa, appearing in the doorway in a towel. 'I left my bag in here.'

'And her knickers,' said Nick, tousled and smirking behind her. He put his thumb up to Patrick behind Rosa's back. 'Rosa, Patrick. Meet each other, you've met, go on – ' and slapped Rosa's backside lightly, turning her to face the bathroom.

'I think you embarrassed her,' Patrick said, turning away from Nick's gaze.

'Gorgeous, isn't she?' Nick said casually, following Patrick closely. 'A gorgeous piece of – '

Patrick was convinced that the girl must be listening at the door and something in him shrank from the thought of her hearing Nick picking over the bones so gleefully.

'Alright,' he said, exasperated. 'I'll work in my room.' And he bent to pack up his easel, but Nick was behind him, suddenly filling the space, almost inside his flesh.

'Christ, can you smell it?' And indeed a strange hot scent was rising in the thin space between them. Patrick was trapped between the wall and Nick.

'What is it?' he managed.

'Her,' said Nick, laughing. He danced away. 'I'll leave you alone, now,' he said, knowing Patrick was watching him. He turned around and wrapped his arms around himself lustfully. Then he was gone and Patrick heard laughter and a door banging. Then the familiar creaking of Nick's tiny bed. Unexplained anger rose in him and he sighed, knowing he was free to paint but unable to concentrate now. He put on loud music, Mozart's *Requiem*, trying to lose himself in the swell.

The phone rang. Patrick waited for Nick to answer it. All calls to the flat were inevitably for Nick except for Patrick's parents on a Sunday morning, equally inevitably. But it rang relentlessly and Patrick, wearily supposing Nick was midthrust, answered it at last.

'Yes,' he said, sighing, to the inevitable young female voice. 'I'll get him for you.' But he was determined not to enter Nick's boudoir. He stood where he was and screamed.

As Nick picked up the extension, Patrick cursed gently and picked up his brush. He stared hard at the canvas, trying to block out the world.

'Can I watch?' a quiet voice said. Patrick closed his eyes and gave up hope for the day.

'Look – ' he said, turning round. She was wrapped up in a sheet which covered all the parts of her body which embarrassed Patrick and she looked not at him but at the nearly blank canvas.

'What will it be?' she said, and her voice and face were at such odds that he simply stared at her.

She curled up into a chair and sat unblinking, her hands smooth on the sheet but trembling a little. He noticed the nails were bitten to the quick.

'You can watch,' he said. 'But only if you're quiet.'

'As a burglar,' she said, and he turned again suspiciously, but her mouth only twitched once and she did not move.

When the tape ended, she got up and turned it over, soundlessly, and returned to her seat. Patrick had forgotten she was there.

'Is Nick still on the phone?' he asked.

She shrugged. 'I like this,' she said softly.

'The music?' asked Patrick, trembling.

'The music and the painting,' she said, seriously. 'It's like a day out for me.' And she smiled at him suddenly, and he found himself smiling back in astonishment, his mouth widening in an unaccustomed manner.

'A day out?' he said, still smiling, and she began to laugh.

'Yes,' she said. 'I just want to soak it all up, see?'

He nodded, not really understanding.

'Like the sun,' she said. 'Like when the sun comes out and there's a cloud there. D'you see now?'

And he did.

'Come and warm the bed up,' said Nick, appearing in the doorway, sulky in his green boxer shorts. Rosa's smile faded. Patrick saw a pulse beat in her throat and her eyes changed as she stood up.

'Thank you,' she said, low, to him as she pattered past. Her feet were small and beautifully shaped, he thought.

'Going out soon, are you?' asked Nick, as he pulled her against him.

'No,' said Patrick, turning back to his canvas. I wonder if she'll ask him who was on the phone, he thought. The light had changed again as she had left.

In the small room, Nick opened the window to let out the stale air. 'Don't let it go,' Rosa protested, fighting with him. But Nick fastened the window and slid her onto the bed again, trapping her legs and winding his arms about her.

'Where have you been all this time?' he asked her, for she had not spoken a word about their past life. It was as if they had not met before but as strangers in a bar. It disturbed and excited him, and he did not worry that it might turn the future ugly, because Nick existed only in the present. The future was for sad people: mortgages and pension plans and dreary mornings where work had to be gone to and children's mouths wiped.

'Where have you been?' he said again, turning her face to him.

'Waiting,' she said, and her eyes narrowed, as if in concentration.

'Waiting for this.' And before he could worry the answer out of her, she slipped from under him and trapped him instead, underneath her body, fierce now, shedding the skin of the sheet from her body and covering him, his hands stretched back under hers, the grey light barely filtering through the grimy windows.

'O God, I love you,' he said as the sun came out and he unpeeled himself from her, stroking her hair. 'I love you like a friend.'

Today is my day off. I have earned it, because they say at work I am looking pale and need to rest. Pale and shiny I am and they have no idea how I spend my nights writhing and why should they? Perhaps they do the same. Prof. Harvey and his terrific thin wife, twenty years younger and American to boot, with all that surplus vitamin energy and plenty of hair. Perhaps. I don't care any more, not for now. Just give me this.

Usually I stay at home and read blankly, eating chocolate mini rolls but with no real pleasure. Today I cruise along Oxford Street, moving smoothly in and out of shops, touching the fabrics, moving among them, trying on everything that feels good and shines. I can't help it, this sorting and touching of shiny fabrics, a moment of pleasure. Is it a bad thing, to sort amongst the fabrics of Marks and Spencer, is it? In my defence I would not say that I am happy but I look as though I am, and surely that must count for something?

''Ere darling,' shouts a man suddenly. 'It's a nice day, the sun's shining. Have these on the house – ' and a pair of cheap silky knickers flies my way. I catch them, to applause. You see? Don't believe the man, he doesn't know. Anyone can look happy, if they try. Don't think that I don't know that, but I smile all the same, it's hard not to.

And then I hear a voice. 'Rosa,' it says, quietly. Real quiet, like it's inside my head, but it's not, it's quiet with surprise, with fear. 'It can't be. Rosa?'

A voice in the crush of Oxford Street. 'You've changed your hair – '

Cold with shock I turn. Lorraine stands there. Lorraine from school, Lorraine *from then*. The cheap silky knickers, a gift given with generous laughter, slip from my hands into the dirt of the street. I see feet trample them almost immediately. In the crush of Oxford Street, Lorraine and her mother are a foot away from me. The hair at the back of my neck is damp and cold. I move backwards, but not fast enough, because they move forward, like in a terrible dream. Only the noise and thrash of life tells me that this is real.

Lorraine is staring, staring like a terrible crazy woman, her hair fluffed up by the wind, her eyes small and scared. 'I thought you were – '

'Dead,' says her mother, staring too. Even with blurred vision I can see their faces. They seem smaller now. How can that be?

'Everyone thought you were dead!' Lorraine cries as I run. 'You're supposed to be dead!' Shoppers block my path and I tear through them, into a store and out the back way, dodging security guards and elderly people. I don't know where I am going. I am just

going.

'Rosa!' she calls. I can hear the echo of her voice in my head as I dip into small Soho streets and out again, weaving through the traffic. I run until the blood has left my head and the breath my lungs and still I run, pounding like lunacy, but the streets seem empty and wide and there is no cover.

I run.

But I still hear the echo.

We thought you were dead –
You're supposed to be
dead

CHAPTER 7

Going back, back.

No –

Further back. Where am I? Heavy with child I walk in the park, I don't know which one. A park in London, maybe, and there are many. I am weighed down with many things but I swaddle my poor burden tight for disguise and survival and I walk through the leaves, counting the leaves. Counting the days. I have never been so lonely. A woman sits on a park bench feeding dirty pigeons and offers me a piece of stale bread. I take it.

'Expecting?' she says, a dry stick of woman, surrounded by bags and dirt.

'I expect nothing,' I tell her, and she cackles, a tinny sound. She pulls a can of Special Brew out of her overcoat and offers it to me. I sip.

'How can you tell?' I ask her because she is nobody to me.

'Way you sit,' she says. 'Like this – ' and God help me, she demonstrates. I turn away, ashamed to feel my face wet in the late sun. When I turn my mother is sitting on the bench beside me. She says nothing until I change the way I am sitting.

'That's better,' she says. 'Are you comfortable now?'

I nod, frozen like death.

'Then I'll begin,' she says, and she starts to weep and weep and *thank Christ I wake up*, sweating and chilled and wanting to be held but nobody is within screaming distance.

How could I have been so stupid?

You think that in the city you can disappear but it's never true. Nowhere is far enough from your own nightmare, is it? Far enough from the recent past. I burrow deep inside me and there is only more, like the endless piece of string. My intestines pulling out through my own mouth showing who I really am but I'm still alive, keep pulling daddy keep pulling. We'll get there in the end, won't we?

If I tell you now will I be brave enough? Will you? Don't turn your head. Let me say something. It might be my only chance, even if the words can only be said from behind my own closed eyelids. Lorraine's appearance threw me. She's not real, is she? Only someone who saw one part of me, denied access to dangerous areas. Tell me that she's not real, that I imagined her like everything else, that none of it ever happened. *Tell me* –

I could explain, if the pieces of me were together for long enough. Listen. Think of a family, although we were never part of one, scattered around the country. Like a body, limbs everywhere, waiting for someone to discover and put the pieces back together again. No. Some things can't be repaired, can they? I don't know. When I came back that time, remember? In the last week, before it all became too big. I can remember, anyway, enough for all of us.

The light was strange, bright and clear and white. The details matter to me because they are all that I have in place of photographs or reality. Leaving London, struggling with the bus, arriving early evening. I creep along in cover of fading light, sneak in the back way like a war criminal. Your surprise nearly undoes me but I don't cry *I daren't* I smile and your mouth is open with surprise. You have got older since I went. How can that be?

'I was passing by,' I say, and you frown in disbelief. Nothing I can tell you that you will accept.

'I wanted a day off,' I say, at last, and you say nothing but go the kitchen, brightening and crisping with usefulness, and you assemble food.

'Have you been eating properly?' you say, and I shake my head, astonished. You can see that I am too pale and bloodless, that I am being eaten away from the inside, nourishing something other than myself. Can you see the words waiting inside my head as well?

You cook for me then, steak and watercress and tiny mushrooms, as though you have known I would appear and marvel. For surely you would not have bought such luxuries for yourself? You never do. I eat voraciously, *I can't help it.* I am starved, the demands in my womb dictating to me eat eat –

Feed me. Caught between the present and the future, I devour the steak. You watch me silently, and you begin to smile.

'I've never seen you eat so well,' you say. 'Is that why you came back early? Just hungry?'

And that's when I start to sob and cannot stop, that you would think your worth is only measured in the food you can give me, that my only needs are those that can be satisfied so easily. We sit on, in the darkening evening, making my return to safety almost impossible with every growing, unspoken minute. You put your hand, trembling and shrinking, on my back and you pat rhythmically. When I look at you, really look at you, I can see how you have spent the time since I left. Your eyes have grown duller and your throat is loose.

'Listen to me,' I say and I would rather have cut my own throat then than said a word more. Believe me. Your eyes change and I can hear your breath drawn in tightly.

And that's when I told you, that's when I ripped it all apart, because I could not help myself, because I was so lonely, because I was dying of loneliness and so were you. That's when I told you that I had no job, no training course, but a pregnancy and a safe house where I might give birth in complete privacy and –

'How?' you said. That's all you said. I tried to reassure you, to tell you that it would all be alright, that nobody would find out, but your hand clutched mine and you were whiter than me and you had not had your say yet.

'How could I not have known?' you said, and I knew then that I had done a terrible thing. 'How could I?' and then I saw you cry, as I had never done before, without sound, like an animal caught in some hideous private pain. I see your face ageing before me now like some terrible dream that we are both trapped in and I have no power to help you. You move slowly so slowly that it agonises me to sit beneath the window and there is *nothing I can say*

is there?

and again I leave but this time we have decided that it is for good and we both know it because there is no way back, is there?

Is there?

God forgive me. We say it is for the best and we believe it, in our separate agonies.

And I go. But I look back. *Believe me.*

And now, two years later, he says, I love you like a friend. There it is. That night we ate and drank greedily all that there was in his tiny fridge and then I made to leave. He never said *don't go* but he never said *stay* either. I need clear directions, see. Silence confounds me. So I repair my make-up and I tear my hair apart to find some sense of order and I make to go, but he stops me.

'When will I see you again?' he says. Standing between me and the door, his nakedness fills me with pity. He is long and white and almost perfect, to my eyes, but then I don't ask for much.

'Don't ask never got,' said my grandmother, but she has died since I went, and I don't know if she got what she asked for. Some would say yes, but they never knew her and I cannot go back to listen to the silence of a grave. Nick is here and he is alive o yes and he moves closer to me and I am water I run down to the source I can't help it.

Don't give up on me now I'm moving closer to the shore if

the waves will let me. Will you wait? I fight them when I can, will you wait? I hear you talking in my sleep but when I wake you're never there, are you?

Nick would have walked her to the tube but she fled, as before, when he wasn't looking. He busied himself collecting condoms. Although she was on the Pill, she was insistent on the thin skein of rubber between them. 'I need some protection,' she said, and he, puzzled, had really no choice but to agree. He heard Patrick's music and it annoyed him. He put on his small, powerful stereo and turned the volume up inconsiderately high.

'Please – ' Patrick shouted from the door. 'I can't hear myself – '

Nick opened the door. He abandoned the spring-cleaning. 'Let's go to the pub,' he said, taking his jacket from the hall.

'Don't you ever work?' asked Patrick. 'You'll fail your summer exams. Won't your parents go mad? Mine would.'

Nick's easel stood unused in Patrick's room. It was an often contested point that although Nick seemed to paint and draw little, he avoided reprimands and letters warning about lack of attendance, while Patrick sat through every class and listened closely to the lecturers and painted when he was not sleeping, yet failed to draw attention to himself. It made him ask why he lived with Nick and not alone, where he could create undisturbed.

'I don't drink during the day,' Patrick said crossly. 'You know that. Why don't you do some work? Unplug the phone and get on with it. Or you'll fail . . .'

Nick thought about that for a minute. 'No I won't,' he said. 'You know who my personal tutor is?' Patrick nodded. Nick inclined his head.

'You're – going out with her?' Patrick said, not believing him.

'No,' Nick said. 'I fuck her every Thursday afternoon.'

Patrick left the room disgusted.

'Anyway,' shouted Nick, 'I do work. I just do it quicker than you and in private and I'm more spontaneous, see?'

'What about Rosa?' Patrick shouted back, regretting it instantly.

Nick smiled inside his room. He picked up the knickers from under the bed and put them with the others in a drawer set aside for his collection. He crept into the hall and dialled Rosa's number, wanting her to be at home, waiting for his call, wondering, briefly, what home was to her. It rang and rang. Patrick appeared, pulling his jacket on.

'Who are you phoning now?' he asked. Nick put the phone down. 'My sister,' he said. 'She's probably at Mass. Coming to the pub then?'

'No,' said Patrick. 'I'm going for more turps, I've run out.'

'I'll come with you.' Patrick sighed, knowing that he would be persuaded to drink unpleasantly warm beer until Nick became bored with his company.

But Nick insisted on going to a cafe where no alcohol was sold, and they sat with coffee at a small wooden table and watched people pass by outside, depressed by the sudden rain. 'Rosa said she liked it here,' said Nick, morose. 'Crap, isn't it?'

Patrick rather liked it, too. There was no service, you bought your coffee at the small counter and they were all over the place but they smiled such an awful lot you couldn't complain. He ate his ginger cake and sat back, thankful that Nick was experimenting to his taste. The girls at the next table were limbering up for a night out, pulling sparkling scraps of fabric from plastic bags and comparing prices. Nick's eyes narrowed in concentration, listening shamelessly.

'Did you see him last night?' said a tiny, dark-haired girl, almost hidden behind a cloud of constant smoke. 'He was a bastard, him. Says to me, says "I'll have that off you in no time." I says, "You fucking won't. Wait while you see me tomorrow." Look – ' and she held her dress up. Patrick, fascinated, watched her pulling the dress out of its sheath, smoothing out the straps and buckles that held the leather affair together. 'Nice,' her companion said, appreciatively. 'You'll trap off in that.'

'I fucking hope so,' said the dark girl, frowning. 'But he's a bastard, him.'

Nick caught Patrick's eye. They shared a moment of brief amusement.

'So are you going to see her again?' asked Patrick, feeling brave.

Smiling, Nick said, 'Is it any of your business?'

'No,' Patrick said, awkward, but he felt it was. 'She didn't seem like your usual type. She keeps running away, doesn't she? Why is that?'

'Why don't you get yourself a girlfriend?' Nick said, and his face quickened in anticipation of malice.

'I have,' said Patrick in spite of himself, and Nick sat back astonished.

'We'll have to have a foursome,' he said, managing to make it sound lewd and frightening. 'We'll double-date. Next week, after I've gone home to see the family and told my usual lies.'

The dark girl went to the loo, walking with challenge in the shake of her insolent bottom. Nick stood. 'Got to make a phone call,' he said.

'The phone's the other way, look – ' said Patrick, but Nick had left, in pursuit. He smiled nervously at the other girl, who was less frightening, but she rolled her eyes and blew smoke at him. He wished he were back in the safety of the flat, with colours ready to be mixed and slid into a creation, and nothing besides. Rosa had been a quiet presence, and he had liked that, but her eyes had changed when she had seen Nick and he had seen it all before. 'Don't hurt her,' he had wanted to say, but it had been impossible that he should say that. 'You seem to be right together,' he might also have said, but that would be impossible too, and besides, a downright lie. He would buy the girl from school a drink and she would ask him about Nick, and that would be that.

After Patrick went home to work on uninterrupted, Nick took himself to the pub and sat morosely alone, thinking about Rosa. He remembered that he had told her he loved her and groaned. Girls at college, who were granted naive and hopelessly unsophisticated were much less trouble. He decided that he would not see her again, although her eyes stayed with him. 'I want nothing from you,' she had said to him, after they had made love the third time, facing away from him. 'What about your family?' he had asked, intrigued. 'Yes. I have one,' she had said, and had gone to the bathroom.

He should have been glad that she was content with so little and gave nothing away, thus causing no emotional cost to him, no weeping confessions of family rows, no tearful pleas for love, but he could not help but see this as a challenge to be taken up. But no, he would not see her again. She had disappeared on him twice in front of Patrick and there were far easier conquests to be made with more public results. 'Fuck Rosa,' he declared, and the man next to him raised his glass to that.

'Terrific,' he said, and fell over.

'What's he drinking?' Nick asked the barman. As he sat slumped with the older man, he wondered briefly if he looked a bit sad. He could be anywhere else right now – why, he was something. He was the Most Shaggable Bloke at art school, one of the girls in his year had told him, blushing, after her ninth snakebite in the Union.

'I'd try you,' she had confessed, laughing.

'Why?' Nick had asked, indolent with drink. He had been stripped to the waist, in the intense heat, slender and lithe and sweating, watching stockier men being led around the bar by girlfriends, hands on their charges' pecs, proudly.

'Dunno,' said the girl, fiddling with her earring. It fell and Nick fixed it back on, gently. 'Thanks. You listen to what we say and you're so – so interested. Oh. I think I'm going to be sick.'

Of course he had taken her home, and of course he had made love to her just in time, just before she had passed out, with the candles and the rosy light and the tape by the bed, encouraging dizzy romance. And of course, in the morning he had been eager for her to vacate the space beside him. Why else did he have a single bed? When his sister Cissy had come to stay, on their parents' condition that Nick chaperone her everywhere, she had looked at the bed and sniffed.

'I,' she had said, solemn and contemptuous, 'would have a great big bollocks of a bed all to myself and roll around in it every night, just because I could.'

'And you would be all by yourself in it, because I would kill any man who touched you,' Nick had said, feeling tender and protective towards his sister, who had had a passion for priests ever since Nick's now ancient interview with the Bishop.

'You would not,' Cissy had said, stretching out her long slender brown legs. 'If you try to stop me doing what I want I will tell mum that you keep girls' knickers in a drawer and have condoms under the bed. And she will tell dad and he will come straight down here and drag you home by your hair. I'm going out now.'

'I'm coming with you,' he had said, shaken by her calm assertion. 'You'll be carried off by men with evil designs upon your virgin body.'

'Sod off,' said Cissy, snaking from the room in a dress of purple satin, impossibly short and tight. 'I haven't been a virgin for three years.' And with this, she had left the flat. Nick's mother had rung minutes afterwards, anxious to check that Cissy was being looked after.

'She's in bed,' Nick had said, hoping that this was not already true. 'I think she was worn out with all the sightseeing, yeh?' Nick's mother wanted to be sure that the flatmate was nowhere near her, and that a state of general chastity was being maintained by all.

'Keep your trousers on,' she said mysteriously.

Cissy had returned home, sly and in one piece, hiding her other life as Nick had done, and reporting well and favourably of her brother, and now a visit home was due. Nick dreaded these visits, which were undertaken as little as possible, and with secret supplies of alcohol and cigarettes and phone numbers to make it bearable. For, since leaving, he had developed a loathing for his family, for that haphazard and occasionally brutal household, for their religious hypocrisy and their stifling effect on him.

The visits were made partly to sustain the flow of cheques which made his lifestyle possible and partly because he enjoyed the women of his house fussing over him, without demanding sex and affection. Lately, however, his older brother and sworn enemy had announced his engagement, to Chantelle, and the family were curious to know why Nick, the next in line to be safely married off, apparently had no girlfriend. Nick doubted that the idea of homosexuality would enter his mother's head, but the time of reckoning had now come, and he would enjoy seeing his brother's surprise and envy, were he success-fully to transport Rosa home, after all these years. It would be controversial, and it would be a temporary sweetener, and the probing questions would cease for a while.

It never occurred to him that Rosa would not grasp, as other girls had done, at the chance of playing sweetheart for a weekend. When he tried to phone her, a man's puzzled voice told him that he knew of no one called Rosa in the building.

Other people probably live here but I never see them. There are three bedsits in this cavernous and yet claustrophobic building, and we share a tiny, vertical shower room, in total darkness, and a yellow kitchen, like an office, with a small oven on a greasy ledge and a metal sink. For hygiene. A tiny toilet, stinking faintly of ancient days and many people passing through, is on a lower level between floors. You take your own toilet paper when you visit, to ensure that nothing is shared, except the phone in the corridor. It rings at odd times, but rarely for me. In the night, I sneak under cover of darkness to the toilet, first making sure that no one else is abroad. It would be embarrassing and very possibly dangerous to do otherwise.

Nobody knows who or what I am, and likewise, nobody knows I live here, except for Nick, and that was a mistake, so when the buzzer for my room sounds I am caught in a cold sweat, unreasonably. It could be a stranger, drunk and lonely. It could be a visitor for the last tenant, who I am informed died, although not here. It could be a Jehovah's Witness bearing me the Way, the Truth and the Light. But I don't want to know, and so I shrink from the door, seeking escape and having none.

Since Lorraine, I have stayed here, barricaded in, with a hefty work of romantic fiction that I have looked at but not read, and tins of cold baked beans and Alphabetti Spaghetti. I could nip down the road for a sandwich, but that would be unnecessary, because what I want is childish, soft food, like that given to an invalid, a box of tissues and a comfort book. I will be sacked from the temp agency if I do not venture outside soon, and yet I stay here, strangely inert like a dead thing. I am shocked into myself, and so I sleep at odd times, hoping the hours and the nightmares will pass, and wake disoriented and scared, my heart pounding. I have taken up smoking heavily, and my tiny room is now blue and stale with the fug.

When the ringing of the buzzer seems hours away, I go downstairs in the fading light. No one there but a piece of paper in a scarlet envelope pushed under the door, amongst all the bailiffs' demands and solicitors' envelopes for previous tenants. Because of these, I am occasionally accosted at the door by a large man with overalls and a cigarette, accusing me of robbery, hoarding other people's furniture and equipment, and so on.

I have come almost to relish these encounters. I am asked

to prove that I am not Greenaway Estates Incorporated, or Amran Trading, or some such fictional company. When I show them my passport – unused as yet, but there is hope (and whenever I travel on the Piccadilly line I dream of stopping on until the end and arriving at Heathrow) – they look puzzled, as if to say, 'But who are you? Who is that?' and I cannot answer their unspoken question, because they are not looking for me. Nobody is, yet.

Rosa

You keep disappearing. Are you there? If you are, listen to me carefully. I like to keep hold of things that belong to me, and you have borrowed my heart. Or some of it anyway. Either bring it or yourself back as soon as you can. I've got a surprise for you . . . Will you come away with me? I want to take you somewhere.
   Call me

Nick

It is my first love letter. I fold it up carefully and slip it into my bra. I don't know why, it's the sort of thing that heroines on afternoon television do. His handwriting is large and careless and flowery. When he wakes his eyes are filled with pain, as if he has been dreaming bad things and cannot face daylight afterwards. I understand that but his dreams are his business.

I scan the doorway for faces and slip out, unnoticed in the teeming world, across the road to the phone box. I dial his number and hear his voice, laughter beneath the message, on his answerphone. It is all I want to hear. I buy cigarettes and put my key in the lock and a hand is on the door next to mine. I know this hand because it has touched my face in the night and entered me and I do not turn around because of that. There is no need.

'Come with me,' he says. 'Put some clothes in a bag and we'll go, now. I thought I'd never see you again.'

His voice has a note of panic and relief. In sudden fear I

open the door, slip inside, and inches of glass are between us but I still stand there.

He is smacking his hand flat against the glass door. 'Rosa,' I can hear. 'What's the matter? This isn't cool . . .' I nearly laugh and turn around. What does logic have to do with my life? His white face shocks me with beauty honey eyes damp mouth long fingers splayed out on the glass like sweat. He's writing something down. Wait. He's going, the note stuck to the damp door with his breath lingering on the dirty glass. 'Red car Kings Cross 6pm or else'.

The note slides down and flies away in the wind as I stand. Three years after leaving the warmth of his friendship, two nights and one declaration, unclear and not answered, and he wants to take me away from all this. I lean against the door and laugh out loud. A passer-by with a buggy sees me and stops. Her child stares at me, solemn and angry all at once. His tiny red face accuses me. 'Are you alright?' the woman is mouthing. 'Are you – '

'I'm fine,' I say, emerging now from my glass shell into the day. 'Thank you.'

The child starts to cry. I watch him. 'You looked upset,' she says, finally, as the child wails between us. Sirens pass us, shrieking, and we barely glance at them.

'No,' I say. 'It's funny. I just found out that I'm pregnant.'

She smiles, puzzlement giving way to relief. 'Nice one,' she says, rolling her eyes. 'You can have him, if you like, save all the bother of giving birth.'

'Can I hold him?' I ask her. She scoops him up gladly and hands him to me, a screaming bundle of limbs. I take him against me, in the dirty street, and he is not quieted. He yells, his face purple with fear and unfamiliarity, his tiny fingers clutching at air. I do not like him. I feel nothing. I smile and stroke his head.

'He's beautiful,' I lie.

'He's a bastard,' she says flatly, her eyes searching the buggy. 'Got a fag on you?' I hand her my new pack and she stands flexing her arms, free of her charge for a moment. 'I wish I'd never had him,' she says, and exhales.

When I go upstairs I smell baby on my collar and a sudden rush of hate for her runs through me, for her, for this reluctant mother, but I –

Had the chance.

What kind of a life would it have been, for you?

We'll see, shall we? Shall we? Shall we play a game? See if we can win. Watch me.

Whores and dealers jostled with lost tourists and backpackers and Nick watched it all, amused, as he waited, his skin crawling with the atmosphere. A wandering drunk accosted commuters and they fixed glazed eyes on the clock.

'Oy,' said a taxi driver, cruising gently alongside him. 'Word of advice, mate. Move on.'

Nick pulled out smoothly before the vice van moved up the road. He was on time, which was hard enough, but to be stood up – and at King's Cross, too, as if he were just anybody, cruising for company. He thought of all the girls he could have asked to accompany him, all easier to deal with than an unknown quantity. He circled around, caught in the slow traffic of working lives, sneering gently at other people sweating in their suits.

As he approached the station again he realised that she was not there and began forming in his mind the reasons why. She had gone mad. She was about to enter a convent. She belonged to a muscular gangster who would beat Nick's brains out if he discovered that she had spent the night with him. She . . .

'Am I late?' she said, sliding into the passenger seat quietly, and he turned to her, seeing her wild eyes and crimson satin dress. She'll have to change before we get home, he thought, and then he leaned across and kissed her swiftly, tasting her skin experimentally. 'You smell wonderful,' he said.

She sat back and he drove off, his heart racing gleefully with lust and triumph. He slotted a tape in the deck and incredibly loud music pounded out immediately. Rosa lit a cigarette and ignored it.

'So where we going?' she asked, and Nick smiled.

'Just enjoy the ride,' he said, watching her stretch her legs out in the car. Patrick's car, loaned under pressure, with many repeated promises not to use the ashtray, recline the seats back too far, litter the floor or fuck on the back seat. Nick had allowed an expression of shock onto his face at this last.

'I,' he had said primly, 'have more class.' Patrick had snorted and set about cleaning the flat ferociously as soon as Nick had banged the door behind him.

Rosa fell asleep almost as soon as they left London, wherever that was. Nick drove lazily, slower than usual, watching her occasionally. Her hair fell everywhere, strands attaching themselves to the seat, Nick's shoulder, the floor. In sleep her face softened and slackened, her mouth damp and part open, her fingers near her face, curled like a child. He stopped the car when they were halfway there, at a service station, and watched her in silence. I should drive on, he thought, we'll be late.

He touched her face: her temple, her cheek, her mouth, his fingers trembling. She grabbed his hand and held it against her, and instead of moving away, he laid his head against the seat and did not move, even when, still in sleep, she laid her head against his chest, demanding that he hold her. Tired commuters and squabbling families milled around them as they sat, silent and still, in the only quiet place in that centre of travellers' discontent.

Rosa woke, suddenly, disoriented, in a place full of strangers. Nick's head was tilted sideways, looking at her, and all around her faces peered into the car. She closed her eyes again in panic.

'Jesus, she's asleep,' said Nick's father. 'Wind down the window, Nick.'

'Leave the girl alone,' said his mother. 'What's her name?'

'You don't remember her?' Nick asked. He was beginning to feel mild worry that he had not woken her forcibly and told her where they were going. After all, she might not appreciate her old hometown any more than he did. He climbed out of the car and ducked out of the problem.

'I know who she is,' said Cissy, slowly. 'It's Rosa, isn't it? Rosa Raine. She left. She used to have terrible spots.'

'Well, she has none now,' said Nick shortly, opening Rosa's door quickly and watching his family notice her legs, splayed beneath the scarlet satin. As Rosa's eyes opened, she caught sight of the boy who used to torment her in the playground and nearly fell out. Daniel caught her first, smirking across at Nick, who stood impassive. Rosa stood upright and blinked at the O'Connor family.

'Oh God,' she said, reaching for a cigarette.

'Well, you've certainly made an impression,' said Daniel, holding out his hand to her. She stared at it with disgust and walked away from him, into the house, followed by Nick.

'She was always weird,' said Cissy, cross that her brother had brought home an attractive creature.

Entering the house, Nick became acutely aware of the religious wallpaper. A large crucifix hung in the hallway along with Mass cards in the priest's spidery handwriting. Rosa did not speak as he tried to explain.

'Now, now, no lovers' quarrels,' said Nick's father, slapping his son on the back too hard. He was a volcanic man, his temper uncertain and intrusive. When Nick was a child, he and his siblings and mother had crept around the father, placating and silent and resentful, as he seethed and thrashed at will. The house had always seemed too small for him, but now that his targets were growing stronger and leaving he seemed to have shrunk by small degrees, his eyes hard and frustrated, seeking pleasure in humiliation. Nick wondered what he would do when there was just him and his wife left, with only her and the walls filled with photographs of the departed children to lash out at.

'Where are we sleeping?' asked Nick, risking wrath.

His father ignored him as usual. 'Will you have a drink?' he asked Rosa, bearing down upon her with a wolfish smile. She sat heavily.

'Whisky,' she said, her face white and her eyes blank and terrified, and Nick was ashamed for possibly the first time in his life.

'You help your mother,' his father told him. 'You're in the spare room, your guest is in the caravan and don't you forget it.' He stared at Rosa's scarlet breasts. 'Now, madam, it's a while since we've seen you. How's your mother keeping since you both went off to that place? We've often meant to call her up and ask how she is but we don't have the number. How is she?'

In the toilet I sit examining my options. The window is tiny and rusted but if I am determined enough surely I can force it and escape. 'Hey,' I hear Nick say softly, outside the door. 'I'm sorry. I should have told you we were coming here.

Don't worry, we can go off in half an hour or so. Remember that pub you were always being thrown out of? We'll go there and stick two fingers up to them. It'll be a laugh. Okay?'

'Yeh,' I say. 'Why not?' My voice sounds fine but my overnight bag is in Nick's car. No matter. Nick's footsteps disappear and I squeeze through the window, even though my nightmares always have me in small spaces, squeezing through tunnels in the dark, not knowing what lies ahead. I hear a knock as I force my hips through the constricted space but I am gone, dry land beneath me, for now, and I flee, onto a back road where no traffic passes. I hear a dull roar in the distance; it is either Nick's father or life. I go where my ears take me.

In a dress like this it is easy to find a lift and hard to avoid a ride. But the elderly woman who stops is brave and she drives silently the few miles to my destination. 'Thank you,' I tell her, and as she stops she says, 'Where are you going at this time of night?'

'Babysitting,' I say, and her face relaxes. No madam, I am not a psychopath.

'I have grandchildren in this street,' she says thoughtfully, and I wonder.

The house is dark and I am outside. Their living room is well lit. I see many things. I see the outline of a woman, bent away from me, perhaps over a playpen. I see a man, with a pipe and a belly, rising from a shabby easy chair. As I press nearer the windows, unseen, the man takes the child in his arms and bounces it. I can tell by the way he holds it that he is uncomfortable with children. I do not blame him. A wailing starts and I shrink beside the porch, bleeding with the night into a black patch.

You wail. I do not think about Nick or why he has brought me here because he cannot know. He thinks it will be a weekend out of town for me. I hear your voice and I am here. I ring the bell.

The woman blinks with the light. 'Yes?' she says. She is scared, I realise, and I wonder if I look mad or loose or, worse, hungry. She's screwing up her eyes, trying to remember where she's seen me before, and forgetting. Good.

'I'm sorry to disturb you,' I say. 'My car's broken down, I wondered if I could use your phone. I'll pay for it, of course.'

'Oh!' she says, her face clearing. 'Yes, come in, of course.'

The living room is bright and scatty, toys on the floor, papers scattered everywhere, her husband dancing with the child on his chest, dancing frantically.

'Darling,' she says, distracted. 'This lady – oh, give him to me – ' And she takes the child from him and relieved, he smiles helplessly at me. He has a moustache and tired eyes, weak and blue, but blameless for all that. A kind face.

'Oh dear,' he says to me, spreading his hands comically. 'I'm no good with him. Perhaps he doesn't like me.'

'Nonsense,' the woman says, her eyes feverish now, like a religious convert. 'Shussh. Shhussh, now, for a visitor.' And the child quietens, his eyes huge, on me. 'We don't get many strangers here, you see,' she says. 'The phone's over there.'

The house is warm, perhaps overwarm, like a greenhouse's artificial heat. It is lush, with cushions and soft fabrics and thick curtains. A dog races into the room and the child pants loudly, a fat baby finger pointing at it. 'Yes, puppy,' says the woman. '*Pa-pee*. Say it. Say it?' But the child is transfixed by the dog and struggles to be released. Fascinated, I watch him crawl and sit in front of the puppy. He reaches out and touches its head, gently. He begins to laugh.

I dial.

'Where the fuck are you?' Nick asks. He sounds angry but I watch the child crawl towards me, the object of fresh investigation. 'Pick me up,' I tell him. I give him the address and hang up, but they are both looking at me oddly now.

'My boyfriend will be here very soon,' I tell them. I place a pound coin beside the phone and go towards the door.

'Oh, you don't have to wait outside,' the man says, bending his stocky body towards me. 'Can I offer you a drink?'

'I don't drink,' I say, lying through my teeth.

'Don't you live round here?' the woman asks, her eyes

always on the child. He is nearly at my feet. I hold my breath. 'I'm sure I've seen you around.'

'Would you like to hold him?' says the man suddenly, and he scoops the child up in a shockingly familiar manner and offers him to me.

Time stands still. Perhaps it is an hour before I stretch my arms out to receive the child, perhaps it is a second. They say an explosion can last for days in the minds of those nearby but a second in reality. Well, reality has no place in this world. His eyes are mine. His hands grasp at whatever is offered them. He rejects nothing, now, but give him sixteen years and he will choose. Will he choose well and wisely? I give him my finger and he holds on for life. I give you life. I choose life when others would have chosen otherwise.

'He likes you,' the woman says, smiling fondly. 'Aren't his eyes lovely?'

'All mothers think that,' the man says shortly, obviously having heard this before.

I stare at them both. They seem like good people. 'Where does he get his eyes from?' I ask, from cruelty and love. 'You are both brown-eyed and he is green-eyed.'

And they both look away, but not at each other, and I know I have crossed my own line. The child clings to my breast, fingers grasping at my dress, and I feel his heat seeping into me like a lover's. A horn sounds outside and I kiss his temple, white and silky and crossed with pale green veins. 'You're mine,' I whisper, like a madwoman. I can't help it. His heat distracts me as a lover never has. 'And one day you will know it.' He sighs, like an angel, and his eyelids flutter with milky sleep. Whose milk? The horn sounds again. I place him on the chair, a soft velvety seat, his mouth closing with tiredness, almost a smile. Will he remember this?

'You've sent him off,' the woman says, not entirely pleased. I can see the frustration on her face, shattered with lack of sleep and worn by unbelievable luck. I know the statistics of adoption by heart. It is no easier to be given a child than it is to relinquish one. There, I said it. To relinquish, to give back, to borrow and return, to give up. Is that enough? I leave, thanking them. At the door, the man presses the coin I left into my palm. The woman is occupied with my child.

'Take it,' he whispers and leans closer to me in the stained-glass porch. 'If you ever get lost again, you know where we are. Just don't make a habit of it, eh?' He laughs.

'Thank you,' I say, and mean it, knowing my child is safe here for now.

As we drive away in silence, all three of them stand at the window, waving nicely. I see his tiny hand held up in farewell.

Me? I would say au revoir, myself, which means *until the next time*. That is what I would say.

CHAPTER 8

Cissy was summoned to take a tray up to the guest.

'It's not fair,' said Cissy, sulky in her black halter-neck dress. 'I never get breakfast in bed. Plus she used to have terrible skin.' Her father poked his finger into the soft flesh of her cheek until he touched bone and she bit her lip with pain.

'Madam,' he said. 'What a little madam we've become.'

'I'll take it,' said Nick shortly and whisked the tray away before anyone could protest. To his surprise, his father winked, rather lewdly.

'You'll have to keep that one chained to your side,' he said, enjoying his son's hostile face.

'Go away,' said Rosa, sitting up in bed. Far from being banished to the caravan for her sins, she had been hastily installed in Cissy's bedroom after Nick had explained that she had a terrible migraine that was making her behave strangely.

'Climbing out of toilet windows?' his mother had said bemusedly. 'For a headache?' But Nick only shook his head, and touched his brow in sympathy with the invalid.

'I bloody won't go away,' he said, slamming the tray down on the pink nylon coverlet. 'What's the matter with you?' But she had already slipped out of bed and stood by the window, watching his father swat angrily at flies and assorted children.

'Your father is insane,' she said.

'Yes,' Nick said, confused. 'I suppose he is, but then so are you, climbing out of toilet windows. Do you hate it here?'

'Why didn't you tell me where we were going?' Rosa asked him, facing him. She was pale, her eyes ringed with black, and her mouth seemed tired, as if she had held one particular expression for too long. But Nick saw her long white legs beneath the sheet she had wrapped around her, and he held her against him, stifling her protests.

'Lie down,' he said, breathing the newly woken scent of her, and pushed her gently back onto the bed.

'Not now – ' she said, putting her hands on his shoulders and heaving herself away from him. 'Not here – '

'Yes, now, and yes, here,' he said, roughly. 'I'm sick of you running away all the time. What's there to be afraid of? You've no reason to run.' And he twisted her underneath him, pushing the sheet away from her, but she was too quick for him.

'You'll have to do better than that,' she said, her face a smooth mask now, but he thought he saw a flicker of hatred, something live and livid, before she shut the bathroom door. If she gets out of that window I'll kill myself, he thought, gloomy.

But she had changed again when she came downstairs to the family. Her face was painted carefully and expertly, and only her hands gave her away, snatching greedily at each other.

'Your mother always had terrible headaches, the poor soul,' said Nick's mother, pouring strong tea and sniffing the milk anxiously. 'It looks off. Never mind, offer it up. Does she still get them?' And Nick thought he saw the mask slip again, but so quickly it made his head spin. She sipped at the tea.

'Wonderful,' she said slowly. 'This is just wonderful. It must be leaves, not bags, mustn't it?' And his mother sat and told her exactly how to make the best tea. Nick left the room, surplus to requirements, and found his father in the caravan, examining the contents of Nick's suitcase minutely.

'What's this?' he said, thrusting a packet of condoms in his son's face. Nick shrugged, feeling his skin boil under the scalding gaze. I'd like to be able to look him in the eye, he thought, one day.

'Bloody art school,' said his father, purpling with rage. 'I'll stop your grant.'

'You can't,' said Nick, feeling bolder as he watched Rosa pick her way delicately across the lawn towards them. 'It's not up to you. The State gives me the grant, not you.'

'Stop your allowance, then,' he said belligerently.

Nick shook his head. 'I don't care,' he said, although he did, very much. This was an old, well-practised argument, but the condoms had been an unnecessary error. 'I'll live on the streets, if I have to,' knowing that he was not equipped for such a life, hearing the childish note in his words. 'I'll steal food from – from Marks and Spencers, or somewhere . . . You can't stop me and I'll never, ever come home again.'

His father stood swaying a little. Momentarily speechless, he made the sign of the cross. 'What in God's name did we do to deserve a son like you?' he said, his yellow teeth clicking of their own accord with frustration. 'What in God's name?'

'Maybe you just got lucky,' said Rosa, appearing behind Mr O'Connor. He turned, caught off guard. He smiled at her wolfishly.

'Ah – ' he said, thoughtfully, spreading his hands flat in the air before him, as if to excuse a moment of unusual bad temper.

But she did not smile. 'You are lucky,' she said quietly. 'You should be thankful, for that. Some people aren't lucky, you know, in the way that their children turn out to be.'

'Stomach ulcer,' said the father, hand at his belly now, wheedling a little. 'Makes me crotchety.' Nick turned his head.

'Drink,' he whispered, meeting Rosa's eyes. She smiled, and he realised then how rarely she did so.

'Yes,' she said clearly now. 'I expect he does.' And she looked straight up at the father, who could not hold her gaze, and then she held her hand out to Nick, offering him a way out. The moment hung in the space between them. Nick saw her eyes glitter with a strange light and then he saw her blink it away and swallow. I could go now, he realised, and almost cried the words out aloud. So simple and so stupidly, blindingly obvious. *I could be free.* 'Come on,' she said, her voice crisp, and he moved towards her, gathering strength.

'Now then, now then,' said his father, breathing hard, his mouth damp with anticipation. He turned his bright, hard, small eye upon her. 'He'll be all yours in a moment, madam. Be a good girl and wait outside, eh?' He was nodding. Nick held his breath in the airless void, watching Rosa coil her anger away neatly. But still she looked at him and still she looked, and it was the older man who dropped his eyes first. Then she looked at Nick, and seemed to clip her gaze with a tiny sharp nod, as if she had decided something, there in those seconds. And then she was gone, and there was only his father's ragged angry heat and him, and a tiny sigh of regret inside him, that he had not taken her hand, whatever it offered. He turned to his father wearily.

In the late afternoon they escaped the terrors of the house. Rosa asked Nick if they could drive deeper into the country. 'Why?' asked Nick, not unreasonably, since he loathed fields and was allergic to most living creatures. 'Let's go into town and laugh at everybody we used to secretly hate. Let's have one drink for every dickhead and every sad fuck we see, and then another for having got away.' But Rosa pointed out that they were beyond that now.

'We,' she said, unbraiding her hair from the religion of the house, 'can rise above that, can't we? We will drink by all means, but not in this place. It depresses me, and you wouldn't like to see that, would you?' Nick thought she smiled a little as she said this.

He agreed and drove off too fast, nearly colliding with a tractor. 'That's the trouble with the country,' he said crossly, and they stopped at a small pub, perched over a golden field filled with allergies.

Sleepy with lager and late, unexpected sun, they sat for hours, unable to stir, watching the light fade and blur. 'Am I expected to go to Mass tomorrow?' she asked him suddenly, breaking the dazed silence.

Nick hadn't thought about it. 'Of course,' he said, surprised. 'It's part of the deal. Isn't it the same when you go home?' He saw her eyelids close once, very quickly, and he was curious. 'Isn't it?' he pushed. She shook her head.

'No,' she said, so low he hardly hear her. 'It's not the same.'

'You're lucky, then,' he said, frowning. 'It's got to be done. Mass. You will come?'

She looked up at him, and the dying sun lit her words. 'Are you happy?'

'Got to go,' he said, dizzy with quick heat. 'Got to go to the bog.' But she took his wrist lightly and held fast. 'What you doing?' he asked stupidly.

'Taking your pulse,' she said, closing her eyes. He bent his head to hers and kissed her temple swiftly, turning her face to him with his free hand, wondering what she wanted. Her eyes were always somewhere else, even in love. Especially in love. His? Oh, his were kept firmly closed, in case he saw something he didn't like.

'Don't make it more difficult than it has to be,' she said, and he tried to drop his hands from hers but still she held on fast.

'What do you mean?' he asked, and he was trembling, not knowing why.

'There's enough bad things . . .' She was searching for her words, for once unsure. 'Things are there, anyway, waiting to happen. Or already in the past. You don't have to always be unhappy, do you? There's a way we could try, see. If we just close our eyes and jump anyway and not care what it's like – d'you see?'

'No,' said Nick, wanting to leave. 'It's getting cold, let's go. I'm bored anyway.'

'But I want something more,' she said, her eyes holding his, her hand hot and grasping at his, and now he was scared, just scared.

'Fine,' he said. 'Fine, we'll go somewhere else, come on.'

'You,' she said. 'I want you.'

When we come back to this silent place, this – this home, it's late and Nick puts me to bed. I ask if I can sleep in the tiny fusty caravan, although his family think my choice is odd. There are reasons. 'You don't want to be out there, all alone in the dark,' says his mother, puzzled and suspicious. Oh, I do. It's that or sit in the house unable to escape questions, and I have no desire to go wandering, not here. Where would I go in this town? I know it better than I want to.

It's not that late but Nick explains that he has been ordered to have a drink with his father in the Catholic Club. Women aren't allowed in the Club. I remember this, but the question remains, why would they want to go there anyway? The priest drinks there, florid and raddled, and so does Nick tonight while I curl up on a hard bed. A strange smell fills the place. I can't identify it, and I overturn blankets and search cupboards in the hunt for the source, and then I have it. The smell of Family. I try to open the door to banish it but it sticks and I am trapped. I open the window instead and cold air rushes in. Thankfully I sleep.

I mean to wait for Nick's return, to see him walking up the

drive, his father's arm a little too heavily on his shoulder, but after midnight I am in a room with four doors and all of them marked Exit and I know I am in a dream. I know this because when I try to open any of the doors they are all stuck, and when I cry out in confusion I can only hear sobbing, far away, and then silence.

A soft persistent sound, outside me. I know that it is late, very late. My watch glows three at me, and when I sit up confused I see a face pressed against the grimy window of the caravan, sliding down, blurred with rain. Dark-rimmed eyes and a hole where the mouth should be. 'Help me,' it says, and wind rattles the caravan now. 'Oh, help me!' I can't move, I don't know where I am, inside or outside the dream. The door opens with a scream and Nick stands on the step, swaying a little, a livid red mark on his cheek. 'Help me,' he says, weeping now, and when I go to him I can see his lashes damp like a child's. I can smell alcohol.

'Are you drunk?' I ask him. He just stares at me. 'What happened to your face?'

'Can I come in?' he asks, stumbling over the step, falling against me. I hold him, steady him. Is this what it's like, then? This sickness in the stomach, this slow tenderness? He bends his face against my neck and I am holding him, his rain soaking into me. I put my mouth to his temple, his cheek, his scarred face, trying not to hurt him, frighten him, close in on him, not yet. I can't be sure.

'I love you,' he says, on a sob, on the end of a sigh, and the words hang in the stale air. I hold my breath for as long as they hang there. He is stronger now. He holds me. Raises his head, turns mine to him, touching my mouth, my eyes, reading my face like Braille and then he says, *will you marry me? I've always loved you, surely you know that. Marry me.*

I do not speak. Something surges inside me. I reach up and touch the wound on his face. 'My father,' he says, turning away in horror. I see it cross his face fleetingly and we hear the dull roar approaching. 'Let's go, now,' Nick says, and I gladly throw my few things together, because I do not want to linger on in this place where I remember too much and think of another life.

'What will we do?' I say, because I have learnt to be practical.

'We'll just go,' Nick says, his face ragged and feverishly bright. 'Drive all night and then in the morning we'll get married. D'you see? We can do anything we want now.' And this time it is me standing on the threshold, ignoring the outstretched hand, the trust that is blindly offered in darkness because he does not know what I want. He smiles suddenly, the sun coming out after a storm, his white face beautiful with power, and I take his hand and we leave the caravan. As we reach the car, the front door opens and a stream of yellow light pours out. 'Now!' Nick says, his eyes wild and afraid. He opens the car door, struggling with the lock, and his father rages out of the house, breath white in the night air, to the car, where he stands massive and righteous. I am afraid, too.

'If you leave this house, never come back,' he says, his eyes red with anger. His wife runs up behind him, weeping.

'Don't say that, he'll go, he will go, look at him – ' she says, ravaged by her children. 'He can't see anything else but her, don't let him go – he's mine! He's my boy – ' and she tries to grab hold of him but he's into the car, locking his door, shouting at me to get in, get in NOW –

Her hands are scratching at me now, her voice a tiny stiletto-thin whip. 'You!' she says, laughing suddenly. 'What can you do for him?' And there is Cissy, standing arms folded in the doorway, hungrily enjoying the drama, her eyes on me as the family hatred begins to gather momentum.

'Maybe I love him,' I tell her, and see the terror in her eyes. 'He wants to leave. It's up to him.' And she gathers her loose mouth together in a pucker of hate and she spits at me. She spits. I am crying now. So much hatred. I wipe my face and wait for Nick to say something. He starts the car. Will we start a life together from this?

His father is panting heavily now, losing spirit. He slumps and I see his age for the first time. Does Nick, I wonder?

A lion with its claws and teeth clipped. 'Get in,' says Nick again, and I do.

As we drive away I see them standing in the pool of light, separate now, too dazed for sleep. 'You don't need to run away any more,' Nick says abruptly, as we pick up speed. 'We'll run together if we have to.' But we are already running and I don't want to run. I'm tired, so tired. Nick is too and he stops the car after an hour, as light begins to appear. We sit in silence in the tiny car, in a lay-by hidden by trees, and look at each other.

'Did you mean it?' I ask him. He laughs, exhausted.

He leans his head on me and as we drift into sleep, he says, 'They needed to be taught a lesson. I taught them, didn't I? Told him . . . told him I would marry you. Seen his face . . .' and then he is gone, with me but somewhere else, while I sit chilled, suddenly wide awake.

When Nick opened the door to the flat, it was early evening and he ushered Rosa in, expecting order and solitude. Patrick almost ran him down in his haste to prevent them opening the living-room door. 'What's going on?' he asked Patrick. 'If you're bloody painting again, forget it, we're knackered. We were in a lay-by until four hours ago and the traffic was shitty.'

Patrick ignored him. 'Just give me a few minutes,' he said, desperately. 'Go and unpack and I'll be out of your way. Please.' Rosa took charge and led Nick, delirious, into his room, where they sat motionless on the bed amid disarray.

'Who is it?' asked Phyllis, bright with anticipation. She had been there for two hours and no sign of the sexy one. Her friend had cried off with a better proposition and while she was content to be the only female in competition, it made things more difficult. 'Got any more wine?' she said, hitching up her skirt a notch.

'Look,' said Patrick, seeing his evening crumbling, 'Let's go out, I've been in all day. There's a place down the road, or we could go into town – '

'Forget it. I'm staying here,' the girl said firmly, and planted her hiking boots on the coffee table. She winked at Patrick. 'Get cooking,' she said, sniffing the air. She belched loudly and examined her nails while Patrick went obediently to the kitchen and stirred the food that he had started to prepare far too early. He heard doors open and close and he stood watching Phyllis and stirring Bolognese and wishing Nick were dead in a ditch somewhere.

'I need a drink,' Nick said at last, staring at Rosa as though she were very far away. She knew that he had glasses still, and wore them when he was alone, because she had found them tucked furtively under the bed, along with other, less endearing items, but she did not refer to that. Nor did she ask, 'Are we still going to get married?'

'Christ, Patrick, give us a – Hello, who are you? Are you Patrick's girlfriend?' Hearing this, followed by a giggle, Patrick gave up on the food and put his head in the fridge. 'Or are you his model?'

'No,' said Phyllis, content now that the light had been switched on. 'I'm Phyllis.' Nick stood faking astonishment and charm, while his bones ached and his eyes were blurry.

'My God,' he said, sinking into the sofa beside her. 'You're Phyllis, that's a strange name. I'm Nick. Phyllis – do you think you could get me a drink?' And Phyllis sat staring at him from the corner of her eye.

'Pat,' she yelled. 'Get this man a drink.' Patrick emerged hot and annoyed from the steaming kitchen.

'That smells good, Pat,' said Nick, winking. 'We're just in time, then, are we, for supper?'

'We?' asked Phyllis, arranging her thighs to their best advantage. 'Who's we?'

'Well – ' said Nick, thoughtfully. 'A friend of mine, you'll meet her in a minute, I guess.' And Patrick saw a brief flash of colour through the sliver of the open door, and then it was gone. A minute later Rosa came through the door and stood uncertainly by the sofa, waiting to be introduced. Nick glanced up at her and held out his hand, smile switched on again, but he made no effort to make space for her, or to include her.

'Phyllis,' said Nick, stroking Rosa's hand. 'This is Rosa.'

Phyllis sniffed and dredged up a smile. 'Hiya,' she said, and Rosa smiled limply. 'You're not in our year, are you?' asked Phyllis.

Rosa opened her mouth and then closed it. 'No, I'm not,' she said quietly.

'Oh,' said Phyllis. 'What course you on, then?'

Patrick took pity on her. 'Come and taste the food,' he offered.

'Mind that's all she tastes,' Nick warned, and turned back to entertain Phyllis. She was not really listening; she was studying his face and hands and deciding whether she wanted him or not. She nodded and laughed as she watched Rosa move towards the kitchen, drifting in bare feet and a scarlet satin dress. Wrinkling her nose, she wrote her off as a lightweight threat.

'It's good,' Rosa said, distractedly licking the spoon. She smiled at Patrick suddenly, and he realised how close they were in the tiny kitchen.

'Is there enough mince in it?' he asked, turning to the sink and aimlessly scrubbing dishes.

'Is she your girlfriend?' Rosa asked, touching his arm lightly. He opened his mouth without a word escaping. She leaned against the sink and dried a dish, waiting. 'We've walked right into the middle of your first date, haven't we?' He nodded, ashamed, hearing Phyllis's throaty laugh drift in from the other room.

'I didn't know you'd be coming back tonight,' he mumbled, throwing more raw mince into the pan. The stench of raw meat filled the space instantly and they both turned away, repelled.

'Ugh . . .' said Rosa. 'Are you mad for her?'

Patrick caught her eye and they both giggled, helpless for a second. He poured them both a drink and they clinked their glasses without a toast.

'I don't know her,' he said, and she smiled again, struck by his honesty.

'And you won't get to know her with us here, will you?' she said. 'Why don't we go out for a drink or something? Give you some time alone.'

Patrick was terrified by the thought of being alone with Phyllis; she seemed to invade every space, trample over it in her hiking boots, contemptuous of weaker people. 'Why don't *we* go for a drink and leave them to it?' he suggested, trying to change the mood. But Rosa's eyes seemed to close inside and she turned, stirring the mess in the pan.

'Listen,' she said. 'I don't think you understand. I'm going to marry him.'

Patrick took his spectacles off and wiped them, astonished and alarmed. 'Er . . .' he said, nervous now, 'Rosa . . .' But she was staring straight at him, her face set and beautiful and quite sure of what she was saying, he could see that, and he completely forgot what he was going to say.

'What's the matter, Patrick?' she said, quietly. 'Aren't you going to offer me your congratulations?'

Patrick took her arm. 'Listen,' he said, frightened and not knowing why. 'He's always saying things – you mustn't take it too seriously – '. He saw her face. 'I don't mean that he isn't – but you must see how he is – '

'We'll see,' she said, holding his gaze. 'Don't you believe me?'

Patrick put his glasses back on, trembling. 'Of course,' he said, avoiding her eyes. She smiled.

'I'll ask him, shall I?' she said.

'No,' said Patrick desperately. 'No – '

'Where's this food, then?' Nick asked belligerently on his way into the kitchen, opening cupboards and drawers, making a great deal of noise, not liking the atmosphere that he found. 'What's going on?'

'We're getting married, that's what,' said Rosa, quite calmly. 'Aren't we?' But it wasn't a question. Nick smiled easily and touched her cheek lightly as he hunted for more wine.

'Sure,' he said. 'Sure we are.'

'Feed her,' he said to Patrick, gesturing to the girl on the sofa. 'And fuck her. That's what she's expecting, so get on with it. Come on, gorgeous, give us that bottle – ' and he seized the wine and kissed Rosa swiftly, leaving as quickly as he had entered.

Rosa followed him slowly. 'Don't think,' she said to Patrick, 'That I won't do it. I have to do it.'

Patrick stared, absurdly reminded of the way she had sat curled up and silent while he painted, the first time he had met her. 'Are you – are you pregnant?' he managed.

Rosa smiled, her mouth a hard curve. 'No,' she said. 'Not yet.'

After the meal we leave Patrick and the girl with the hard, careless face alone to their fate, because that's what it feels like by then. I see Nick's hand on the girl's blunt squat thigh, being friendly, and her small hard eyes sizing him up. He's out of control. He needs someone to make him see how short our lives are and that we can choose what we regret. He won't regret marrying me. I'll see to that, if trying will be enough.

'I'm going to bed,' he says to me, when we are safe behind the door of his small room. 'You can come if you like.' I take this to be an invitation and lie beside him, my hand fitting in the curve between waist and hip, smoothing the plane of taut white skin, my body slotting behind his precisely. But his hand stills mine and he yawns. 'No,' he says, cutting a path between us, and I rise from the bed and watch the moon rise.

'Are we really to be married?' I ask him, and he moans. 'Are we?' I sit beside him, persistent.

'Mmm,' he says, sleep slurring his words.

'We fit together,' I tell him. 'There are a hundred reasons and more why we should marry. Besides,' I add, as a postscript, 'I love you.' He starts in his sleep and kicks me.

I leave, listening covertly but with the best of motives at Patrick's bedroom door; strangely I smell Vic rub and can hear only shuffling and furtive creaks, no moans of ecstatic pleasure or protestations of undying love. However, it is a first date, I remind myself and him silently, and leave. On my way, I see Phyllis's push-up bra abandoned on the floor and fight briefly with a desire to shove it down the toilet, letting it wind its charms around the U-bend instead of Nick, hoping that she will be gone or satisfied by the time he wakes. No matter, he is mine now.

Back at my room, the darkness is everywhere. I find a letter, my second. My temping agency say that they will have no option but to erase me from their books if I do not recover soon and make contact. Well, that's nice. We will be sorry to lose you, they add, and the controller has added, 'Take care! Absolutely sincerely, Adelaide.'

Erase me, rub me out, what do I care? There are always ways of making money, of living, even if those ways may be unpleasant. Love has led me astray, temporarily, and my world has shifted. In time to come, you won't know or care how I made the money to pay the rent, will you? Nobody will tell you about this dark room and the turning of the handle in the night. I am glad for that. Things will improve by then, just you see. Wait and see.

On the train I buy a coffee and some cigarettes and see a couple having sex in an otherwise empty coach. I choose to sit elsewhere. The last of my money is gone, for now, but I don't care. We are thirty minutes from my destination. We pass through dead and dying countryside. A redundant pit lies abandoned by the tracks as we slow down, its outline frozen forever in the minds of passengers. Or perhaps they don't see it, engrossed as they are in having sex or eating their British Rail sandwiches. Perhaps they marvel at this quaint relic, point it out to their bored restless children who would like to play on it, dismissing it from their minds as they speed past, onto the next view. Fields get flatter.

My stomach fires up and my hands sweat cold. Twenty minutes. I don't know what I'm doing and yet I do it, like a mechanical doll, smiling at the ticket collector, the old lady with white gloves who sits opposite me, neatly. Her face tells a story but I don't want to hear it, not now. Isn't that what we all say? Not now. Some other time, but I'm sure you had a fascinating life. Just not now. She catches my eye and we both look away, just in time for politeness.

'Lovely day,' she says, as you do, and I agree, startled, because until now I have not noticed. But she's right. The sun is coming out and the fields are filled with light, early light that they push back at us. A train passes us crammed with unhappy commuters and this train is nearly empty. Nobody wants to come here, you see. Not even me, but they all want to leave.

'Going far?' the old lady says, shedding her gloves, and I see her hands. They are entirely covered with burn scars, a livid mass of raw skin. I pull my eyes away from shame.

'Yes,' I say. 'I'm going home.'

Ten minutes. But when I get off the train I don't have to go anywhere, don't have to get on the bus that'll be waiting. I've done this often enough, in the last few years, oh you wouldn't believe how much of my pitiful salary has been spent on these futile journeys. Getting off at stations all along the way, then crossing the bridge and getting back on the next London train, willing it to speed all the way. I've never got as far as this before.

I've never had anything to take with me, before.

On the bus I watch all the passengers, scanning them for signs of familiarity. None. There's no reason why they should recognise me, though, since I am completely different. I wear my hair long and dark and coloured lenses have turned my eyes from green to blue. My body has changed in shape; there are no curves left, only angles and lines, and my deportment is that of an unobtrusive woman, not a plump scared girl. There is nothing about me which would jog the memory of anyone who knew me well. If I had my way I would wear discreetly labelled classics, but my present fortune demands grey and caramel, blending me into the background. The bus slides into the garage and we are here. Home.

And on the long walk down the hill, the abattoir still sends its great spurts of poison into the air. I hold my breath from memory. The houses still lie squat and red against the flat parched earth. Another planet. It's not as though I expected anything to change but my thighs are damp with sweat and my body chafes and perspires, turning the cheap smart outfit stained and crumpled. The roads lead away to the sky, to the house, but nobody is here, nobody intercepts me on my journey. Nobody to say, 'Alright, ent seen you around for a while. How are you? What you bin up to?' People pass me without a glance because I am anonymous, a beige and grey person with sunglasses and a slightly hesitant walk. That's all.

At the door, I lift the knocker before I remember that I still have my key. But I don't use it. I knock on the door, once, twice, three times. Gently. There is no answer. You can't be out, because you never are, not at this time of day. Fear begins to creep into my throat. A face appears over the fence, from next door, a stranger's face. 'Who are you looking for, love?' she asks, her forehead corrugated in the sun. She carries a child. My mouth is dry. She puts the child down and he wails on and on and on on on while she stands there.

'Does he usually cry like that?' I say. I think of you.

'Yuh,' she says, sniffing. 'He's teething, that's all. Stop soon, he will.' She considers me. 'Mrs Raine?' she asks. 'That who you looking for? Ah, she's gone,' she says, 'Not here any more.'

I nod, over and over, like a toy dog. 'Do you have an address?' I ask her. The child is still screaming, his face livid.

'NO!' she shouts, over his increasing noise. 'Oi!' She slaps him and, strangely, he subsides into quiet misery. I can't wait any longer.

'Where's she gone?' I ask. 'You must know – have some idea – '

'Sorry, love,' she says, taking down her washing. 'She put the house on the market and left, never said anything to me. Just goodbye and she hoped I got nice neighbours. That's all.' She scoops up the nightmare and carries his wails inside.

Covering the door with my body, I turn the key in the lock. Inside the hall the air is musty and cold, despite the heat outside. I go into the living room and stop dead, my flesh crawling. Nobody lives here but the room is as it always was: neatly arranged furniture and a newspaper on the dining table. It is six months old. For some reason this upsets me, that nobody has thought to hide this away, no estate agent, no seller or buyer. In some way I am sure that there will be a forwarding address, a note, something –

As I go towards the kitchen, I sniff the air. A different smell here. It can't be, but it is: a delicious, warm baking smell, as if someone is in there, pulling out a tray of cakes, ready for the child home from school. I am paralysed where I stand. Coming home to see golden creations on the table awaiting inspection: fairy cakes for the Brownies, a Victoria sponge cake hot and sweating, leading me by the nose back to another life. I am sweating cold and I know it can't be but I move towards the kitchen in a dream, inhaling the past.

I can't imagine where it can come from until I see the wasp slowly cooking on the light bulb where it has landed, helpless and fried.

She has left the light on.

I run from the house, shaking and shaking until I reach the stream. I am going the wrong way, towards the land, not towards the town. I turn back, past the empty shell of the house. I run up the hill, breathless and drawing in lungfuls of air, stinking dead air, who cares, until I reach the estate agency and I stop outside to smooth myself down.

'There's a couple for sale in that road,' the agent says, pulling out a sheaf of details. There it is, a picture of our house.

'This one,' I say. Vacant on possession. 'Is this – does this mean that the owner is gone already?' The agent hides a yawn. It is lunchtime nearly and he is thinking about the pasty he will buy, the pint he will hurriedly throw back. I know this town.

'There's no damp,' he assures me. 'The owner has looked after it well.'

'Owner,' I say. 'The owner. Where is – the owner now?'

'Would you like to view the property?' he says wearily. It is one o'clock.

'Look,' I say, desperate for information. 'I'm a cash buyer. I just want to know the history. Humour me.'

He sighs. I'm losing him. Where are you? 'Mrs Raine – '

'Mrs Raine,' I repeat stupidly.

'Mrs Raine,' he repeats, as if I am deaf and stupid, 'moved out of the property several months ago, for personal reasons. She has instructed us to – '

'Yes. But where is she?'

'I'm afraid I can't tell you anything more than that,' he says, astonished.

'But you must know where she is,' I say. I must be shouting because all the people in the office are looking at me. I lower my voice. 'I just want to get in touch with her to discuss the house,' I whisper. 'Personally.' He clearly wants me out of here, now, and I don't blame him. I want me out of here now too.

He slams a piece of paper in front of me. 'She's moved right out of the area,' he says, finished with my fraud now, and I stare at the words.

Mrs Raine
c/o 21 Embassy House
Avenue Walk
Radley Bay

I don't think about the wasp any more, nor about the kitchen light. All I can think about is that you are gone.

CHAPTER 9

Patrick enjoyed the mornings when nobody else seemed to be alive. He had been up since seven and had gone out for the papers and milk, but he had seen no sign of Nick for a day or so. He made coffee and stood in front of his painting. 'Oh dear,' he said out loud. 'Why don't you love me?' It isn't working, he thought, and looked at it carefully, touching up the eyelashes . . .

The assignment was a portrait, in any style, using oils, and he was trying to paint Phyllis from memory, rather than embarrass himself by asking her to pose. A week on from their first date he was still terrified of her judgments. The heretic thought that she was better matched to Nick had crossed his mind, but that was as far as he had got.

He heard a giggle, a small girlish noise, and then the click of the door, and he busied himself with the canvas. Nick came through to the kitchen and headed for the fridge. Patrick tried to radiate silent disapproval. 'How you doing?' said Nick, and when Patrick turned around he was standing, drinking orange juice thirstily from the carton, his white throat gleaming with fine sweat. 'Has she called?' he asked.

'Of course she has,' said Patrick, wishing she hadn't. 'I don't like lying to her, Nick.'

'Then don't,' Nick said sharply, his face hardening. 'Nobody asked you to, did they? I didn't. Did I ask you to lie for me?' He was close up now. Patrick could see the pores in his skin and the circles round his eyes.

'No,' he said, softly. 'You didn't ask me, but occasionally I do things because I think I should. See?'

Nick considered this. He backed off and smiled a hard, tight smile, his mouth a line of dissatisfaction. 'She's the Disappearing Woman, isn't she? Someone should sell her to a circus.'

'Will you marry her?' Patrick asked, his mouth dry. Nick laughed, a real laugh this time, and flung his arms around Patrick suddenly, squeezing him. 'Want to be best man?' he murmured. 'Want to watch my life a little longer?' And his hands moved down Patrick's body, lovingly, for the moment.

'Nick,' said a voice, plaintively, from elsewhere. Patrick coughed in the heavy silence. He was speechless and his skin cold with disgust, for the first time since he had known Nick. He pushed the other boy away. 'What do I tell her, then?' he asked. But when he turned around Nick had gone.

Patrick?

Is that you, where are you, shall I call you back?

No, no. Listen. It's – I'm in a church. Well, just outside. It's difficult. Don't tell Nick. That I'm in a church, I mean.

I didn't know you went to –

No, nor did I. It's not Mass. It's something else, just a visit. A sort of returning. D'you see?

No, not really . . . You're not in London?

No. No, I'm hours away, Patrick. I know he's not there, or if he is –

– out. Research.

Thank you. Thank you. Do you ever play games, Patrick?

What?

Do you believe in games of chance? I do. I just wondered. Sometimes I think –

Yes?

We ignore things we don't want to see, don't we?

I don't know. I can't –

Like going through red lights in the middle of the night.

But why would –

You think no one'll ever catch up with you. But they always do, no matter how you try to do it right.

I played poker once.
When?
With Nick, here.
Who won?
Who do you think?
Stupid of me. I'm sorry. Do you love him, Patrick?
Nick? I suppose so. Sort of.
Then don't tell him that I rang. Will you do that?
Are you alright, Rosa?

But she had rung off by then, and he wondered why she had spoken to him at such length, since she must have plenty of friends. Patrick knew that anyone like her, like Nick, couldn't be lonely, since he considered himself beyond hope, despite the presence of Phyllis. 'Do not think,' he said to the fridge, 'that I am fooling myself.' He went back to the canvas, where her face sat, more successful since he had decided that she should be turned away from him slightly, in repose. He had ten days to complete it, technical work and all. Tongue between his teeth, he went back to the eyelashes.

That evening he met Phyllis in the Union bar. She sat on a stool, her thighs brazen and stocky in cycling shorts and boots. 'I know my legs are crap,' she had said to him, as she had walked naked to the bathroom in full light. 'I just don't give a shit.' He was the one walking towards her candid gaze, stripped down by her bulbous eyes.

'What shall I get?' he asked, as he neared her.

'God, but you're romantic,' said Phyllis, examining his scruffy jeans and trainers. She had never meant to end up with this half of the partnership, but she had, and there it was. She took what came to her as her right. 'Half of lager,' she added.

'What happened to that girl?' she asked, hours later, as they sat warmly sweating over their fourth drink. She was onto pints now, with a student chequebook. The Union accepted them wearily, knowing they were worth nothing. 'Rosa. What happened to her?'

'Why?' asked Patrick, emboldened by drink.

Phyllis shrugged. 'Seemed a bit – weird. Not his type, anyway, is she?'

'Shut up,' said Patrick, suddenly angry, knowing he should not have said a word. 'Don't talk about her like that.'

'Just making conversation,' said Phyllis, intrigued by his temper. 'Just . . .'

'You don't need to pass the time,' said Patrick. The lights were flashing on and off in the bar and in his head. 'Let's go home.'

'Cool,' Phyllis said. 'I've got some handcuffs in my bag. Let's go.'

It is cool and dark where I am, like death. The dead surround me, in their slipping tombs and inscriptions from centuries ago. The flowers wilt because she no longer tends them and standards have slipped. Even I, the heretic, can tell that at a glance. An hour ago the priest approached me. He is young and slender. He is a replacement. 'Can I do anything for you?' he asks. I nearly laugh. Yes, Father, you can tell me why I'm here. You can tell me where they've all gone. His face is puzzled.

'You can give me confession,' I say, and I can't believe such bitterly wrong words have slipped from my hidden mind.

'When do I speak?' I ask him, confused. He stops.

'Whenever you want,' he assures me. He is gentle and puzzled and he is a priest.

'It's nearly three years since my last confession,' I say. I wait for the sharp intake of disapproval. I know priests alright. When none comes, I say, 'Did you know a Mrs Raine?'

There is a silence then. A sigh and, 'All confessions are sacred and confidential,' he says.

'I don't want to know what she said,' I say, my voice harsh now, in this place which echoes with disappointment. 'Is she alright?'

'Who are you?' he says, and his voice is scared . Everything is wrong, and I know that he is very young and still learning. Thank God.

'I don't know,' I say, for once speaking the truth. 'You tell me, Father.'

In the Presbytery he offers me a brandy, which shocks me. He smiles shyly. 'You need it,' he says, from very far away. Oh I drink it down and sit, watching him, examining this place, this secret place. A priest's home. An ancient, disapproving housekeeper will emerge soon to tut at my brandy glass and whisper to this priest, who tells me he is called Richard. He came here from Essex because the old priest died.

'From drink?' I ask, and his expression shames me.

'From age,' he says, firmly, and as I look away he winks.

'Is she alright?' I ask. I have to ask although I have no right and his hands fold themselves in the black cloth.

'I think so,' he says, his eyebrows knitting. He pours more brandy, for me and for himself now, and I tense. 'Most of the parishioners here treat me like a hairdresser,' he says. 'They tell me their problems. The day-to-day ones, not the really bad ones. Then they sigh and leave, as if they've purged something.'

'Have they?' I ask. If it takes time it takes time. I can wait. What, after all, do I have to go back to? I've been here nearly three days, in the church, in the woods, by the man-made lake, hiding. Nothing has led me further than this.

He smiles, almost like Nick, but sadly. Nick would never smile sadly, but then he is without the burden of God. 'They'd probably do better getting a shampoo and blow-dry,' he says.

'Why don't you tell me all about it?' he asks, drawing the curtains from the street. A thoughtful man. His hands are ugly, blunt and squat, but his face is honest. How else should a priest's face be? I've known priests with faces like weasels, faces like cat's arses, face that have had wood chopped on them, but this face before me now nearly disarms me. He is offering luxury of a kind and I have forsworn that, for now.

'Why don't you tell *me*?' I suggest. 'And then I'll be gone.'

'I only spoke to her once,' he says, watching my face. 'Not been here long, but I saw her with the flowers, one day. Weeping over them.'

He turns his face away now, to give me privacy. I've no time for that. The words leap out of me like fish. 'Did you ask her why?'

He frowns. 'Of course,' he says, amazed. 'She was looking for a place of safety. She came in here to feel what she could not feel at her home, and I – ' He moves away, straightening objects. There are not many. What, after all, would he collect, apart from other people's sins? 'I could not help her,' he says quietly.

'Why not?' The bitter taste at the back of my mouth slides against my tongue. 'It's your job, isn't it, to help people in distress?' His hands twist. I see small details. It's all I see. 'Is she alright?' I shriek. I can't help it.

'She was leaving, for a new life, to make a new start. That's what she said. There's really nothing more I can tell you. No – ' He fends me off. 'I don't know where, or with who, or anything more. I'm sorry.'

I absorb this in silence. There's something I've forgotten isn't there? 'But why was she weeping?' I ask.

He turns. 'Oh – ' he says, relief in his face. 'She was happy,' he says, finally. 'She said that she was happy at last.'

'You've passed two and failed three,' Nick's personal tutor said. Her eyelids were purple with fatigue and Nick stared at her mouth, seeing her age for the first time. What was it like, he wondered, watching students year after year and wishing you could have your chance again? But he only wondered briefly.

'Yeh yeh,' he said, impatient to get to the point. 'Not a problem, I'll re-sit in October.' He stood up, ready to leave the small fusty room.

'I'm afraid it's not as simple as that,' said Ani. 'You've failed to deliver assignments – important ones. What's happening to you, Nick?'

He shrugged, feeling sick. The night before, and the night before that, and if he didn't have a drink soon he knew he would start to feel very bad.

'My parents . . . girlfriend . . .'

Ani sighed. 'Why don't you see the college counsellor?'

Nick sucked his cheeks in and thought fuck that but nodded and agreed that he should do just that and could he have an extra week and then he'd deliver all the late projects and *where the fuck was Rosa these days anyway*?

'Okay, ten days, that's more likely, yes? But you have to understand

– wait, wait, come back – that if you don't get yourself sorted out we will have to let you go.'

'No', said Patrick, furious. 'No way. Do it yourself.'

'Come on,' Nick said, smiling desperately. 'All I'm saying . . .'

Patrick turned back, rather pointedly, to the paintings stacked up against the wall ready for college. 'See these?' he asked. 'That's what I've spent the last year and a half doing.'

'But you've not submitted them yet,' Nick said thoughtfully.

'No,' Patrick admitted. 'I'm not there yet. But I've done the work.'

Nick flicked through them. Portraits of Phyllis, a landscape he didn't recognise, line drawings. Other stuff, but he didn't bother with that. 'So? That's your career. End up as a graphic designer for Tesco. What about me?' He didn't see Patrick's face because he was examining the last drawing. 'Perspective's out here,' he pointed out.

'Thank you,' said Patrick. He was smiling. 'That's you,' he said. 'That sketch. It went wrong because you couldn't sit still. You're a better artist than me, Nick, you know it, but you're – '

'Lazy.'

'Scared.' They stared at each other.

'Sister, you're blushing,' Nick said, making it worse.

'You're going to fail, Nick,' Patrick said, and he was not smiling now. 'What else is there? You can't go back home, you're not – '

'Look, relax, I'm living,' Nick said, easy now, his face bland and smooth, a mask of certainty, his heart racing. 'Meeting Rosa tonight. There, that shut you up, didn't it?'

Patrick was alarmed. 'But I'm seeing Phyllis tonight,' he wailed, seeing a repeat performance of the double-date fiasco.

'I'm meeting her somewhere,' Nick said. 'Somewhere where she can't make a scene, hopefully.'

Patrick wanted to ask Nick about Phyllis, about why she sighed when he entered her, why he could not look at her face after he had loved her. In the morning he longed for her to tell him something real but she bounced out of bed like a Christian. 'Get us a bacon buttie,' she had said, pulling her knickers on, and he turned his face away and said nothing.

'Rosa's back then? So, is it really serious?'

Nick smiled and shut the door. Back from where, he wondered. His mother had phoned the night before, trying to catch him in. No words had been exchanged since the showdown and he preferred it that way. 'Is he still getting married?' she had asked Patrick piteously and he had stammered that he didn't know, he would tell Nick to call her, but he was working really hard and . . . Why do you think I wanted a flatmate like you, Nick thought ferociously. If I were like you neither of us would really be alive. Would we? He lay down on his prison-hard bed and imagined his next painting.

At school Linda Blair had been the most outrageous teacher. Art was a sin then and all the nervous rebels had signed up for it accordingly. 'Listen to the music and just let yourselves go,' Linda had growled, her leather trousers creaking close in the darkness. Black curtains at the windows and strange sounds coming from nowhere, the smelly darkness and the rustle of the wind at the artroom door and

Paint said Linda, turning the lights on.

But Nick had already started.

And now he couldn't pick up a brush without hearing *You'll never make it. It's been a waste of money for us.*

His father.

Look at Joe, twelve grand a year and a fiancée. Is it a phase?

His mother.

You're going to fail, Nick.

We will have to let you go.

He picked up his jacket and slammed the door. Ten days. I can still do it.

'Three paintings?' said Rosa, frowning. 'That doesn't sound possible.' She looked unusually rough, Nick thought, uneasy. Her black hair was matted to her forehead and her eyes had not yet met his. He touched her cheek. Her skin was hot and clammy and he moved his hand carelessly, away from her. 'Why don't you just get on with it?' He shook his head.

'I have to be in the mood,' he said, looking around the bar. Her choice, because he had been an hour and a half late. When he turned up, she was still standing against the church pillars, a study in frozen boredom. 'I thought you'd have gone long ago,' he said, without apologising.

'I had nowhere else to go,' she said simply, her eyes empty, and it chilled him. *I don't want to hear that, he thought, tell me something else. Make something up* . . . Now they sat in an overheated bar with pink lighting and sofas, where her thighs sank into his without choice.

'Where've you been?' he asked, without thinking. 'I've tried to call you.'

'No you haven't,' she said, smiling at him in a mirror. He watched them reflected.

'No. I haven't. Do we look right together?' he asked, considering them.

'I don't know,' she said, looking directly at him now. 'Do we?'

'Yeh,' said Nick. 'We look alright.' A blonde girl with a nose ring hovered in the background. He wondered briefly . . .

'Do you want to know where I've been?' she was saying now, her voice flat and white like a noise in his head.

No, he thought, I want the neon lights to come back on and the rain in our eyes and you a mystery to me still. 'Of course,' Nick said, stealing some of her drink. 'I want to know everything about you, don't I?'

'Help me, then,' Rosa said. Her voice scared him.

'You want another drink, is that it?' he said, ignoring her hand reaching for his.

'Nick,' said the blonde. 'I thought you drank vodka?'

Later, Nick wished that he had done what he originally intended to and stood her up entirely. Rosa had not looked at the girl for a second and he felt her gaze on the side of his face like heat.

'Go away,' said Rosa. 'We are talking.'

'Shouldn't that be, I am talking?' said Nick. The blonde giggled and sat on Nick's arm of the sofa.

'I am talking too,' she said.

'Is that a film?' Nick asked her, and she put her hand on his arm and whispered to him, 'Is she your girlfriend?'

'No,' said Rosa. 'I'm his wife.'

When he laughs in disbelief I know I have lost him, for then. I am drunk with fear and beer and I relieve the girl with the nose ring of her red wine and throw it at her and run, run, run before the barman catches me. I saw somebody do it in a film and there will be no romance while she is gasping like a dead pike and Nick stares and strangers laugh in horrified ways and hide their bad teeth behind hands clogged with London dirt. Napkins will be offered by Australian barmaids in the smelly toilets and nobody will understand but Nick.

There will be no romance but she is a symptom of a disease and tonight there will be no emergencies. Do you understand? When you read me in years to come you will see what I tried to do. Does that imply that I believe I will fail?

No. No, because –

Where are you?

If I listen hard enough and the wind is moving in the right direction I can hear you crying. Is that a sin and, if so, whose sin? Mine?

Where am I?

Listen. Once upon a time there was a boy who sailed the seven seas. No, he did. He saw the sunsets and the mountains and the hills and he thought: I would like to live in a place where the grass is green and the sun is red and the sea is blue all day long and in the night I can swim with the fish and they will guide me. And back home a girl waited for him, and she had hair red as fire and eyes green as jealousy and a heart that beat like a pump and she thought: I would like to live in a place where there is no sin.

And so it came to pass that he returned home and on dry land he took the girl into his arms and said, come with me to a place where the grass is green and the sun is red and the sea blue all day long. The girl's eyes grew dull and her heart grew heavy with fear, because yes, she was frightened, and she said to him, I cannot. And he was puzzled. Who would not want to live in such a place? But she smiled and swallowed her tears and sent him on his way, waving him farewell as his ship sailed again, and as the ship sailed out of sight, towards that red sunset, she touched her stomach and was glad that each wave took him further away.

And whenever the tide came in, she wondered where his ship had docked and if he noticed the colour of the sun or remembered the fierceness of her eyes or wondered why she had cried when she said no, you must go.

If, sometimes, you see a woman waving out to sea, on a calm day when there are no boats that you can see, why, think of that sunset, in a different country, a steamy heat and a wild sky elsewhere and do not laugh at her. If you see her cry as she walks along the shore, picking at shells, then see her flat stomach and her stiff walk and hurry home, home safe to the lighted windows, yellow with safety and love. And if she disappears in the seconds that you turn away to draw breath from your running, your frantic running, be glad.

Do you know these stories? I am trying to tell you something that I cannot tell you in another way. We squander life sometimes because we do not know and I have spared yours but you will not see that, will you?

Where was I? A bride without a groom. Well. That is no matter. I will not say that I want you because I have no rights, like a prisoner, but you are still mine.

All of you.

Now. Back at the flat Patrick opens the door and his face says

o

he's not here but, uh, I do believe he was going to –

'Yes!' I say, brightly. It is not too late for a social call, I think. 'I left Nick in the bar. He met a friend.'

I would say, if asked by a lady with a clipboard and a survey, that I go to great lengths to avoid danger. I step over drunks in the street carefully and I cross the road when large numbers of men are singing rude songs after a match, my eyes down and my hair caught back inside my collar. My windows have strong locks upon them, oh yes, and my door is fastened with many chains and bolts. What could frighten me now, you might ask? So why am I shaking?

'Madness,' Patrick is saying, from far away. 'Sheer madness.'

'I agree,' I say, snapping back into now. 'Plans have to be made, after all. People alerted. Dates made.'

Patrick is uncorking wine. Thwack. 'I hope he can make it,' he says, lines appearing on his forehead. I laugh.

'Me too!' I say. The reluctant groom at his reception. The wine drips slowly.

'Or he'll be thrown off the course, definitely,' he continues.

I continue to smile. My face aches with rarely used expressions. 'He'll be home soon, I expect,' Patrick says, but red wine is difficult to get out so I wouldn't bank on it.

His paintings are stacked up as though they are waiting for something. If they were mine I would display them somehow, proud and fierce. I touch them. 'They're beautiful,' I say. 'Oh, here's your girlfriend. Are you still seeing her?'

Patrick looks embarrassed. So do I. He clears his throat and I take off my shoes because I have beautiful feet. It's something, isn't it? 'Yes . . .' he says.

'Are you sure?' I ask him, because he looks confused.

'Shall I put some music on?' he says, and I ask him if I should go, is it difficult, and he practically sinks to his knees, a supplicant on Saturday night. 'No,' he assures me, fiddling with tapes, dropping them. 'I don't have anything trendy, though, nothing that you'd probably – '

He pushes the right button eventually and some music shrieks out that he tells me is by Dvořák, something that he wrote when his young daughter died. 'If you don't like it . . .' he says, biting his lip. 'I'm not very trendy.' He laughs. There is sweat on his upper lip. I lie back because when Nick is not here I feel comfortable like this. We listen in silence to the beautiful music that I don't understand, that makes me want to cry.

'I don't think I'm very trendy either,' I say, to lift his mood. He is sitting with his knees up around his ears. If he were mine I would touch him lightly so as not to frighten him but all the same the music is something.

At two o'clock we have barely touched the bottle and barely spoken and I am content, for now. Increasingly I think of you in secret in silence inside me and this is good, do you see? Patrick the best man and me.

At three o'clock I know he is not coming home. I have

known for hours, for days. Patrick's hands move in tiny detail over a huge pad of paper as I languish here, unable to move. 'Don't move,' he says every now and again, when I shift my legs or arms in a kind of sensual adjustment. 'O don't move,' and so I lie. It is embarrassing, being drawn, but only if you think about it. It's the longest someone has watched me for a while anyhow. I would tell you that I had become invisible but you might think that all I thought about was myself.

Four o'clock. Tiredness has passed us by now and Patrick has shyly put glasses on. 'Nick wears them as well,' I say, for the sake of it, and his pencil wobbles. He stares.

'He does not,' he says, astonished. 'He can't.'

'Well, he does,' I tell him, annoyed. 'Since he was little. A little monkey with glasses.' My deep and prior knowledge gives me some lead to secure me to the ground. I know him.

'I'm sure you're right,' Patrick says quickly. He is very nice about everything. 'Just never seen them.' He looks worried about this.

'Probably,' I say, 'he never needed to with you. Probably he always wanted to see things the way they naturally were.' Patrick's face clears a little and he keeps drawing. Me. I'm a model, now. Isn't that a thing? It's a bit like being in Confession but better because you actually want to say the things you never should. Nobody drags them out of you.

'I said I was his wife,' I tell Patrick. Don't ask me why. He listens without pretending to, and if he doesn't hear it's not because he doesn't want to, it's because he's absorbed in your left eyelash or something. It's soothing.

'Are you?' he says, without looking up. Maybe he will make me look like a side of bacon or a black square or something. I don't mind. I will show you and you will know that somebody wanted to draw me. Once.

'No,' I say. 'But since I will be and soon is it really a lie?'

Patrick thinks without stopping. I can feel it because it's what I do but different. 'I think it's an untruth,' he says, feeling the way with his words. 'Do you really think that he will – '

I have to stop him there. 'Is the drawing good? Is it

working?' I ask him, and he has to go along with me. 'Can I say anything to you or are you drawing my mouth right now this second?' He shakes his head.

'Your – probably your neck, or – '

'Are you in love?' I ask him, changing my mind at the last second about what I say. I'm almost enjoying this. He's not. His fingers tremble on his 4H and I see him swallow.

'Can we – it's – can we not . . .?' I take pity on him with silence. So thick I can taste it like iron. I am sick of silence and words clog up in my head like traffic. We are both moored in this loneliness, I think, but, aching, I stay where I am. When a room is full of bright goods and souvenirs it is always full but here tonight this room echoes metallic as though we are leaving soon. My words clang.

'I have a child,' I say, and tiredness hits me as I say it. And now Patrick puts his pencil down and rubs his eyes. He does not say a word but he sits just across from me and to my shame I start to

Cry. I don't mean to. *I'm sorry.*

So sorry and 'Where?' says Patrick, his face unchanged.

'Where?' he asks. I look at him now. His face is calm and tired and honest and not beautiful. His eyes are weak from the light and can meet mine. And even though he may not want to hear he will listen to me now.

And so I tell him.

Nick stood outside the door and he heard the words, heard the sobbing and put his hand on the door handle. I should go in now, he thought, and now, or now, but from what he could hear, there was nothing that he could say and he knew that if he were to enter now Rosa would become someone else within seconds. A child, he thought, and his body was bent over for a swift moment. He took his hand from over the mouth of the blonde and ushered her back out of the front door.

'What's going on?' she asked, after she got her breath back.

'Your place,' said Nick, down the stairs already, away from chaos.

'You're joking – ' she said, as they stood in the street, dismal and badly lit, waiting for a cab.

'No,' said Nick grimly, walking backwards, wanting to get far away. He hoped the blonde lived across the river, or further. He would pay, it didn't matter. He stared into the distance. On a really clear day you could see the City, the river even, on this straight road. Tonight, yellow lights glinted miles away.

'See you,' said the blonde, and before Nick could move she had jumped into the only cab and disappeared. He stood still, not knowing what to do. Home was only a few yards away, and his bed, narrow and uncomfortable and shared, of necessity, tonight, with a girl whose mystery could be shared with Patrick but not him. And I would have married her, he thought, almost believing it himself, as he walked on. A cab stopped and he got in. 'Euston station,' he said, and sat back. It never occurred to him until he got to the station that he had been spared.

'Jesus,' his father said. 'Where the hell are you? It's eight in the morning.'

'Yeh,' said Nick, shivering at the station. 'Will you pick us up, dad?'

'Are you single still?' said his father.

'Yeh,' said Nick with bitter emphasis, but all the same he knew that there would be breakfast when he returned, and a bed, and his mother fussing over his white brow, and sweaty clothes whisked away to the wonderful machine that made everything clean again. Nick lit a cigarette gloomily while he waited, knowing his father would speed gleefully, triumphantly to meet him and then spend the journey berating him.

In the morning, penance done in the temporary form, he borrowed the small car from his mother after some wheedling and drove to the small city nearby. He hated the relentless push moving past the car, clutching boyfriend or girlfriend or whining child and bags and unhappiness. He parked the car, found a phone and called his own London number. There was no answer. He smiled and retraced his steps to a large hotel on the very outskirts of the city, nearly in his home town, with a dull concrete façade. He went inside. I am going insane, he thought, as the daylight faded to a false, cushioned night. His feet sank into the soft, hideous carpet and small, obvious lights everywhere replaced the greying sun. 'Canihelpyow?' said the receptionist, inevitably, and Nick smiled, helplessly.

'Yes,' he said. 'I hope you can, I'm in need of some help,' and her cold blue face lifted to his in question.

Patrick knew that Nick had come back at the wrong time and prayed that he wouldn't come in and upset everything. Rosa had not heard anything; she had told her terrible story regardless of observers. He was sure about that. Yes. He could have thrown the door open and shouted: Nick! You should hear this and not me. He could have asked her not to say what she had to say and he had not.

'I am evil,' she had said, and he had leant across to her but she had moved away, arms locked around her body, locking him out. 'I must be. Don't you see? There's nothing else I can do, is there?'

'No,' he said, urgent, forcing her hands from her face. 'No – ' but her hands waved him away, and his words were rain in the wind.

'Do you see why I have to have him?' she said, and he saw. He saw her arms blue with the cold inside her and he thought, Nick will warm you with his frantic heat if you don't tell him. That was before he heard the hiss of his sigh in the corridor and could not tell her that he was already gone. But he kept on drawing.

By six o'clock he had the first full sketch he needed and he was tired. He spoke to her about perspective and angles and he knew he was lightheaded. 'I'm inventing it all – ' he said to her, surprised.

'I've been doing that for years,' she said. The tears came again, and this time he moved closer to her and clumsily went to put his arm around her, as a friend, as a comfort, but she moved away from his arm and took his hand and put it to her face and he felt the dampness of her cheek. This is life, he thought, without wanting the thought, it's what Nick talks about, it's happening, and now – and he put his mouth against hers but she moved just away and he tasted her tears and heard her say, from a distance, 'Dear Patrick'. His evening had begun with Phyllis, her face flushed with drink, saying, 'But I don't think you really want me here, do you?', knowing that he could not say, 'Yes I do,' and take her in his arms. And home he had come, alone, expecting Nick to flounce in with Rosa in his hands, bunched with expectation.

And now he knew that he should take control of the situation, but Rosa simply lay down where she was, tired from her story, unknowing, and he covered her with a tablecloth.

'You are beautiful,' he said as she slept, and she stirred, restless, her hair over her face, fighting already, but he did not know that. He tiptoed to bed, alone, turning over and over in the space until he fled through dreams, chasing Rosa, only the soles of her feet pale and visible to him in his night blindness. He knew that she would be gone in the morning.

In the art school they will not let me through the door unless I can prove who I am. Oh, well that's difficult alright. It occurs to me, madly, standing at the door facing a security guard, that if I were to drop dead right now, nobody would be able to identify me. You would not recognise me now, because I have changed myself the better to hide a secret. Perhaps you know this, wherever you are now. People keep disappearing; it's as if they are all moving about me while I, trapped in a dream, try to call out. Here I am! Here – look at me. But when you turn and look, confused and maybe alerted by something in my voice, you do not see a face that you know any more. If I try to find you, will you always be one step ahead of me?

'You have to be a student,' the guard says, bored. His uniform is grey and so is his skin but his eyes are black and they look past me. I agree with him but he will not move and I see Patrick enter, pass in his hand, paintbox under his neat arm. For some reason I duck away, not wanting to be seen being refused entry. I slip outside the college and catch sight of myself in the glass window. I am pale and thin and on the edges of poverty. It's no surprise to me that Nick has taken to blondes without this stench of failure already upon them. In a few years they may know this bitter taste too, but for now he gobbles them up. He has always known that he wanted to be a painter, and Patrick has probably known that he would always be a sidekick, and me? I have always known that I would be someone else.

And now I am. Lurking outside an art school, hiding in the bushes outside the house where a child plays, creeping through an empty home where wasps congeal and old newspapers rustle in the stale air. What does Nick want? Success, money, the brightening of eyes and the apparently casual turning of glances as he moves through his life. I want none of those but that goes without saying.

All I want is you.

To my agency. The woman smiles terribly nicely at me but terribly she tells me that I am unreliable. I tell her I have an illness but am better now and would love to resume work. Her eyes slide away from me. 'So sorry . . .' she murmurs. She bites her nails. 'A difficult time . . . No opportunities just now but do call back, won't you? Oh – ' she calls me as I head for the door. 'I hope you recover properly soon,' she says, smiling again now that I am leaving. Thank you. So do I.

When you have exhausted all immediate solutions, sometimes it is better to sit and think. I find myself doing this more and more lately. There is a bench just off Oxford Circus, behind the madness, where office workers who are probably lonely sit and unwrap their lunch, furtively. One sits next to me and takes time to ease his sandwich from the plastic. It looks pink and tasty and I am hungry. 'May I have a bite?' I ask him. He backs away, wild-eyed. If I had a mirror might I understand why he is frightened? 'I'm sorry,' I call. 'I just wanted something to eat.' He walks away quickly, disassociating himself from lunacy, but a woman approaches me and offers me an apple. She comes too close and I can smell ham on her breath but I take the apple all the same.

'Are you alright, love?' she asks, sympathy oozing from every pore. I nod and start in on the fruit. It tastes strange to me, as if it has been doctored with blandness. 'Is life getting you down?' she asks. I nod. My mouth is full.

Two nurses walk by and a builder yells at them, 'You can come and take my sperm count any time – ' The woman leaps up.

'Follow the way of the Lord,' she says, and people scatter away from her instantly, smoothly, as if she is a bomb site. 'Repent of the flesh – ' but her audience has fled the square, and there is only me and an apple core.

In the department store the assistants pass me over with a glance. I am not smart but I am not a threat either. I pick three dresses to try on and all are over eighty pounds each. The scarlet is best, as always. I don't know why. It clings to my bones and the woman watching me in the communal mirrors nods. She is trying on a column of pale-blue satin, stretching and moulding it to her curves. She looks wonderful. 'I look enormous,' she pronounces. 'You're lucky. Your boyfriend will love it.' I smile and twirl for her. 'Is it for a dance?' she asks, bending to strip. Her breasts heave from the dress, white and round and glowing.

'It's for my wedding reception,' I say, and she smiles, charmed. We discuss marriage for exactly one minute and I wait for her to go, while I slip the red underneath the black. I like this store, because they do not believe in security tags: ladies like to try on clothes without the inhibiting rasp of metal and plastic marring the silks and satins of their evening wear. I quite agree; it is why I especially enjoy shopping here. No money ever changes hands because serious women always shop on credit.

I lied. It is not for my wedding reception at all, of course. It is for the wedding.

Oh yes. The store announces it is closing and as I step outside the liveried doorman thanks me for shopping with them. 'It's been a pleasure,' I assure him.

All I have to do now is find the bridegroom.

CHAPTER **10**

Nick went to a phone near the hotel. The sun beat down relentlessly but the sky and the city were still grey and the faces of shoppers were ringed with tiredness. He thought suddenly of Rosa's bright dresses in this landscape. 'You're there,' he said, laughing.

'I live here,' said Patrick tersely. 'Where else would I be?'

'In the greatest city in goddamn Europe,' said Nick, teasing, 'you could be at the theatre. The cinema. A bar, a cafe, a restaurant . . .'

Patrick sniffed. 'Rosa's not here, you know. What am I supposed to say to girls when they ring up? You should have left me a script.'

'I've got a job,' Nick said. There was a silence then. He thought fast and delicately. 'Well – not exactly a job. More like a commission.'

'But you've not even delivered your assignment yet,' Patrick said, already panicking. 'Are you losing your mind? What about – '

'Listen, listen,' said Nick, his hands shaking. What was he doing? He banged his head against the wall of the box several times and saw two teenage girls giggling at him. They wore cheerleader skirts. 'Didn't you hear me, dickhead? I've got a commission, I've already got what we're supposed to spend four years working for. Is that "Congratulations" I hear? Is it?'

Silence, then, 'Congratulations then.' Patrick's voice sounded tinny, as though he were far away.

'Is this a bad line?' Nick asked, his voice gleeful. 'Anyway I'm coming home. A last weekend before the big time.' And with Patrick squawking in his ear, he put the phone down. 'All yours,' he said to the girls, opening his arms wide. 'You did want to use the phone, didn't you?'

'Talking to your girlfriend?' asked the boldest one. The other collapsed behind her with nerves. Nick smiled at them.

'Do you know a bar where I can go and drown my sorrows?' he said.

'No,' said the bold one, staring at him. She adjusted her bustier and gave him her meanest look.

'Well, I do,' said Nick, walking off.

Come ON,' said the bold girl, dragging her sidekick desperately. 'Look at him, he's boss, come on – ' and they ran after him, screaming and giggling on their stacked platform heels. Nick slowed his pace.

He's not at home. Patrick is a bad liar and this time he is telling the truth. 'I could come round anyway,' I say, and I hear him hesitate, his mind ticking over. Of course. How stupid of me. His girlfriend ... No. In search of a living I replace the phone and go two miles into the city to a hotel bar where an over-friendly boss once took me in the hope of sex. He went away empty-handed but I like the bar. The waiters are old and slow and speak little English. In fact they speak little and I enjoy the view of London since it is fifteen floors up and a high wind tonight.

In my new red dress I am a scandal and men watch me through their gin and tonics. My wedding dress. I see their drinks faintly blue with quinine and order a Coke. I cross my legs as though it is what I do for a living. Where can he be? How can a person propose and then disappear without trace? It is not possible and neither should it be. The wind shrieks and hunts round the building and my sighs are lost in this sound that attracts all attention. Good.

'Ever been to Chicago?' says a man at the next table. I shake my head. There is nothing I suppose that I need to say except Yes and Please and My God, It's Enormous and One Hundred Pounds, things of that nature. And there is really nothing he needs to tell me either except his room number but he tells me all about the tallest bar in the world in his home town and how dangerous it is there.

'Really?' I say, with little enthusiasm. I am not here for the conversation and I am not very good at this, having never done it before.

'Yeh!' he says. 'You ever been to the States?' I have not. Thank you but I am terrified enough of my own land. 'You want to go,' he says, sitting down with a groan.

'No, I don't,' I can honestly assure him. He laughs. 'You British – ' he says. I laugh too and wonder how to tell him that I am expecting money.

'Listen – ' I say, uncrossing my legs. They ache.

'So are you working?' he says. He signals the waiter. I am ashamed. If he thinks I am one of the great unemployed – and I truly am – will he give me more? It all seems so simple so far. 'Would you like to go somewhere else?' he says.

Two hours later we are in a different hotel. His suite is lavish but bland and I do not know where I am but I will be able to afford the cab fare home although we have not broached price. I guess that is my job. 'I'm married,' he says. I feign surprise, shock, I come over all British. 'No,' he says, 'You don't understand.'

He shows me a picture of his wife. She sits smiling at the camera with a small girl beside her and a boy scowling at the sun. She is in a wheelchair and she is tiny. He tells me that she met a truck head on as she was driving to pick him up at the airport. 'I'm sorry,' I tell him. I don't know what to say now. 'A hundred if you want me to stay the night' seems horrific even though the woman in the photograph could be his sister. How do you know what to believe when no one can bear to tell the truth, even yourself?

'We take separate holidays,' he tells me. 'She goes to her sister in Alabama, I come to Europe. I've got to lie down, I'm real tired. Please don't think me rude. Talk to me.' And he falls asleep instantly. I stare at his wallet on the side table. It bulges . . . I take something from it and tiptoe to the door.

'If you need money,' he says sleepily, 'take it. I'm a dumb tourist . . . There's over two hundred bucks in there.'

I close the door quietly and hear his breath settle into sleep.

But I slip the photograph into my jacket. The family photograph.

You think he will wake and miss it? He has the real thing, back home. Don't forget that. He can't.

'Don't forget the wok,' Patrick shouted. 'It's yours.' He had no use for it and neither had Nick but now that he was leaving he wanted nothing there of his. In preparation he had sorted out all the mixed-up mutual items from the shared rooms and set them aside, shaking with anger.

'It's like a divorce,' said Nick, emerging from the bathroom. 'You can keep the soap. And the shower curtain, but I'll take the box of condoms.' It's all mine really, thought Patrick, but he kept quiet. His blood was simmering and ever since the phone call he had felt his heart beating at a very fast rate.

'Have you told Rosa you're leaving?' he asked.

Nick picked up a brush. He touched Patrick's face with it lightly. 'Keep the wok,' he said. 'You can cook yourself up a life with it.'

'I have one,' said Patrick, his ears turning red with knowledge.

'A stir-fry kind of life,' Nick said, laughing with effort. 'A bit of paint, a bit of Phyllis, a bit of phoning home every weekend. I'll send you a postcard from Freedom. It's a wonderful, wonderful life . . .' and he wandered from room to room, singing.

'This commission must be something, to leave college for,' Patrick called out, desperate to know how he had done it. 'Didn't they want to see any of your recent work?'

Nick smiled carefully. He packed his paints away, barely able to remember what it felt like to hold the brush. Fuck art school, fuck sitting in front of a board of hasbeens and justifying himself. The last time he had painted it had been because he had felt the colours seep out of him with nowhere to go and he had worked for hours, not seeing time, not feeling hunger or tiredness until the pale light crept into his filthy room.

'I can't just do it because there's a deadline,' he had yelled at Ani, despairing, knowing that he would sooner walk out this minute than fail. Or be failed, because they had told him already that he had to submit the assignments or forfeit his place on the course.

'You scraped through last year,' Ani had reminded him. 'No second chances any more, Nick. This is it. There's still time.' Time, with Rosa screaming at him, clawing at him until he felt that his skin would tear away from his bones, asking of him. Asking.

'Help me,' she had said, eyes wild and hands clammy against his. But I can't, he had wanted to say. Don't you understand? And she had a child, somewhere, and all he wanted was to be gone from here. Reeking of failure.

'You're lying,' said Patrick, standing in the doorway. Nick looked up. He locked the paints away in their box and stood. He realised that Patrick was taller than him but it had never seemed so before. Patrick smiled with astonishment. 'Where's the job, Nick?'

Nick left the room and went to collect his bags from the kitchen. A red mist swam in front of his eyes and he shook his head to clear it but it remained. When he turned Patrick stood inches away. 'You're a fool,' he was saying, but the words seemed to come from far away. 'And I envied you.' He saw Patrick laugh, his eyes widening with disbelief.

'You wanted to be me,' Nick said, shaping the words with difficulty. 'Everything I had, you wanted, because you believed everything I told you. You sad fuck. Even your girlfriend drew the short straw. She came round here for me, don't you understand?' And now he was shaking, all of him, holding his body upright with effort.

Patrick was still smiling. 'I don't care!' he said, waving Phyllis away.

Nick frowned. 'You don't exist,' he told Patrick. 'Look at you. When you walk through the streets, who sees you? You're one of the invisible people.' He picked up his bags, loaded down and sweating. He saw Patrick dimly, saw his expression change slowly to alarm, through the mist of rage and hurt. 'What?' he screamed, scared now. 'What?'

'What about Rosa?' Patrick cried, as Nick started to move towards the door, his heart beating oddly. Slow, then fast fast fast slow, an uneven dance. He knew if he could get through the door that he would be out. And he would never look at another painting again, not as long as he lived. When you're gone, don't bother to look back, he told himself.

Patrick's voice was quiet now. The words echoed in the hallway they had never bothered to paint, the hallway where Nick's conquests had been persuaded to stay. 'I'll paint for you,' he said.

Nick did not look back. How pleasant it will be to walk from here now, he thought, with the words of humility fresh in his mouth and how bitter how bitter he will taste them after I am gone. He stood, making Patrick stumble through his plea.

'I'll see that you get through the exams. That's what you want, isn't it? Take one of the paintings and hand it in tomorrow. Nobody'll know. It's – it's a different style for me.' And I must have known that this would happen, Patrick thought. Have I always wanted to save him?

Nick dropped the bags without turning, his smile back for real this time. He lit a cigarette, the door still propped open with his foot. 'What's in it for you?' he asked, grinning now.

'No,' said Patrick, uneasy. 'You don't understand. I'm doing you a favour, aren't I?' Nick tapped ash onto the floor. The hours ticked by in seconds. 'Aren't I?'

Nick walked over to the stack of canvases piled up by the wall. 'Let's have a look at what I'd be getting.'

He turned over Phyllis, badly. Patrick's grandmother, his father, a still life drawn diligently from class, a huge aubergine – 'Not that,' Patrick said hastily. 'I didn't mean that one' – the life-class model, skin sagging and mouth drooping with resignation. And then Rosa.

Rosa again. Rosa asleep, her hand near her face, warding off evil dreams. Rosa awake, staring uncomfortably straight at the artist.

Nick went to the kitchen cupboard and brought something out.

'Oh no,' said Patrick, regretting his offer. 'No. Absolutely not.'

Nick sat down. 'Get us a beer. I'll cut.'

Patrick did as he was told, automatically. 'But what are we playing for?' he asked, bewildered.

'If I win, I take the paintings,' said Nick calmly, without looking up.

'But you can have them anyway,' Patrick cried. Nick shook his head, shuffling the pack over and over.

'I don't think you understand,' he said. 'I don't want to take them from you. I want to win them.'

'But what if you lose?' asked Patrick, his head spinning. He put the beer down. Nick grabbed his wrist and held on. He still did not raise his eyes from the pack of cards.

'I won't lose,' he said, his long fingers splayed out on Patrick's skin.

'Okay,' said Patrick. 'What if I were to win? Put it that way.'

'Oh. Well,' said Nick, considering. 'That ain't – what do you want?'

'Tell me where you're going, what this job is,' said Patrick, rubbing his sweating hands on the back of the sofa. Nick shook his head. Patrick stayed silent.

'Okay,' Nick conceded. 'Tell me what you want and I'll give you the number where you can reach me.'

'Rosa,' said Patrick, before he knew what he had said. Now Nick looked at him. His face had changed again.

'Oh,' he said, enjoying himself now. 'That's how it is. That's how it is, then.'

'But you don't want her!' Patrick cried. 'Do you?'

'Don't I?' said Nick. 'You don't know what I want. Have you fucked her?' Patrick was trembling. 'I don't have to do anything, don't you see? She's mine, anyway. She'll always be mine, whether I want her or not. Cruel but true. That's how it is.'

And then he dealt the cards.

It is dark and still and, if you care, I am by the river. The sun is waiting to rise, holding itself back from me or perhaps that is just my fancy. Many things are. The smell of badness also rises from the dirty water but I linger all the same, taking in lungfuls of reeking air before the crowds come to gaze at nothing. There are steps and as usual I go downward, onto the stones, watching a small boat chug past quietly, like a secret. If I swim out fast enough will I catch it?

No. I step into the water, my skirts lifted high to protect my scarlet dress. Nick is here, in this city, now. The water is cold around my legs and the current pulls me lazily out but I resist it. I am stronger than the Thames! See. A larger boat is moored by the wall, swaying with overlate revellers. The disco lights still shine as I wade along towards it in the shallows. A lonely figure leans over the side of the boat, waving at somebody. The city is beautiful in this light, for a moment.

'Wanna come aboard?' says the figure, and to my surprise I climb up the rope ladder it proffers, without thought. I am light-headed for many reasons. As I climb, the face of the speaker appears. I am blinded by the floodlight for a second. A young man, maybe eighteen. A ponytail, narrow eyes, and as I reach the boat, a towel wrapped around his waist and nothing else . . .

'I swam,' he says, helping me over and onto a seat.

'Good for you,' I say, and I mean it. He looks glum.

'They had to throw me a life jacket,' he explains. 'And then a brandy, for shock.'

'Let's have another,' I say, daring, and he produces a bottle. The party rages on around us as we sip at the bottle, not speaking much. We are suspended in time as night slides away.

'Are you married?' he asks, noticing the ring on my finger, and I smile. I show him the photograph. 'Who's the woman?' he says. 'Your mum I bet, what a shame. Nice kids though. Your bloke looks alright. If I were a sober man I'd show you what for.'

'I bet you would,' I say, and he falls asleep. Oh yes I have this effect on men lately. In his sleep he stirs, shouting nonsense, and I take his hand and stroke his sweaty hair and take the bottle still half-full from his pale hands and leave by the front door this time. I hail a tired cabbie from the Embankment. 'Bethnal Green,' I say.

'That'll cost you, love,' he says, whistling with anticipation. Yes. A twenty-pound note was all I took from the dumb tourist. Am I not worth that? You will tell me in time, I know.

At the flats I hesitate. 'Your choice, darlin',' says the helpful cab driver. I hand him the twenty and walk to the main door. I cannot bear pressing the buzzer again only to hear Patrick apologise for being there. A couple emerge, snogging, and I push inside before they are quite gone. 'Alright, alright, mind me girl – ' says the man, but I am up the stairs, a brittle anxious bride.

The door is closed but not locked, jutting imperceptibly in the breeze that hums around the block. Turning the handle, I hear the low murmur of voices. Do I want to go in? I don't know. Later you may judge me for this but understand that I don't know what to do. I am making it up as I go along. Don't we all do that? Even Nick. Even Nick.

Of course I go in. But quietly, so quietly. Understand? They are playing cards. Poker? No women there, then. I squat outside the living-room door. 'Is that right?' Patrick says, his voice scared. Nothing from Nick, yet.

Then, 'Did she sit for you?' I freeze but my veins run alive inside me.

'Not exactly,' Patrick says, and I want to slap him. At least give him the option of jealousy.

'Oh, shit,' Nick says, and I sink nearer the ground, with relief. But he is scooping up the cards now, his back taut with hunger. I know this. I can see no cash on the table but I know he will win. Doesn't he always?

'I won't be coming back, you know,' Nick says, dealing again. 'Don't give my number to anybody.'

The wind blows behind me. My back aches and I rise, careful not to creak. Who's winning? Can anybody join in? Nick loses the next hand and frowns. 'How long are you planning to go on?' asks Patrick. He picks up a glass of water while a collection of beer bottles lines up alongside Nick. I see his eyes flicker over the cards.

'Pass,' Nick says. 'As long as it takes.'

'No,' Patrick says. 'Best of three.'

'Got to have a pee,' Nick says, and I back into his room in darkness. His familiar smell and the sound of his piss. He is drunk and he will fleece Patrick. I briefly consider emerging like a sad ghost to warn the loser but instead I lie down on the bed, trapped in time. The window is open and the room feels empty even in pitch blackness. If I feel my way around what will I catch? The scent of other women. I am not stupid, whatever you may believe.

I can wait until he comes to bed, victorious. I will be the only woman here, then.

I can wait.

'One game to you, that was luck. Two games to go,' said Nick, his vision blurred by beer and his hands unsteady on the cards. They seemed to slip out of his reach. 'These cards are greasy. Change them,' he commanded, drunk and irritable.

'Are you driving?' Patrick asked. 'You can stay if you like.'

'I pay you rent, don't I?' Nick said. 'I'll fucking stay alright. More beer.' And he tried to work out what he needed to get. Numbers flashed inside his head like roulette wheels, flashing past, out of reach. Now red now black now nothing.

'You haven't paid me rent for months, Nick,' Patrick said, weary. 'Other people have been keeping you, haven't they?' His own words shocked him. He's going anyway, he thought, isn't he? It will kill Rosa if he goes. And then – a noise, a soft noise, in the flat.

'Ready?' asked Nick, and he had slicked his hair back with water. If I put my hand out to you now and told you that you did not have to leave, who would I be betraying, Patrick wondered? Which of us?

Nick bent over the cards. He smiled and turned one over. His smile grew. 'Well – ' he said, his head cocked. You're familiar to me and I have loved you, Patrick thought. 'Your call,' Nick said, waiting. I like it when you wait, he had said, in the past.

'Are you going to marry Rosa?' he asked. The room seemed to get smaller with every second. Nick said nothing. Patrick passed.

Nick turned over a new card. 'Do you want to hear it?' he asked, his fingers idling on the cards. Life was outside now, not in here. I'm already gone, he thought.

'She is beautiful,' Patrick said quietly. The shouting would come later, when he had lost, alone in the dim new light. 'There is nothing – ' he spoke now with difficulty. 'There is nothing she could do that would be wrong.'

'Do you want to hear or not?' said Nick, sounds roaring in his ears. His voice carried in the room. His fingers tensed on the cards in front of him. 'Turn yours over,' Nick said. He looked up. Patrick's eyes were red and glassy. He's in love, Nick realised, astonished, but who with? Not Phyllis, surely, not –

'Please, just tell me what you're going to do about her – ' Patrick said, barely glancing at his cards. He turned them over for Nick to see.

'I'll tell you this,' Nick said casually. A door creaked in the wind. 'I've won. I'm feeling lucky, now. One to go.'

There is nothing that she could do that would be wrong. O Patrick you do not know the half of it. When we were twelve we played a game with daisies, pluck a petal he loves me pluck a petal he loves me not and whatever you're left with –

When my sailor left he left me with you and then I left and now there is nothing that is right. The darkness pulls me

nearer to sleep but I drift halfway there, dreaming of muddy water and hands dragging me down. For some reason a voice tells me that I will fail all my exams but this is no surprise. A church under water and seaweed on the bridegroom's suit. The bells echo in the lake around us. I wake briefly to silence and then
something
pulls me
under –

'One left to go,' Nick said, yawning. He stood up and walked to the window, pushing it open, flooding the room with sudden cold air. He unbuttoned his flies and bent into the approaching dawn.

'No,' said Patrick, horrified. 'Don't you dare – '

But Nick was already pissing out of the window. 'There's nobody down there,' he said. He turned suddenly, still shaking himself off. 'I'll marry her,' he said. 'If – '

'I don't want to hear,' Patrick said, shuffling the cards, moving his eyes back into his head back into the past.

Nick came nearer. He stood in front of Patrick with his flies open, swaying to distant music. 'When I win, I'll marry her.'

'What?' asked Patrick, astounded. 'You can't marry someone because you win a game of poker.'

'Why not?' asked Nick. 'People get married because they're pregnant, because they want to be able to fuck in peace, because they want to piss their parents off. They get married to get a fucking council house, for Christ's sake . . . What's wrong with leaving it to chance?'

'How will that make her happy?' Patrick cried.

Nick laughed. 'Happy? I won't make her happy anyway,' he said, and he was sober now. 'Nobody can make her happy.'

And he sat too close to Patrick, taking his face into his hands. 'Remember?' he asked, sly and sad, and Patrick remembered the taste of him, of salt and beer and sweat and a heavy, thick sweetness, his eyes closed, a blind tasting.

'Don't,' he said despairingly to Nick. 'Please. Don't do this.'

'You see?' Nick said, dropping his hands. 'I can't make anyone happy. Not even you.'

'Deal,' Patrick said, and there was urgency in his voice now. You're beautiful, so beautiful, he had said to Nick once; and it had only been once, but now Patrick put his hand against him, pushing him away.

'Deal,' Nick repeated, distant and cool once again. His mouth tightened and he dealt.

When I wake it is days later but the clock tells me an hour or so. I creep to the door and hear them still playing. My boys, I think fondly. They are playing macho tonight, like a stag night. Yes. That is an oddly comforting thought. I will have my last night, too. There will be no girls shrieking, no men stripping down to their burnished thighs, no gin and tonics and throwing up on a dancefloor somewhere in Watford. But I will have my night all the same.

Soon it will all be over. I take off my scarlet dress. It smells of the river. I peel down my stockings and sit in my black bra and knickers. They are cheap but attractive. They suit me, then. I can make them work. Soon Nick will be here. Quietly I feel beneath the bed, feeling for evidence of a past that I know has existed. Oh. No sheaves of letters, no photographs of smiling shy girlfriends with their clothes off, nervous of the camera. I smile into the darkness, although the light is heading towards me. Not yet. I lie down, my pulse racing with certainty. If he is tired I will be content to lie beside him, my arm draped across his side. He will lie like Jesus, long and thin and white. If it does not sound beautiful to you, think of me. I don't ask for much. I told you that already.

There is nothing here now except me.

Waiting

'Turn over,' Nick said. His cards were good and he was tired. 'Let's get this over with.'

Patrick moved into the kitchen to get beer. 'I want whisky,' Nick called, his voice small and petulant. 'Isn't it time we drank whisky?'

Patrick looked at the sun. It was barely there but he could see it. He felt strong and marvellous and he poured beer and whisky like a bartender.

'Ice,' Nick said plaintively. 'Can I have ice?'

Patrick sat heavily. 'Listen,' he said. 'It's almost daylight. Let's forget this, it's stupid. We're drunk, let's go to bed, come on.'

Nick laughed with surprise. 'You're keen,' he said, wiping his damp mouth. 'No way.' His blood was racing. 'We should do this more often. This is good – '

He turned over his cards. They were good. 'It's funny, isn't it' he said. 'I don't even need to win, because she's mine anyway. She's always been mine, and I've always wanted to get away. Know what my dad said to me?' He tipped his whisky back. 'More,' he said, and Patrick moved off, out of sight. He had to shout now, but that was alright, wasn't it?

'He said, "You've always been a loser to us, whatever anybody else thinks of you." "Keep writing the cheques out," I said, "and you'll still have an artistic son." I'll put some music on, shall I?' And he leapt up, sorting through the few remaining tapes with disappointment, wanting music to fit his mood, high on winning. 'Maybe we'll go to America,' he called to Patrick. 'You can get quickie divorces there, you know?' And he put Dvořák on, loud. It filled the small room and Nick winced. 'Come on,' he shouted, victorious now. 'Bring the bottle.'

Patrick closed the fridge. The sky was watery with morning. I'll lose it all, he thought. How did this happen? I should have known.

The bottle sat between them and for the first time Patrick took a glass and filled it with whisky. Nick nudged him. 'Listen,' he said. 'It doesn't matter. Turn them over anyway, who gives a fuck? It's just a game.' Patrick put his hand on the cards. 'Funny to find out that you fancied Rosa though,' Nick said. 'Always wanted a bit of whatever I had, didn't you? Still, it's been a laugh, hasn't it?'

Patrick stood up, his head pounding. 'Yes. A laugh. Got to go to the loo,' he said, unsteadily.

'Turn the cards over first,' Nick said lazily. He lay on the couch, his mouth parted and moist with relief.

'Why don't you do that while I go?' Patrick said, trying to escape before he threw up.

'No,' Nick said. 'Stay there.' And he turned the cards over.

Patrick had won.

Nick's hands moved away from the cards slowly and he picked up the bottle of whisky and held on to it tightly.

'You can't have won,' he said matter-of-factly. 'You never win anything, you, do you?'

'I did not win,' said Patrick. 'Forget it happened, just – '

'You cannot have won,' said Nick, and he was smiling. 'It doesn't mean anything, does it, if you win?"

Patrick stood, swaying. 'Let's just pretend it never happened,' he said, fear spreading through him. I must get to the bathroom before something happens to my brain, he thought.

'You?' said Nick, and he threw the bottle through the window, the plate-glass window that spanned the room.

The glass between you and me is thin and yet it keeps you alive. I pray to a god I don't believe in but surely now here he will do something to save you from the
glass

I sit up. In here? No, it's

Voices

Patrick is shouting.

I run into the living room but they don't seem to notice me. Nick is sitting on the sofa, shrunken like a dead man. Patrick is holding up three cards. He is laughing but like a death has just been announced. When he sees me his face changes and I realise then that I am in my underwear but he doesn't seem to notice that. Nick stands up like he is drunk and without seeing me he walks towards the door, still without seeing me.

'Nick,' I say, but it is like a dream, and he moves slowly.

'Let him go,' Patrick says, and I trust him. What else is there? Nick has some strange moods and –

Nick opens the door and he has not even seen me. Is he sick? His face has changed and there are two bags in his hand. 'Look at me,' I start to say but –

'There's your winnings,' he says, and the door clangs shut like a metal word.

'What about the wedding?' I scream, and Patrick is there, holding me. Holding me back.

'He's gone now,' he says. 'Where are your clothes?' He covers me with a shawl from the couch. I am at the window. There is Nick, look, he is getting into a car and now –

'Stop!' Patrick says, and I am struggling. 'Please stop, I can't stand it – '

He is shaking and I am shouting, I must be shouting because he is holding me, his hand nearly over my mouth, pulling me back hurting me. I do not understand. So Nick lost, and left in a huff.

'He lost,' I say, and Patrick nods dully.

'How much did you hear?' he asks me. His face is white.

'Well, I heard that you won,' I say, although this is not strictly true. Patrick has moved away from the broken window. The stench of whisky fills the room and I kick aside the smatterings of glass that have fallen. I bend down to examine the window and he seizes me, pulls me away just as a huge shard falls where I was. He is crying, tears caught in his throat like a backlog. I can hear him grasping for each breath. 'You did win?' I ask. He nods, shaking. 'You won!' And I am glad that somebody has.

'Yes,' he says, his hands digging into me. 'I won.'

CHAPTER 11

Like a lover, Patrick phones the number he has been given and then puts the phone down in fear before anyone can answer. To his surprise, sweat appears on his stomach, snaking through the clean T-shirt. He checks the bedroom, but Rosa is still asleep, in his bed where he placed her, wearing his dressing-gown, her hair a dark shape on the pillow. He calls again and when a voice tells him what he has reached, he gives Nick's name, out of shock and curiosity. 'I'll just put you through,' she says, laughter in her voice, as though she knows something, but Patrick has already put down the receiver.

Back into the living room he goes, his eyes blank and his hands still shaking. The glass lies on the floor still, glinting in the sunlight, a river of ice. Patrick means to clear up before Rosa wakes but he is turned to stone. He picks up his pencil and finds a sheet of paper and he begins to shape the scene before him. The cards strewn across the table, some crushed with anger. The dark stain of the whisky. Nick's white face against the wall, eyes dark with disbelief. And Rosa, the missing piece, her image in black and white stacked up against the wall waiting to be filled in.

Waiting.

He hears a sneeze and sighs, putting down the paper, half filled in.

I'm ready,' Rosa announced, stretching her arms above her head, hidden in Patrick's vast dressing-gown. Patrick stared. Ready for what? 'How did you get in here last night, exactly?' he asked, as she climbed out of bed. His bed, that he seemed not to have inhabited since all was calm, the present ticking along, a known quantity.

'The door was open,' she said, yawning. 'So I just came in, on the off chance.'

'But you didn't have any clothes on,' Patrick said, confused. Had he imagined it all?

'Oh,' she said, dismissive. 'I went in the river and got wet so I took my dress off. Got any milk?'

In the living room she could not go past the glass any more than he could. She fingered the giant shard that had threatened to decapitate her. 'He really went, didn't he?' she said softly, and Patrick nodded. 'But he'll be back,' she continued, turning to him. 'He'll have to come back, won't he?' Patrick put the kettle on, unwilling to lie any more.

'He's a bad loser, but he won't stay away for long,' Rosa said. She sat at the small kitchen table and lit a cigarette.

'You should give up,' Patrick said sternly. 'It will kill you.' He took the pack of twenty from her listless fingers and crumpled it up into the bin. Rosa watched, eyes round with amazement.

'Thanks,' she said, and he nodded again. As he watched her, she stubbed her cigarette out and sat thinking while the kettle bubbled. 'I have things to do,' she announced. 'Got to get a job, I'm broke. Can I use the washing machine while I'm here? I'd better get home before my landlord does, I owe the rent two weeks ago.' She hesitated. 'Can I borrow a fiver?'

'How much is the rent?' Patrick asked wearily. She held up both hands twice. 'Twenty?' he asked.

'Two hundred,' she said, shaking her head. 'It's okay, I've got plans. I won't be there for long, will I?' Patrick was utterly amazed by her faith.

'You can't be sure that he'll come back though,' he ventured. Her fingers touched his face lightly and he saw her eyes. 'If he doesn't come back then I'll just have to go and find him, won't I?' she said, and he saw that it was not faith but a blind, desperate need. Absurdly he wanted to say *but you're mine now, you belong to me, I won you –*

'You'd better stay here then,' he said, turning away from her gaze which saw past him.

'You'll help me?' she said, and he spread his hands out, hoping it would say enough.

'Will it make you happy?' he asked, and she smiled and slipped her thin arms around his neck.

'Thank you,' she said, not answering him. 'After all, you're his friend as well, aren't you? Despite a silly old game,' and kissed his cheek.

He sighed. 'Sit down,' he said, angry suddenly. 'I'm going to make breakfast.'

I don't even taste the food but I gobble it down because I need it and Patrick is such a little housewife, always wanting to make it safe, keep everybody calm. To work. I make a list. It is a short one. I plan that in the church of my youth I will tie a knot and all the rope before it will be burned away. I should like it to be soon, very soon, because only then can I come back to you and tell you what I have done and what I am now and you will see that I am not without redemption.

And then at last I will belong.

The dress hangs like a bloodied skin in the wrecked window, hanging up to dry. Will I shock the priest? I'd like it small, you said, and we giggled about your family wanting to kill me, slowly, a lingering death. Me too, I said. There's no point in inviting scores of friends when we can have a party afterwards, in London, safely far away. He does not need to know that there are no friends. The party can be just for us. You can't get smaller than that, can you? Just the two of us.

Because soon there will be three.

It's time to go to work. I settle on Friday for the date, since time is of the essence. Patrick is in the living room, cleaning up the broken night. He is a nice man. He does not like to win, but I do, and he shall feel the benefits of it o yes. I walk into the room, behind him.

'It's time to go to work,' I say, and as he turns round I shed the dressing-gown. His mouth is a black hole of disbelief. I pick out the sketch of me from the stack and hold it up to him, to enlighten him. He is slow sometimes, you see. 'You've got the sketch,' I tell him. 'Now here's the colour version. This is painting by numbers, fill in the gaps.' And I lie back.

The first morning, she lay back in the hard chair in her underwear. Patrick was disconcerted by the amount of skin on display and he asked her to put on a wrap.

'But you're always painting nude models, aren't you?' she pointed out, reasonably enough. 'What's the problem?'

Patrick couldn't exactly say, but it was there, and he insisted that she cover up.

'No,' she said firmly, smiling and sitting back, legs twisted underneath her, and that was that. Patrick had no will left to argue any more. He was tired and confused and his blood raced unevenly.

He began mixing paints to her flesh tone. The models at school were women that he did not know, had not seen sleeping, had not touched or wanted to touch. And you had not won them in a poker game, a voice said, but he pressed it from his mind and brushed fierce strokes onto the new canvas, seeing her faintly mocking gaze under his eyelids. I won't tell her, he decided. It's not my place to tell her.

'This is my rent money,' she said, when he gave her a short break, stretching deeply, hands spread out into the midday sun. 'Will it do?' And she stood behind him, while he covered the canvas with his body. Her hands on his shoulders, hunched over him, her hair in his face. 'Does that feel better?' she said. 'Does that feel good?' And he said yes, his throat closing over with fear. Her fingers dug into his flesh until the skin throbbed with hot pain and still she kneaded, deeper and deeper.

'Have you told Nick about your child?' he said, desperate to divert attention. Her fingers still kneaded, softer now.

'What child?' she said, puzzled. 'What on earth are you talking about?'

'But you told me – ' Patrick said, scared now. 'You said you had a child.'

Rosa's hands massaged his spine now, gentle, hypnotic. 'Oh, I make up a lot of nonsense when I've got a drink inside me,' she said lightly. 'It's best not to listen to me at all. Is it time for me to go back to work now?'

That afternoon he painted without speaking and Rosa chattered brightly, her voice receding as his brush scraped along the canvas. 'And it seemed right to buy the scarlet because I look best in red, don't you think?' she finished, and he nodded. He put his brush down, confused. 'What's the matter?' she said, rising from the chair, alarm showing in her face.

'Listen,' Patrick said quietly. 'I don't think you understand. Nick heard you say it, too.'

'Nick heard me say a lot of things,' she said, arms crossed, half-smiling, puzzled. 'So what?'

'Nick heard you say that you have a child,' Patrick said.

Forgive me. I deny you twice and hope that there is no occasion for a third time. We all know what happens then. Just give me until Friday and then it will all be over, don't you see? The road will close over the chasm and we can pass to the next point. I don't want to pretend that it will be easy but I can't wait for much longer. You'll understand, won't you? You'll see.

After I have explained why I lied, Patrick looks more comfortable, after I have told him that I had a miscarriage and I still find it hard to believe that you aren't here with me, that I still count the years as live ones. He is even more sympathetic and we carry on, because I tell him that it will upset me even more if he does not complete his assignment. His, and mine. Mine.

Ours. I am shifting in the chair now because my bones have set like ice but he is quick to notice my pain and he leaps up, comes over to me. His glasses are sweating. I have long ago shrugged off the wrap lest I boil alive like convenience food and I lean, resting my back. 'Am I wrong?' I ask him, because he is squinting at me. Too close. 'How do I look?'

'You are always beautiful,' he says quietly, and I feel ashamed somehow and sit up and do not speak for the rest of the afternoon. The only sound we hear is the faint scrape of the brush. The glass still lies where it fell, shining in the light.

'Go to Confession,' Nick's mother said, watching him in the hall mirror. 'Your hair is too long, get it cut,' she added.

'Don't nag me or I'll leave home again,' said Nick, and his mother's eyes watered. She crossed herself faintly and made a cup of tea.

'What will I confess?' Nick shouted through to her.

'Lust, greed, sloth and rudeness,' she said immediately.

'Okay,' Nick said agreeably, surprising them both. 'Lend us a tenner then.' His mother gave him twenty out of gratitude and he left the house, taking her car keys. He had no intention of going to Confession, of course, but now his mother would feel immensely more at ease. The house was fully occupied just now by returning offspring and he was sleeping in the spare bathroom, the caravan being off limits.

'I'd sooner fire the bollocks thing than have you sneaking girls back there,' his father said. 'Look what it led to last time,' and Nick lowered his eyes and gritted his teeth, because the next day he would be moving out, although he had not informed his parents of that. Just passing through, the temporary son. So tonight he would skirt around the confessional and celebrate his last night of freedom, small-town style.

Nick had called his old friends as soon as he landed, but something strange seemed to have happened to all of them, as though lethargy had passed through the pipes instead of water. The conversations went the same way:

Hi, it's Nick, I'm back home for a while, let's have a drink.

Pause. Yeh, uh, listen – uh, can I call you back? It's not a good time, I promised her I'd cut the drinking down . . .

I can't get a babysitter at this notice, what planet you living on?

I've got no money anyway and how dare you ignore me for two years, you bastard . . .

Why don't you come round though anyway because me mum'd love to see you again . . .

Er . . . sorry, Nick who?

And he already missed London. He sloped into a dark pub and bought himself a drink, wondering why he had come back. It wasn't too late. He could go back and take Patrick's painting and move to a different flat, start over. Nobody need find him, after all. I could do it, he thought . . . But he preferred to think that he could have done it, but chose not to.

'Buy you a drink, gorgeous?' a voice said, and he turned, surprised.

'Nicola,' he said carefully. 'Fucking hell, are you still here?'

Nicola had been his first real passion at seventeen, a lanky, sly girl who had got religion and insisted on remaining a virgin. Her dark hair had covered her eyes and she wore no make-up, but her mouth was huge and pink and it intrigued Nick. With a mouth like that, she's got to be up to something, he had decided, but for once had been spectacularly unsuccessful. Now she had enormous breasts and yellow hair, with a small tattoo on her white plump shoulder. 'Still a virgin?' he asked her, and she smiled lazily.

'Buy us a cider and I'll tell you,' she said, and her eyes trawled the bar for other men. Gladly, Nick thought, relieved by her casual glance. But you couldn't tell, could you? Rosa had seemed nicely mysterious and gently ironic, impossible to get hold of until a desperate remark, a family row had led her to believe that they were going to run off and start frantically nesting. Did you love her? Patrick had asked, quietly, one night, and luckily the phone had rung. I'm twenty, he wanted to scream, don't hold me responsible for anything.

Don't ask of me. There's nothing to declare inside me.

There's nothing, inside me.

'Pint?' he asked, and Nicola's mouth stretched wide with satisfaction. She scratched her crotch without shame as he went to the bar.

The next day I rise early, astonishing myself. I examine my face. My eyes are feverish and my skin damp with a fine spray of sweat but I will paint fine, I expect. Brides are always nervous when approaching the Big Day, I read it in a magazine. Don't get me wrong. I am not desperate. I am determined. That's all.

Patrick's painting will tell you who I am. I am attractive, intelligent, a young woman who does not turn heads but is still worth something. There is nothing wrong with me. You could not pick me out of a crowd but that is not your problem, since I shall pick you. Wherever you are. When the time is right, you can depend upon it.

All you have to do is close your eyes and hold your breath.

This time he stares at my mouth for a long time, lips pursed, until I can feel his breath on my skin, faint and clean. It is disconcerting, as though he is a plastic surgeon, measuring me up for the knife. We'll cut just here, do you think? Whittle me away, every passing day. He stands over me, narrowing his eyes, narrowing mine, his naked eyes large and trusting. I want to speak, to break the silence, but something stops me. How strong must you be to live without love? I asked that once, inside my head, and the answer comes back to me now, only now.

Strong enough to close your eyes hand over your mouth pinch the bridge of your nose and stop up your ears. Tie yourself in knots and nothing can get in. *Get out* –

I have spoken aloud and Patrick flinches. There's no time. He bends over me and I realise then that he must not be hurt, that he may win at poker but lose at everything else and yet – his face is close and I am weak with hunger and I reach up and touch his mouth. It is tight and ungiving and he takes my hand gently and replaces it by my side. But I see, I see that his body is trembling faintly with fear with alarm but also with something else that there is no word for. He leaves the room slowly like an old man and I hear his bedroom door softly close. Here I come.

Inside, he has closed the curtains against life and he lies facing me, expressionless. He could be a client and he could be a corpse but he is Patrick. He sighs and I lean down slowly, yes very slowly so as not to frighten him and bend my mouth to his. I know even in the dark behind my eyelids that he will be there and will not move away at the last second like Nick might do – as a joke, and I will cure Nick of his jokes, but now this is all there is in the world. His mouth tastes of peppermint and clean boy and eagerness and he moves his lips too desperately but he learns by mine quickly.

I take his hands then and guide them down until he reaches for my breasts impatiently, sighing again, cupping them in his damp hands, feeling his way in the dark. Slowly, slowly – downward he travels, fingers warming to me, growing accustomed to the shape of me. I take his face in my hands and slide my tongue into his waiting mouth o he is sweet now and he moves against me, his feet curling around mine, holding me there. We are still and moving at the same time. I move my fingers down, down, over his shoulders, wide and thin, his body an economy of space, to his nipples, tiny and hard.

When I put my mouth to them he makes a noise of surprise and I have found an undiscovered country.

Later, when we rise to continue our painting, he is not distant. He is gentle with me, you see. He holds the pencil against my nose, my cheekbones, the length of my eyes, the angle of my jaw, measuring me intently, peering at me carefully, with attention to detail. He has learned the exact shape of my mouth, the slight scar under my left eye, the tiny mole under my chin, the space between my temple and brow. He is learning me. And all the while, this music pours out at us, music that he tells me was written for a funeral. Not the stuff Nick turns up to fill a room, music I don't understand, with hard shapes and angles and hurt, jagged edges. Music that hurts me, screams at me that I am alive. No, this is music for the dead. And it is beautiful.

CHAPTER 12

When Patrick rose the next morning he realised that he had not been out of the flat for days and the air was musty and pungent. He recognised the smell now. A new start, he thought, and almost laughed out loud with surprise. He called a glazier to repair the window, careless for once of the cost. He called his father and told his mother that he had met a girl.

'Is she nice?' asked his mother, assuming that he was sleeping with her.

'I'm seeing a lot of her,' he answered cautiously. His parents had always been something of an oddity to him. They neither interfered nor ignored, but he always felt that on the occasions they had met Nick they had watched him wistfully as he bounded about their house, while the son they worried about and could not quite understand sat tightly, his limbs awkward.

'Use condoms,' said his mother, and Patrick blushed, thankful there was only sound and no picture. 'I suppose you're blushing now,' his mother added, and he closed his eyes, feeling old-fashioned.

After the call he woke Rosa. 'Come on,' he said, taking coffee to her.

She groaned. 'No,' she said, hidden beneath pillows. 'Go to college.' But Patrick pulled the covers off with a most uncharacteristic briskness.

'We,' he said, standing taller, regarding her uncurling limbs, 'are going out.' Rosa raised her eyebrows at him. 'At least, I think we should,' he amended. 'Go out.'

Rosa smiled weakly. 'You mean like a hen night?' she said hopefully.

He had confided to her on the bus that he never bought clothes for himself, feeling stupid in shops, and she had taken up the idea with a sort of vague, distracted enthusiasm, instructing him on every outfit he had tried on. But she had wearied quickly and was now visibly wilting. 'Levis?' he had suggested, and she had grimaced. 'But Nick wears them,' he said, not understanding, and she had handed him three pairs of chinos and pushed him into a nasty cubicle with doors like a mock Western saloon. 'People can see my legs,' he complained, and she snorted, perhaps with laughter.

'I wouldn't worry,' she said. 'I'll stand guard, alright? Get them on.'

By the eighth shop, Patrick was despairing and Rosa said that she needed a drink. 'Is this how you were with Nick?' said Patrick, irritable and sweaty from too many shop assistants with contemptuous eyebrows. 'I bet you weren't.' She came up to him, close, so close that he could see the sun reflected in tiny points in her eyes.

'Don't ever mention him,' she said. 'Do you understand that you shouldn't? It's not a good thing to do. It's a jinx.' He agreed, surprised and a little fearful, and they sat in a pub near Oxford Circus, silently sipping at warm flat beer.

In the ninth shop, Patrick found some trousers and a couple of tops that were pressed upon him by an assistant whose name badge said 'Jojo, Clothing Consultant. Please Ask Me For Help'. In the cubicle, he could see through a slit in the door that Jojo was watching him quite openly.

'I'll take them,' he declared madly, although they would bankrupt him. When he looked in the mirror he was surprised to see a different reflection from the one that usually depressed him. The heat, the loud pumping music that he abhorred, the expensive clothes and the unfamiliar boy in the glass made him see how he could be someone else. But as the assistant went to the till to start preparing the sale, Rosa pushed Patrick back inside. She took Jojo to one side.

'Listen,' Patrick heard her say, 'Don't sell this shit to him.' Jojo murmured something and his hands parted to show the distance between himself and Rosa's hysterical behaviour. 'But he can't afford it, and you can see it's wrong for him.'

Furious, Patrick emerged hastily and shoved the clothing at the bewildered Jojo. He then produced the credit card that his father had guaranteed. Triumphantly, he paid, and followed Rosa outside. 'What's the matter?' he asked her, confused.

'It's not you,' she said, her hands gesturing. 'All this, it's not how you are.' He saw sudden tears in her eyes.

'But they looked alright!' Patrick cried. 'Something happened to me and I look different, I thought that's what you'd *want* . . .'

He took her hand, but she would not look at him. He began to smile, all the same. Maybe there were other things that he could do, now. He began suddenly to run along the impossibly crowded street, pulling Rosa along, crushing her hand as she tried to struggle free. 'You're hurting me!' she shouted at him, but in the thick knots of people her voice was lost and he gripped her tightly, ignoring her squeak of pain and she gave up, gathering momentum with his infectious energy. At the junction with Poland Street he stopped suddenly, before a taxi ran them over, and they turned to each other, breathless and choked with fumes.

'What the fuck – ' Rosa said, coughing with the unusual exercise.

'That guy – ' Patrick said, still beaming. 'Jojo. He was something, wasn't he? Hey? Jojo?' And he laughed out loud, excited to see her smile, if reluctantly, and he kissed her swiftly, stealing her, going with her rhythm this time as she pulled him down into the plunge of Soho. 'Down here – ' she said, turning into a narrow dirty street, littered with rotting fruit and vegetables, the stink of refuse filling the thin air. 'Here – ' and they stood outside a bar.

'You want another drink already?' said Patrick, still smiling at her. 'No,' she said, her face still and wiped of expression now. 'This is the bar where I first met Nick. This is where everything started.'

Patrick stood breathing heavily, drops of sweat forming on his lip. 'Let's go,' he said quietly, turning back to the main road. He wanted to get away from the winding streets, with their peculiarly silent throb, their anticipation of danger. 'Let's go home.'

Oh, I wanted to go in, to walk through the door, and when the glare of the sun had died, uncover my eyes and see him still standing there, his eyes curious and amused, his mouth twisted with certainty and boredom. Amuse me, make me look twice. And if I were Nick, that's what I would do. But

Patrick's hands fell by his sides as he walked slowly away and the bent shoulders did not say follow me, they said I have already forgotten why we ran as if a tidal wave was behind us and we went faster still than that. I watched him for a minute and then I ran after him, because I will have all the time in the world to look at Nick and remember that day, won't I. Won't I?

In the flat there is a new window. Patrick is not given to sulking and he is excited by the shiny glass, unstained by tears and whisky and breath. We stand and look out over London, seeing mostly tower blocks and a glimpse of Canary Wharf flashing forlornly for nobody except as a warning. A warning of what? My eyes are playing tricks again and my mind is rewinding even as we stand here.

'I love you like a friend,' he said the first time, while the wax ran down the candle and the light was snuffed out just in time to save me. 'I love you,' he said the second time, and then tears ran down his face and he was sick. But the third time he said, 'Marry me, I've always loved you. You will, won't you? You will – ' He was so sure. And so am I. So am I.

Patrick is behind me now. I had almost forgotten him, but I can feel him hovering. His new clothes have not yet given him the confidence he has already paid for. I turn to him. '*Fuck me,*' I say suddenly, and the words surprise both of us. It is a crudeness I had not imagined to use with him, but it works, wiping out the sudden sharp pictures reeling through my vision. Now Patrick blocks out the sun and I can see only him, black and white, his mouth an open patch of red. He pants like a dog and I begin to unbutton my shirt but now he is hungry, yes, and he falls upon me, pulling me back from the line of sight and nearly down to the floor but no not here, the carpet is stained by other memories. He scrabbles furiously for me. I am burning, his eagerness scratching at my skin like stubble.

'No,' I say, and his face slips into shame, but I slide to my knees, 'like this,' and I touch his skin, pulling his shirt loose, stretching the material with a kind of anger.

He is hot, hot like fever and slightly damp, and the rise and

fall of him is against the palm of my hands. I undo his jeans
and find flesh quickly while my head is still empty. I take him
in my hands and he stutters a sound then I put my mouth to
him and he gasps and rears back in surprise and then I know
that no one has ever done this to him before.

It's all that I can give him. It's not much, is it, in return?
When he comes he says my name over and over, over and
over, like a wave, quietly, holding back but unable to hold
back now. I can't say anything, of course, but afterwards,
when he stands with his head bowed, cheeks burning, I rock
back on my heels and look up at him. I make shapes with my
mouth, practising words, knowing I must warn him, must tell
him not to want too much, but before I can complete them
he says, 'It's like the running feeling, like you – ' He thinks.
'Like you know you'll never make it, you're out of breath and
it's too far but then you suddenly know you can go for ever
until you get to the edge of the cliff – ' He stops then,
awkward with his damp limpness and the window glaring at
us with the remains of the day.

'And then what?' I ask, smoothing my clothes down. You
won't find me on the edge of a cliff, oh no. He is helpless,
seeking words. I pull out the unfinished portrait. I cannot tell
you what I see in it. What a gift he will give me, when the
time comes, although he does not know it yet. What a gift of
gifts.

'It depends on how high the cliff is,' he says, touching the
painting.

'No,' I say, cruel suddenly. 'That's not good enough. What
do you do?'

He turns me round like a doll. 'You jump?' he says,
questioning, and his eyes are dilated like a hypnotic, like a
worshipper. If he gets the right answer will he win?

'I don't know,' I say. 'Do you?' He touches my temples,
brushes his hand against the side of my face. How can it be
that two men can touch you the same way and so differently?
I have no answer.

'Yes,' he says, finally. 'And I suppose you have to have
faith that you will make it.'

Faith. I always believed that would be a good name for a child, but what's in a name? I gave you one and somebody else gave you another and that is the one that you answer to. They say that if you change the name of a dog they will never answer you, but children, I imagine, must be more sophisticated. It was all I could give you and it wasn't much. 'Let's go to bed,' I say, and it is a fine antidote, I am discovering. It is best to be flippant and jolly about it so that he does not take it seriously.

'It's too early,' he says, sternly, and sets the painting on the easel. 'I have to submit this soon, there's a lot to be done yet.' He goes to scrub his palette and I wonder what he can be thinking of. This is not for his art tutor to peruse and criticise, not for the dull dirty walls of a studio and the embarrassed giggles of the students, envious and unsexed, with bad skin. I shake my head to clear it of unpleasant realities and we get to work again. Would somebody pay me to do this? I am becoming expert at it. If you're very quiet and very good and never complain then you shall have a big reward. It's usually the other way around in life, isn't it?

He strokes my shoulders with paint, he tells me. He likes to describe what he is doing. It is endearing but it interrupts my dreaming. 'What do your parents think about all this?' he says, gesturing around the room, at us, at the painting, at my life.

'My parents,' I say, playing for time.

'Mine seem to be glad that I've met a girl at last,' he says, laughing apologetically.

'Have you?' I say, surprised, and he laughs.

'Don't tease,' he says. 'Have you told them?'

'Look,' I say carefully, feeling my way. My words live inside me, they are too hard to belong out in the open. I remember your beloved face, stretched tight with pain in the unforgiving light when I told you what I had done. What had *you* ever done to deserve this? 'Patrick, I have to go soon,' I say, and he is confused. But the wedding day won't be delayed, and I have been slothful and fed on good things and lulled into believing that everything will be alright. 'Do you know where Nick is?' I ask him, and he looks uncomfortable.

'No,' he says. 'He took all his stuff though, so – '

'Not all,' I tell him. 'He left a suitcase in the wardrobe, full of clothes and photographs.' I have checked of course, conducting a thorough search of the flat as soon as I could. 'He must have told you where he is. He's got to go to college, hasn't he?' And Patrick's face is shadowed by the light and something else.

When I stand, stretching, for my official break, I see that Patrick has finished the face and is now working on the neck and shoulders. 'It's done,' I say, a secret thrill warming me.

'Only the head,' he says, surprised. 'I've got to do hours more yet.' But it is finished, can't you see that? I take his hand and lead him to the bedroom. He has the taste now and he is willing, although concerned that we get another sitting in before the light goes. I promise, I tell him. And then the doorbell rings.

'Can I come up?' the familiar voice said, hesitating, and Patrick wondered at the change. He felt victorious as he stood by the front door. Visitors had to ascend many flights of stairs to get to the flat. Before he opened the door he heard Rosa's voice, crossly. 'Whoever it is, tell them to sod off. Is it Mormons?' He pushed the bedroom door to, softly.

'Alright,' said Phyllis, breathing hard from the stairs. She ducked her head with embarrassment, and Patrick hurriedly ushered her in. He showed her into the living room and prayed for peace to continue. 'Sorry I've not been round,' she said, sitting neatly on the couch. Patrick was so astonished by her solemnity that he made her a coffee and sat in silence with her while she tried to find words.

'Are you alright?' he asked, genuinely concerned.

She looked away. 'Yeh, but I'm pregnant. It's okay, I'm sorting it, it's not a problem.'

Patrick swallowed hard and looked at her. 'Er – is it – how do you know?'

Phyllis laughed, a hollow metal laugh. She sniffed. 'It's not yours, don't shit yourself.'

Patrick felt that some response was expected of him all the same.

'Whose is it then?' he asked. 'I mean – are you sure it's not me? We were –'

'Yeh, but we used rubbers, remember?' Phyllis said, her voice completely expressionless. 'It's Mike. He's a graduate, he came to show us . . .' her voice trailed away. 'Oh, never mind, fuck, I just wanted to talk. She sniffed again. 'I smell pussy,' she said, and Patrick winced.

Rosa walked in, seeing the other girl. 'Oh,' she said, her face hardening.

'Oh indeed,' said Phyllis, putting her cup down. 'I haven't come to cause a scene. I'm up the duff, that's all. It's not his,' and she sat on, watching Rosa's face change from suspicion to sympathy and then to a terrible blank fear.

'What will you do?' asked Patrick, his forehead corrugated.

'Well, I'm not going to have it, that's for sure,' Phyllis said. 'So I suppose I'll have an abortion.'

Rosa walked into the kitchen and poured herself some wine. She stood propped up by the door, watching. Phyllis's bland white face had sharpened despite the slight weight she carried, her movements slower, more careful, as if she were dimly stirred from within. But her eyes were watchful, distracted by the scene she had walked into.

'How old are you?' Rosa asked her.

'Nineteen,' said Phyllis. 'So what? I should have been more sussed, I'm not blaming anybody. What would you do?'

Rosa sipped her wine carefully. 'If I were you, I would go now,' she said. Patrick watched confused. 'We are in the middle of something important,' she said, smiling insolently at Patrick.

'So'm I,' said Phyllis, but she stood heavily. Her eyes were dark with mascara and tiredness. 'Still getting married?' she asked Rosa as she made her way to the door. It did not seem to be said with malice.

'Of course,' Rosa said. 'I'm sure Nick would want you to be there, but it's going to be very small, you see. Very private.'

Phyllis stared at her and shook her head. 'D'you know something?' she said. 'You are insane. Do you know that?'

Rosa smiled. She drained her glass. 'I read somewhere that pregnant women often have hormone disorders,' she said. 'It gives them mild delusions. I have to go now.' And she disappeared into the kitchen with her glass, barely making a sound on bare feet.

Patrick showed Phyllis to the door. He patted her arm ineffectually. 'Listen, if there's anything you –'

'Patrick,' Phyllis said. 'I know you mean well but fuck off. I'll be alright. It's her you should worry about.' And she was gone. 'I'll come and see you when it's all over,' she shouted up at him, and he could hear her heavy tread on the stairs, echoing down the flights until the thick metal door clanged. When he went back inside, Rosa was lying in his bed, asleep, her arms flung out.

He went to the phone and dialled the number he had been given, confusion raging behind his eyelids. When the breathless operator answered he asked for Nick by name and the phone rang five times.

'Yeh?' Nick's tired voice said. 'Who is it?'

'It's me,' Patrick whispered. Everything resounded in this metallic hall. He put his hand, shaking, over the phone, cupping his words into the mouthpiece like a secret. 'It's Patrick. What are you doing there?'

Nick laughed. 'I'm back at home,' he said, and he sounded as though he were in a desert. Words rang back at Patrick, mangled and distorted, somebody else's conversation.

'Are you coming back?'

'Why would I?' said Nick. 'I like it here. I'm free. Get on with it.'

'Never?' Patrick asked, and all he heard then was the sound of a phone gently replaced and the dull singing of wires, then the operator's voice. *Please replace the handset and try again, please replace . . .*

In his room we lie apart, unusually. For in this short space of time, when I should be searching, I have lain here for many an hour with his legs trapping mine, his heavier body over me, his regular breathing. No nightmares here but he blinks a lot. I do not see that as a sign of major psychopathic disturbance and yet tonight he lies asleep but twitching, his arms thrashing occasionally. Once I have been hit in the face and once is enough. Now that I am sure he is asleep I get up silently and pull his jeans on, creeping into the living room for one of the cigarettes which I have taken care to hide in the kitchen drawer.

Nick? It's me. Pause. Patrick. Are you coming back? Betrayal is everywhere, but I have no complaint. If it were me I'd do the same. When they took you from me your skin was white paper and I counted the blue veins that ran through it. A pulse beat at your temple and your eyes never met mine except once. I held you in my arms and you screamed, knowing what I had done and was about to do. You screamed and we were alone. That's how I found you. Don't ask me now, I'll have to tell you later.

Are you coming back? Pause. Never?

However, thanks to British Telecom, I may now access Nick, there within reach, although I am peculiarly unable to act. But today is Thursday, just, and we are to be married tomorrow, I have decided, so there is no time for sensitive delays and small details. It is true that I have conducted most of the arrangements myself but that is the lot that often falls to the woman, is it not? I drag the phone through the living room, straining the wire. I press the redial button.

It rings. And rings, and I am nearly asleep before a voice answers, a nearly automated voice, telling me where I have reached. I press the receiver. It must be a wrong number. There is no other explanation. But when I redial there is the same hateful voice. 'Hello Millbarn Hotel and Restaurant, how can I help you?' I ask for Nick. 'I'll try to connect you to his line,' she says, and then a distant line rings, from a haunted dream. I replace the receiver.

He is there. And I know where to find him. He is, somehow, mystifyingly, at the only hotel in the town where we grew up.

Are you sleeping, my fine beauty? Can you dream me?

Because I am on my way.

I take very little with me. What will I need? My bag and a few cheap items of clothing. I leave a note for Patrick, because despite this, he has done nothing wrong to me. I don't know what to say to him so I make it short. I leave it against the easel because it seems appropriate. After all, without me he can still paint. He is clever enough to fill in the gaps. I sit smoking through the pack until the clock says five and I can expect to get a train from Euston, and I slip from the flat. What's that you say? Guilty?

The light is thin and I am scared, yes. There are no cabs but I can walk. There are not many miles between me and everything else now. I think of Phyllis, her tired eyes. She is strong and I hate her. I think of Patrick, his long legs stretching the sheets to capacity when he wakes hot and alone in the surprise of the morning. But by then it will nearly be over and I will shed my skin of guilt at an altar by tomorrow evening. Patrick gave me unconditional adoration and I gave him a lesson.

Take what you can while you can. Only the first lesson is free. That's all I can say, right now. It is not much but it is all there is. I reach the city and cross over, swerving into the West End. The light is yellow and as I reach Trafalgar Square, empty and littered, the ghosts of a thousand children seem to crowd the grey stone floor, their hands outstretched to the birds of the air. Their white legs in the fountains, turned blue with cold and faces red with excitement, caught on a thousand camcorders. Their screams of pleasure and fear rend the air, dividing it, and I walk through the middle, up onto roads that lead me eventually to the station.

When I look back, the children are leaving, their parents leading them away, their backs turned to me. Their hands stretch out, waving me goodbye. But I don't wave back, because I can't promise anything. I move forward, into the future.

And now there is silence.

CHAPTER 13

The shrill of the phone cut into Nick's sleep, punctuating his dreams, restless versions of the truth. He ignored the ringing and sat up, disoriented. I still don't know where I am, he thought, and then he realised why. He did not choose to linger in the small bed, little different from the one in London, or the camp bed on the floor of his parents' spare bathroom. A bed was a bed, and the only difference could be who was in it. There was an abrupt knock on the door and Nick swung his thin legs onto the cold lino. He searched for a cigarette and found, disgusted, that he had none.

'You're on in half an hour,' a voice said from outside the door, inches away, and Nick sniffed in response. Through the window traffic blared and fumed, and directly under his room was a car park where every single vehicle seemed to be beige or grey.

'Where d'you think you're going?' said Nicola from the bed as Nick tiptoed to the door. She lay facing the wall and as she turned over, her body appeared to be permanently squashed into the shape she had been forced during sleep. Nick was reminded irritably of Tom in the cartoon, and he resisted an urge to mould her back into the shape of Nicola – curves and an abundance of flesh.

'You'll have to go,' Nick said, face puffed and bleary with sleep. If anyone catches you I'll get the sack.'

Nicola sat up, sullen. She burped, her face still wearing last night's make-up, although it had slipped a few inches. 'I'm not a slag, you know,' she said, and Nick winced, wanting her gone so he could concentrate his mind.

'Of course not.' He smiled at her from under his lashes. 'But you do see, don't you . . .?' And he leaned forward to kiss her, tasting her stale perfume and early-morning breath. If she tasted the same on him, she did not remark on it. She reached for him to pull him down, but he pushed her away, still kissing her, edging delicately from her. 'You're very tempting,' he said, as he moved from her, 'but I really do have to go now. I'll call you later on, okay?'

She pulled her clothes on, suddenly eager to leave the room, the daylight making her close her eyes. 'Yeh,' she said, 'probably.' Why not? He was a considerate lover and good to look at even in the morning, although she sensed that she was not. In this town men who remained available and not brutish were something to come across, and if he did not last long, he was at least a welcome diversion. What else is there, Nicola thought, in this bloody place? He opened the door for her, always polite, and as she passed through she kissed him again, a lingering, wet, sultry kiss. Nick smacked her backside smartly and they went down the corridor in different directions, Nick willing her to remain undiscovered.

As Nicola glanced back, she saw him wipe his mouth furiously with his sleeve, heading for the showers. I feel sick, she thought, and she knew that she would not see him again, even if he were to call her. She suppressed the need to scream and left the building with an urge to go shoplifting.

Nick sang along loudly to a dance tape while he shaved – with a proper razor to keep his skin smooth. He had always suffered terribly with acne and now feared waking with a red itch anywhere on his face. Not aftershave, that was for losers or anxious men, but some lotion. He washed and conditioned his hair, recently cut, and now he worked it with gel and a mousse preparation, bought in London at a salon. How did you manage to stay beautiful, Rosa had asked him once, with genuine curiosity, after a night spent telling each other their life stories.

When he had told her about his father's casual and predictable violence she had studied his eyes, his pale, easily marked skin, the long fingers, touching his ribcage when he pointed out the few scars. If he had exaggerated a little, his occasionally defective memory was partly responsible, and her expectations encouraged him. As if she wanted to say something, but wanted to hear him tell her first.

He searched his mind vaguely, but he could not really remember that she had told him anything, anything at all, now that he thought about it. Briskly he outlined his eyes with faint liner, imperceptible to most, and examined his pale form in the blurred mirror before leaving.

He did not think about Nicola at all, until he straightened the coverlet in his room and removed the condoms now stuck firmly to the rug. He was surprised and relieved at how easy she had been to get rid of. I'll call her later, he decided, and then, *maybe*. The room stank.

In the last few weeks, before Nick disappeared into his temporary retreat, I bought his time to some extent. Not that he had to be persuaded, you understand, but he was busy and the lure of dinner or a drink or two was what it took. I didn't mind, not really. There's always a price and you take what you can get in this life, don't you? I did. I do.

As I approach the High Street, I see myself a hundred times over in shop windows, which is the really terrible thing about small towns. There are so many reflections and nothing else to look at. Not many people, not enough. The butcher, the baker, the furniture maker. None have customers, and I stare at them all, willing someone to remember me, to allow an expression of puzzlement and then recognition to slide over their face, to stop me and ask me how I am, although it is not in my interests for them to do so. In London I enjoy the blankness of faces, a thousand strangers passing in the course of a day, but here I long suddenly for someone to tell me who I am. How are you who are you what did you say?

It doesn't matter. I am fanciful no doubt as the day is long and the road is a straight one, lined with memories like trees. The post office, the bank, the cheap dress shop where tarty skirts can still be purchased, and when I pause at the window I see the younger sister of a schoolmate serving at the till, bored, eating chocolate. Her sharp eyes stare back at me for a moment and I hold my breath but she looks away, dulled by her life, and takes a customer's money with resignation. I badly want to go in and seize her arm and say, where is your sister now? But that would mean that I cared to find out, and there is only one reason to be here again. Women my age pass me by with two children: one in the pushchair, crying silently, pale and straw-haired, one clutching sweets and wandering near to the traffic. Their faces are fattened and softened, eyes constantly pulled in the direction of screams and tiny noises, like instinct tugging at their stomachs.

The town has changed. Yes, I dawdle. I want to examine every change, to map the way it has altered exactly and know what it means. Where the Olde English Grill stood, offering cheap omelette and chips, dirt in every crevice, is now a Tapas bar. The menu features Sangria, Jugs Of, and Spanish Omelette . . . I try to imagine the seventeen-year-olds crowding in, eager to jostle at the bar and sip tequila. Jo-Anne's Hairdressing Salon is still here, the site of my monthly torture by fringe-cutting, but the windows are blocked with white paint and a new sign is being hoisted over my head on ladders and large men. I duck for luck and walk on.

The clock tower chimes, and that is a surprise, because it never used to. Everywhere the colours are bright but not garish. When I grew up here all was muted shades, but now I see blue and red and yellow and green, and awnings announce small cafes, and a delicatessen, and the previously fabulous Italian shoe boutique has become a smart Levi concession. Now I am here and beyond the miraculously operating clock tower is the Millbarn Hotel, which is neither a mill nor a barn, but a dull building in pale-flesh brick, with a large circular car park enclosing it. A hotel, and the only one in this town.

Beyond that is the long road or the short cut to the small church of our youth. And beyond that is darkness, because the town ends there, in that darkness.

I could walk for ever into that darkness.

'How many?' Nick asked. He was sweating and the man with him noticed the dark stain on his back as he walked in front, through the huge hall.

'Three hundred,' said the man. He lit a cigarette and then, as an afterthought, offered one to Nick, who hesitated and then took one. 'It's no big deal, really,' the man said, as Nick blew smoke rings. 'All you've got to remember is that if they're drunk, they'll be happy. Happens every week.' Nick nodded casually. He wiped his face quickly as the man turned away.

'Can Nick O'Connor come to front desk please?' asked the receptionist over the PA system. Nick pointed his fingers, gun like, at the man.

'I'll be back,' he said, with a bad Arnie impression and a confidence he did not feel. He felt like running out of the hotel screaming.

When he saw Rosa standing there, he did not want to run screaming from her. He admired her profile and the fall of hair that lay about her shoulders and back and he walked up to her without a sinking of the heart. 'Hi,' she said, and he smiled and kissed her, noticing that she drew back slightly from the smell of grease.

'I've only got ten minutes,' he said and drew her away from the front desk out into the forecourt.

'What are you doing here?' she said. They sat on a grey concrete wall watching traffic.

'I'm working,' said Nick, holding his hands up. 'Trying to make some money, that's all.' He did not mention escape because her eyes were brilliant and she had not tried to touch him. 'I've got to go back in.'

'When do you finish?' she said, her face serious. 'You're so far away from London. We need to meet up later.'

'Yes,' he said, stretching his already tired face in agreement. 'Does Patrick know you're here?' he asked. *You belong to him, he thought, has he told you yet what we bargained for? You were the –*

'Patrick?' she said, puzzled. 'What time d'you get off?'

Eight, he said, edging towards the hotel doors in his uniform. I'll see you then, she said, and as he pushed thankfully through the glass doors she shouted something at him. *What job are you doing anyway?* But the words were lost to the winds and he slipped through the corridors to his boss, to finish sorting out the arrangements for the wedding reception. He contemplated not appearing later, but he knew Rosa. She would turn up at reception and bang her fist on the desk, making wild shrill sounds until he was brought to her. 'Your girlfriend?' asked the manager.

'Just someone I used to go to school with. Show us how to fold those napkins again, I've forgotten.'

We go to dinner. I sweep him off to the only other restaurant in town besides the Tapas Bar selling Sangria, Jugs Of. An Indian place, which previously would not have been tolerated here. People would have complained about the smell of curried foods drifting towards their Barratt Homes half a mile away and the decor would have been unpleasing to them, the faces of the proprietors too unfamiliar, however polite and accommodating. Now ageing couples and foursomes dine here, on the plush banquettes that smell of vicious air freshener and lager rather than chicken madras and lamb rhogan josh. His face is white amid the rosy splendour of the walls and the spray of artificial flowers almost separates us but he chose this table, not me.

'You've come a long way for a short date,' he says, smiling but tired, and I smile, confused. Why wouldn't I?

A trip out of town, he says. I laugh and show my teeth but I would go to Africa to see him for ten minutes. Never chase a man, my grandmother said to me once, spectacularly, before she died. You don't want to be out of breath, she said, and shortly after expired. I don't see why this thought should come to me now. We order some wine and a crowd of lads pile into the place, making the waiter anxious. He smiles too much, you can always tell. They settle near us, pissed. 'Oi, Gandhi, bring us some poppadums,' shouts one and grins at us, foolishly, at the wallpaper, at anything. Nick leans back.

'So how are you?' he says.

'Fine,' I say, 'considering.'

'Considering what?' He tastes the wine he is offered, although I expect I shall be paying, with the twenty I borrowed from Patrick. 'Mmmm, that's great,' he tells the waiter, and I reach out to touch his hand just as he draws it back, to light his cigarette. My timing is out.

'Considering that you disappeared,' I tell him.

His face says nothing. I scan it. 'But I'm working,' he says, and he raises his now full glass to mine and leans forward.

'Shall we drink to you?'

I hold my breath and my glass aloft. 'To you,' he says, and we press our glasses together thinly, delicately, so as not to break the tender glass. In the public toilets I have dressed carefully, to wear what would please him but not trying too hard, so as not to anger him. You may laugh, but I hope you will not. I hope in vain that you will see how scared I am, how sure I am, how it must all be right. A thin narrow line to tread but I am a tightrope walker and there is no net beneath me to catch my mistakes.

'Do you still want me?' I ask him. I flip upside down on the wire, my hands outstretched. If he catches me I'll make it, but that's what training is for. It's all down to timing, isn't it? You save the triple somersault for last, when the crowd begins to rise for an encore and your heart soars, the clapping marking your rhythm for you. He cocks his head, but that isn't good enough any more.

There is a little silence, during which I plot my slow descent.

'Of course I want you,' he says, filling my glass before his. I am pathetically grateful for this courtesy. We expect less than we deserve, always. You know that, you expected that I would not fail you and do not close the door quite, yet. 'Who wouldn't?' he says thoughtfully. 'You are beautiful.'

Is that all? I am disappointed, for the first time, I confess, because I expect more than this. I am tired and I long for honesty but not here. I call for the bill for food which he has devoured like a rabbit, his front teeth working, and I have ignored.

'Can I come back with you?' I ask, and he looks up at me, his eyes shadowed with tiredness and I long to reach out and touch the skin under his eyes so tender not silk but soft damp elastic and he laughs, a harsh abrupt sound.

'When does your last train go?' he says.

'Later,' I say. Later, much later. Now is not the time to mention the church, obviously, we are not relaxed enough. Nick goes to the gents and I buy a secret bottle of wine to take back with us.

In the street, he weaves against me and takes my arm. 'We're going to talk,' he says, as we reach the hotel, and he steers me away from the reception desk. We go in the

Tradesman's Entrance and we giggle as we reach a room, a dark musty room, and he turns the light on, and we work at the cork, still giggling, out of breath. I perch on the bed awkwardly and Nick stands.

'So talk,' he says, and he is watching the clock. The room is littered with boxer shorts, tissues, human remains. I have some time to play with but not much. I stand up near him. Not too near. He doesn't move. Good. I am still, very still, my body held within itself. I watch him but he does not move. Despite myself, I grow impatient. Time ticks away and we linger as if we possess liberty in some way but we do not.

Then I lean forward and I put my hands against his thin chest and I feel his heart beating and the room is after all very small and we are together, close together, and I can't say whether he kisses me or I kiss him but we kiss I close my eyes and my skin welds against his how I have needed this! And I feel him stiffen against me and I can't help myself after all

You do want me, I say, and before the words are cooling in the air he is pulling away, into the light, saying unfamiliar things to me.

'I'll sleep on the floor,' he says, his face blank and scared, and it takes me minutes to realise.

It's bad luck for the bride and groom to spend the night under the same roof. And this is his version of it. He wants me to go, but I won't give in to tradition. No. I'll sleep on the floor, I say, although I want nothing less, now.

No. He is adamant that I will sleep in his bed and he takes a pillow to prove it. 'It won't matter soon,' I say, but he is religious sometimes and he turns his head and I love the nape of his neck to distraction and I agree. The light on, he lies on the hard floor as I undress completely and slide into his bed, hold my breath for other perfumes and lie still.

'Promise you won't touch me?'

I can hear his breathing from the floor and I lie as near the wall as I can get, a sliver of a human life. I'm barely here.

'Promise?' he says.

Yes o yes I do –

The light goes off and we breathe with the generator running beneath us, its throb a hungry distraction to sleep. I am on a hill and he is beneath, the light I now see casting itself blue over him, lying white and thin under a pale gaze. In the first days of your life you were blue and tiny in a space made for you, just you, and I watched you thrash under a yellow blanket. Then, surrounded by others, your cries were indistinguishable.

'What?' Nick cries suddenly, thrusting his hands from the floor, fighting air. 'What? What?' Caught in the blanket of half sleep, he climbs into the bed, his bed, and I am thankful for his timing. I break my promise.

I slide my body against him, holding my breath still, over him. He groans with sleepy petulance but I cannot help myself. I wind myself around him, kissing his skin, stretching my hand down and sliding him inside me. I move slowly so that he does not quite wake and I can feel his heart fluttering under my hands. 'Cold,' he says suddenly, and then he turns me over swiftly and lies in me, moving like in a dream. Now he won't let me kiss him but I breathe shallowly, lying on the surface of a riverbed. I think he comes but I can't be sure, but he pulls out of me like shock and sits upright, running his hand over his face, turning the light on. He looks scared and young and then we both look down and there is blood everywhere.

The bare bulb of light shows us the blood slick like a snail trail on his thighs my thighs the bedclothes and his limpness.

I've never seen him move so fast. His face changes, hatred flashing across his features before he runs out of the room to the bathroom. I hear the sound of him being violently sick and the shower runs full blast for a long time.

When he comes back I am shivering. His face is set hard, lips white. He picks up my clothes with his finger and thumb as though they disgust him. 'Put them on,' he tells me.

'It's just my period,' I say, but my voice is thin and weak in this room, which echoes, throwing my words back at me.

'You're going,' he says. 'Now. Out.'

I pull my clothes on with shaking hands, tights sticking to

my damp and bloodied thighs. It is 2 a.m. Where will I go, I ask him. He shrugs and holds the door open, not looking at me. He can't look at me. His hand is tightening on the handle, wanting it to be over already but I don't understand.

We are going to be married tomorrow, I say, and he laughs, with surprise, I think. It's hard to tell because my senses have shrunk. Marry you, he says. I leave the room and he follows me out, locking the door. He leans close to me and I know he realises now that he has made a mistake.

If you ever come near me again, he says to me, I will call the police. Do you understand? Before I can tell him that the church is booked, he knocks on the door of the next room. Where are you going, I ask him.

I will not go back in there until it has been cleaned of you and you are gone, he says, his mouth slatey and grey. Now go. The door opens and he walks inside and slams it shut.

Then I hear the key turn inside and silence. There is a corridor ahead of me and I stumble down it until I find a door that leads away from this place.

Outside, nothing moves except me and the wind. There are no trains and no buses and the people here have buttoned themselves into their neat homes. Are they watching me from behind their printed curtains? I don't know. There is no money and now the rain starts as I stand at the deserted bus stop. Blood is running down my thighs, oozing like a stain.

A car slows beside me. Police. *What's up love?*

They see only the blood and the tears and my face and they think that I have been raped. When they ask me to explain exactly what has happened I cannot quite tell them.

I have to get in, don't I? Anything else would have worried them. Besides, there is a strange relief in being taken away.

At the police station, they sit me next to a lolling drunk who vomits on the floor in front of me. A woman police officer wants to talk to me but I explain that I would rather just go. Go where, love? they ask, and they are kind, but it isn't their kindness that I want. It is the kindness of a razor that I want and if I had one I would use it now, quickly.

It is 3 a.m. now. When their backs are turned I rise and

walk out and start for the train station. It is closed and it is cold and I sit outside until it opens for the 6.15 to London, stinking of my own blood and rottenness.

I want to die.

CHAPTER 14

The painting stood against the wall, its eyes following the viewer around the room. There were other portraits, other aubergines, other bold and strange abstracts, but Patrick saw nothing else. His eyes burned, and he had been up all night. He had drunk half a bottle of cheap wine and some very old and stale bitter, and all he got was sick, but the racing fear had subsided a little, and now all he could feel was a hangover, which was an unusual experience, although not one he cared for.

He had called Nick as soon as he had woken the previous morning and, waiting to be put through, he had known that he would be lost for the right words even if he were to reach Nick. *I'm ringing to warn you? To ask you not to* – No. And the flat tone of the receptionist had told him that there was no answer. He's probably not up yet,' and there had been just a faint hint of knowing smugness. Is she with him, Patrick wanted to scream. Has she found him again, what has he done –

'Yes,' said Ani, the tutor, her crisp voice suddenly close to him. 'It's good.'

'I know,' said Patrick, and Ani was surprised, because he was not a student to acknowledge his own worth, however lightly.

'Why isn't it quite finished?' she asked, and he stared at the painting, a face rising out of lines half filled in with lack of inspiration.

'The model disappeared,' Patrick said, heat rising into his face.

'I see,' said the tutor. 'There's something slightly wrong with the eyes, though. I'm not sure . . .' She walked past it, concentrating.

'Too staring?' Patrick said, not really caring at that moment. 'Too beautiful?'

'No,' the tutor said. 'In fact, the problem is that there doesn't seem to be anything in them at all. It's rather eerie. Apart from that, the execution is excellent. Well done.' And she moved on to study the aubergine. 'You're a good student, Patrick, you'll do well. Have you thought about where to go next?'

'Nowhere near vegetables,' Patrick said, thinking, dully, a good student. Not amazing, not brilliant, or outstanding, but a good student who would do well. Would he be a good husband, a good father, a good worker? A boy without complaints, without too much greed or with too little ambition, content to accept what he could have and equally what he could not? 'Maybe I'll be a graphic designer for Tesco,' he said bitterly, and his tutor laughed.

'That's an insult to this school, although it might suit some,' she said. 'Stay away from commerce and advertising. Both will dilute your talent.'

'What do you suggest, then?' he said. 'Artists don't starve in garrets any longer, do they? Should I start collecting bricks and dead sheep?'

'No,' said Ani, who did not dislike teaching, but was sometimes wearied when students changed personality between lectures. 'You should paint this girl again. If you can find her, of course.' And she saw the usually dull and calm Patrick shudder just a little, as if he were gripped by a sharp ache.

'How can I paint her again?' he said, miserably. 'She's gone off with Nick.'

Look,' Ani said, gently now. 'This is no good, no good at all. She must be important to you. This work has something tremendous about it, don't you want to seize that? My Christ, if I were you – ' and she shut up then, because her own desires were no business of his.

'Did you used to paint?' Patrick asked her, eager to get away from the subject of Rosa. 'What did you paint? Were you good?' and he ducked his head, with shame. 'Are you good? Can I see?'

'You know what they say,' Ani said lightly, pulling an urban landscape further into the light. 'If you can, do. If you can't, teach. The light is good here, is the perspective meant to be this way?'

'But you're a good teacher,' Patrick said, bewildered, seeing his tutor grimace.

'Exactly,' she said. 'So I'd better teach you about perspective again, hadn't I?' And they bent their heads over the painting, which was indeed not his best effort. And if Ani's hands were not quite steady, neither of them appeared to notice it.

When I reach the flat it is late morning. I hope that Patrick will not be there but when he is I am glad all the same. His face appears tentatively and he does not ask questions but looks at me, slowly, taking it all in, because I have not made any attempt to clean my rotten self up. Why would I? On the train, commuters averted their eyes and wrinkled their noses and a guard asked me to stand in the mail van, but I could not speak or move and so I sat on, like a rat, in my own filth and rancour.

You think this is too much? You think, maybe, that I could have made the effort? After all, it's not so bad, really, is it? Come now . . . But Patrick runs me a bath without words and brings me some chocolate melted into a cup with warm milk and even when I climb out and am sick instantly he puts me to bed while he cleans up. I snuggle in bed, a sick child, an invalid, a daydreamer, the warmth of the bottle at my feet turning my body to sludge and mush. My brain floats above it all and Patrick sits by the bed, watching, while I drift uncertainly.

If I could speak I would say simply, *Thank you.*

When I wake, it seems as though days have passed. I do know where I am but I don't know what to do now. I do not list what I have not got but there are no arrows leading to Your Next Move. In the living room there is a gap where I was. 'Where am I?' I say, testing words, and Patrick looks startled. He touches my forehead but touch is repulsive to me and I shy away. 'I know where I am,' I tell him. 'But where is she?' When he understands, he looks puzzled, faintly alarmed, and a lock of hair falls into his eyes. Two days ago I would have pushed it aside, taken his head against my breasts, but now I want to take a razor to his head that no more locks shall fall, as Nick's did, although artifice and not shyness was the cause there.

When he tells me what he has done with Me, I do not scream. 'It belongs to me,' I tell him, since he has not understood that already. 'It's mine.'

'How can it be yours?' he says. He frowns. O I know what you have done, between you. You have stolen me. 'I painted you. I don't – what have I – '

He comes closer to me and I slap him, hard, across the mouth. He springs back but I o I am ready for more. There is blood and shock on his face and I am confused, disoriented. There's something I have to remember, something –

'What happened?' he says. He puts on his glasses, touches his mouth gingerly. Poor Patrick. Patrick must not be hurt. That was what I had to remember, but –

'Did you see Nick?' he asks, his voice low, considerate. Patrick is nice, isn't he?

'I'm sorry,' I say, and I am. 'Are you hurt? – does it sting? – let me put something on it.' But he tells me that it's alright, he'll live. He is absurd, blood like jam smeared over his mouth, glasses at an angle.

'Nick,' he says. 'Did you see him?'

'Oh, Nick,' I say. My voice is coming to you from a different planet. 'Yes. I'll move out soon,' I say, although this is disconnected from our conversation, and there is the tiny matter of money, job, life, etcetera. It doesn't seem real to me but I know that I must go soon.

'Move out? But you were covered in blood,' he says. 'I nearly phoned the police – '

I laugh. 'They've been informed,' I tell him, for reassurance. 'I have been to the police station.' I want to be alone now, but I can hardly ask him to leave his own flat, although he would. That is why I do not ask because I have hurt enough people and everything keeps going wrong however hard I try to make it right. Next thing I know he's bringing me brandy.

'Try and sip it,' he says, his eyes myopic. Sip it? I ask for vodka and while he is gone throw back the brandy anyway.

'I've been thinking,' he says, nervous as always. 'My tutor says that I could really make something of . . . this,' spreading his arms to indicate the easel and palette, the fragments of charcoal and glasses of dyed water, the scraps of sketches. Plans for a life. Lucky Patrick.

'Yes,' I say. 'That's good and I'm pleased for you.'

'No,' he insists. 'I thought – if you – you don't have to go anywhere, we can stay here – '

We?

' – because there's money, not much, not riches, but I get enough – my dad'll give – and there's always work, isn't there? Not that you have to, but – ' He is sweating, he always does, but his forehead is shining now and his lip, a white damp blur of skin, too close to me too close. ' – And if we were, it would make me so hap – I haven't told you, how I f-feel, but I'd never hurt you – ' Why do men always say this? Do women say, But I'll Never Hurt You Jim? I don't think so. 'Nobody has to know, if you don't want – I know there are things you haven't told me, but I could make everything alright, I'd look after – '

'Patrick,' I say. 'What are you talking about?'

'I want to marry you,' he says, and he wipes the moisture from his mouth. 'I want you to be my wife.'

'I don't think you understand what you're saying,' she said, taking more vodka.

He watched the level of the bottle. 'Don't have too much of that stuff,' he warned her. 'You're not well.'

He saw her eyes turn on him savagely and she drained the glass and refilled it. 'What do you know?' she said. 'You've gone mad, Patrick.'

But he felt his body alert and sinewy and if he were alone he would have run his hands over himself, feeling the taut skin, the pumping blood, the aliveness. To feel something, he thought – 'No,' he told her, removing the bottle. 'I'm not mad. I know what I'm saying, I've practised it for days in my head. It might not be perfect but it would work, I know it would, think about it.' He leaned forward. She leaned back, but it was a shock, wasn't it?

'I've never wanted anything before,' he said, looking fully at her. Her eyes glittered and her skin was white and smooth and he knew all about her. 'The past is gone,' he said madly, words tumbling from him now. 'I'd never treat you like Nick did. I don't want anybody else, I even stopped seeing Phyllis because I couldn't stop thinking about you, what your mouth would taste like, how you'd feel, how I could . . . love you,' he finished lamely, ashamed of his need. 'What more could you want?'

'Do you know what Nick thought of you?' she asked, and as she reached for the bottle, her mouth opened and she hissed the words at him. 'Christ, you fool, he felt sorry for you, he said you were the only virgin left in captivity.'

'He used you!' Patrick cried. 'He asked every girl he brought back here to marry him. It was one of his – '

'I won't hear this,' she said, shrinking away from him.

'Don't you understand?' Patrick shouted at her. His face felt hot and wet but he could not stop now. 'It was one of his lines. It always worked, on the second or third date he'd say, will you marry me, you know I've always wanted to, ever since the first – '

'If you care for me at all, don't tell me any more,' Rosa said, forcing out the words and he saw her eyes close with trying to shut it out. You must hear this, he thought, and he knew it was not to be said.

'Do you know why he left?' he asked her, and the light was fading outside. The new glass made the view perfect and he barely heard her.

'He will always be mine,' she whispered. 'He'll come to save me, you'll see. What else is left? There's nothing . . .'

He knew that he should stop but something else was inside him now. The invisible man, Nick had called him, and they had both laughed the first time he said it, but in the street outside Patrick had been elbowed aside while Nick strode ahead, unencumbered.

'He left because he lost at poker,' he said, sickened now, remembering Nick's face, glowing with the anticipation of winning, knowing he surely would. Don't I always, he had said, after the second hand, but best of three, remember. And he, like a fool, thinking it would stop him leaving: don't turn them over, Nick, it doesn't matter anyway, does it?

I could let you win, he had thought, but the bitter taste inside him had risen in his throat like bile and he had won, in the end.

'So?' Rosa said, her face sure and distant. 'He's a bad loser.'

'We played for you,' Patrick said. 'And he lost. And then he left, and he won't come back.'

Rosa sat very still.

'Can I paint you again?' Patrick said insanely, seeing her in a series of portraits. Maybe in a gallery, their triumph together. The artist and his model, the artist and his inspiration, the artist and his wife . . .

'And you won,' she said. 'You won me, is that it?'

'Yes,' Patrick said. His legs had turned cold and he realised dimly that the bottle of vodka was spilling down his jeans. 'I'm soaked,' he said, laughing nervously. 'Look at me! I'm asking you to marry me and I'm – soaked . . .'

'The thing is, Patrick,' Rosa said, her hands in her lap. 'I don't love you.'

Patrick absorbed this in silence. He swallowed. 'I don't expect that you could, right now, but I think we could – '

'I am going now,' Rosa said, standing up.

'You can't,' said Patrick, appalled. 'You're drunk and you've got nowhere to go.'

Rosa smiled. 'The seaside. I think I shall go to the seaside. A nice little break by the sea. It will do me good.' She picked up the bottle of vodka and capped the remaining liquid tightly. 'Mind if I take this?'

'I love you,' Patrick said. 'Where are you going?'

Rosa yawned. Her gums were pink and her eyes tired. 'If I go now I will catch the next train to Radley. I know all the train times off by heart. Sad, isn't it?' Patrick sat, his legs wobbly. 'When you played poker, what would you usually play for? she asked. 'Assuming that you weren't putting girlfriends up as the prize, that is?'

'Rosa, please, don't do this – ' Patrick rose to go to her.

'No,' she said, holding him away from her. 'Keep away from me. What would you play for? Money? How much?'

'We hardly ever played – once or twice. Maybe for – records, or – '

Rosa was holding the front door open now. 'What was the most you played for?' she asked. 'Five – ten – what? I'm curious.'

'Let me come with you,' Patrick said, desperate now. 'I can be ready in a second – '

'How much?' she said.

Patrick bowed his head. 'Nick used a five-pound bag of ten-pence pieces,' he said. Rosa nodded. He heard her laugh, a quick, sharp, cutting sound like a knife and when he looked up the door banged in the silence and she was gone.

So. The water is cold on the train. I am used to trains in my life. They take me to all the places I need to go, isn't that a miracle? After ninety minutes I have sipped the vodka away and we slow down, pulling into the place where the journey ends. Will you be glad? You, in that seaside place where the tide never came in. Does it disappoint you, still?

My bones ache, and I examine my skin in the tired blue light of the tiny toilet. I see no marks but there are teethmarks under the flesh, tiny scars nibbling away at the bone. Is this how you felt? Did you crumble inch by inch, getting smaller? I'm sorry. I hoped to have better news to soften my arrival but I cannot even promise that.

No one else alights here because it is the end. A tired British Rail man stands waiting for me and my ticket but there is only one of us present. Me.

'Late,' he says, as I panic.

'Can I give you a cheque?' I say.

'Late, that train,' he repeats. Under the bright shout of his torch I cannot see him. There is nowhere to run and I smell whisky. 'Where you staying?' he says, and he turns the torch off.

A bar with no name, where he knocks three times and the door swings open, a blast of sound struggling to get out. I am so near now and he will buy me what I need for the last part of this journey. For a price. He buys me a tequila because it is easy to lip-read the order when he gets to the bar. In the half light he is forty, short, with blond hair cut like a soldier and a dirty beard. His eyes are small and hungry but he is in no hurry. I excuse myself after the third tequila, go to the Ladies and am neatly sick, like a cat. I work out that I am eight streets from you, half a mile. And I am drunk, and I have no money and no portrait and no husband.

At the hotel he says stays open late he takes a room and payment is stayed like execution until the morning, which alarms me. Endless corridors and I know that the floor would still be slanted and the walls narrowing in upon us if I was sober. I smell piss as he puts his hand over my mouth to quiet my fall. The room is small and shaped strangely with a view only of the kitchens. When I point this out he laughs harshly and says that he is paying for the bed not the view. I think he is paying for both but opinion costs extra.

I have forgotten his name but he turns the light on and I lie on the bed because that is all there is in the room. He lies over me and the breath is squashed out of me. He undresses me and I lie like a corpse while he plays with my breasts. They are small but they are breasts and he grunts, apparently satisfied. He is undoing his flies. I move back on the hard bed. It squeaks. His cock is long and thin and very red, like an angry Peperami. I could bite it off with one snap of my long sharp white teeth but I am here of my own free will. What's that you say?

I won't come to you with nothing.

I am dry. 'It's alright,' I say, terrified of being left alone with my inadequacy. 'Go ahead.' But he takes me at my word and he moves down, down, down, until his mouth is against me and I am caught in the gap between pain and indifference, could be something else, his teeth catching at me, a glancing blow. I gasp and he scrapes back up my body, pushing himself into me, heaving and struggling and sighing angrily, finding me rough and tight and still dry.

And then he is there and it does not take him long and he lies, spent like a fish on my skin, and I can smell him again, but it is not whisky this time. He pulls out of me quickly and shreds the condom from his body. His eyes slide away, not with shame, but with blankness, and he pulls some money from his pocket and lets it fall on to the floor.

He adjusts his British Rail uniform. 'Thanks,' he says. 'That was alright.' And he is gone, and when the door closes I pick up the notes and see that he has overpaid me.

And I am alone at last.

Patrick is scrubbing the kitchen. Isn't this what women do when they are angry? No, it is just what women do. But Patrick doesn't think about what he is doing. He scrubs the floor and the dirty wounds of the cooker, its mouth a gash of crusted junk. Nick's junk, Rosa's junk, other people's lives, messy and full. The phone rings and rings but he is immersed in the cracks between the tiles, devouring dirt like a Christian.

When the kitchen shines like glass he stands up, breathing hard. Nobody lives here now, only him. In the shower he scrapes and tears the flannel over his long white body until he is red raw clean. There are no windows in his bathroom and he likes it that way, used to like it, but now there is nothing left, not now that he has scrubbed the dirt away.

When he goes to the phone it is silent and he is puzzled. He must have imagined it but he picks it up anyway and there is nobody there. He dials the station. There are trains there are planes there are buses. 'Hello?' says the operator, testily. 'How can I help you?' But Patrick can't decide yet exactly how she can help him. The windows are still dirty and he hasn't even touched Nick's room yet.

He starts to cry and the expression in the plate glass stops him, reflecting back at him. In the bedroom, Nick's bedroom, he sees the empty space, feeling underneath the bed for memories. There are things there and his hands touch them but he pulls back. He lies on the bed in the dark, touching himself, feeling his shape, but he cannot stop crying, the tears tasting salty in his mouth, his nose blocked. He imagines Nick lying over her, his hands finding her with confidence in the dark. He knows that Nick prefers the dark because it is his territory.

Where are you, he asks, but there is no answer because he is alone.

He stands and pulls the portrait of Rosa from Nick's cupboard. If you had asked me I would have given it to you, he thinks, and he stares at the eyes that have no meaning.

'I would have given it to you anyway,' he says out loud, frightened suddenly of the silence that will no longer be broken by anyone bursting in the door, telling of adventures, asking for loans, demanding drinks.

And so he packs a small holdall, because he is Patrick and he is sensible. A toothbrush, a change of clothing, a flannel. And he rolls up the painting, although it hurts him to do so, and he calls a cab.

It's nearly dark when he finds the snaking road that leads to the sea. He passes a score of amusement arcades but nobody seems to be having a good time. The faces swim red and yellow and he stops abruptly in a pub populated by a few old men and several morose couples and orders a pint. 'A pint of what?' asks the bemused barmaid, and Patrick's head swims, but he points at a tap and the barmaid shrugs and folds her arms, as if he is a lunatic.

'Give me a whisky,' he says, emboldened by his task. 'Have you seen a girl in here, about twenty, lot of hair?' he asks, and she stares at him.

'Yeh,' she says, making her eyes big and round with amazement. 'Matter of fact, I have.' She hands him the whisky and he drinks it too quickly, choking a little. She winks at the landlord.

'When?' Patrick asks, gesturing for more whisky, his blood racing to keep up with his new drinking pace.

'All the bloody time,' the girl says, laughing. 'Every girl in this town's got big hair.'

With his holdall, Patrick walks down the bright tatty street with its neon-lit chippies, families falling silent and morose over the mushy peas and ice-cream. He goes into every one and stands, a forlorn figure in his pressed jeans, his eyes wild. He smells of drink now. In a bar called Fella's, he thinks finally that it might be Rosa's kind of place. It is murky and smoke-filled, and scruffy men with tattoos line the bar. There is a band, white boys with dreadlocks and bad music. His hands shake and a thin spotty man offers him drugs. When he leaves, he is drunk. He begins on the hotels, although he knows that she has no money. As he heads for the third, his steps are faltering and his legs do not seem to be going where his brain tells them to.

And then something hits him out of the darkness. 'Sorry, mate,' and a burp, and all Patrick can make out as the stranger helps him up is a British Rail badge on a jacket, and the rasp and click of a lighter before the man goes on his way. And now he can smell the sea because it is suddenly immediately before him and the air has changed. The pier lights are turning the water green and white in patches and the screaming of girls is hidden by the rush of the waves.

When he goes down to the beach, curiously the sea is not there.

The sound of water fills his ears but the tide is going out and the water is halfway down the bay. It seems to be raining and he puts his hand up to ward off the drops but the air is clear. His face is wet. He puts the holdall down for a minute and forgets why he is here.

'I'm at the seaside,' he says, and a young couple passing by giggle at his drunkenness.

I pee in the wastepaper bin standing up, because there is no toilet. A nice man, to have brought me to a room with no toilet, I think bitterly, and count the notes again. It is late and I am not drunk enough for comfort but too drunk to go knocking on a door. Am I? I sneak out, while the night manager sleeps like a huge guard dog, his thick lips hanging open.

I know this town because this is where we watched the tide move out of our grasp, all three of us. I remember that, but I do not remember why. You always hated it, though, didn't you? It was no holiday for you. You sat stiffly in a deckchair, counting the hours until we could leave. Why are you here, now, then? It is one more of the things I do not understand. I climb the hills in the dark, smelling the flowers. The sea races out beneath me, as I ascend. When I stand in the street where you live, I begin to tremble. I am bringing nothing with me.

When I find your house it is bigger than I had thought it would be. There's no lights on, but then I can't see the back. When I go to the door, there are five bells. No names, just bells. It is 3 a.m. now, and my head spins. I do not want to alarm you, nor your neighbours. I know you. I know that you will keep yourself very quietly here, here in this odd place that you hated, in a life where you have no daughter because we have both agreed that is for the best, and no grandson because he belongs to someone else.

So I cannot know you, then, if I know that none of these things seem like you. Nothing makes sense to me any more. You never told me if it hurt you, that you would never see him, or that I would not either. You never said . . . We said hardly anything and yet we said it all. I run through my mind, as I have done ever since it all began, what you will say to me,

now. How dare you? or, what do you want? Somebody might
see you. Or the worst of all –

Who are you?

In London the night is thin and light and faintly orange but here, out
here at the edge of the world, the sky is dark and thick, hiding
everything. 'I want to go to sleep,' Patrick says out loud, but he
finds himself walking along the shore, his feet wet now. The water
runs away from him like Rosa and he runs to catch it, laughing a
little, breathless, giddy. The tide is leaving a thick creamy scurf
behind.

Patrick kicks at the seaweed and he can see now, beyond the end
of the pier, an island, a dark thin flat shape of land with a few tiny
lights. It looks very near and the bay is shallow, his legs barely wet,
ankle-deep. Then knee-deep and, suddenly, a jolt of swirling water
and a hiss of tide, and he can feel the chill now. It pulls at him like a
drug. 'Rosa,' he says, but no one laughs this time, because no one
can hear him now. When he looks back the shore seems very far
away and the island near, so near. He has left the bag on the shore,
but only for now. He'll come back for it, later.

The sand is sucking at his feet, slowing him down, dragging him in.
He shivers, but strangely he feels warm where the water covers him,
up to his waist now, creeping up his chest. It's only the air that chills
him. Then he feels the cross-current, although he does not know that
is what it is. It is only then that he realises, through the drunken mist
that warms him, that he cannot get back to the shore or ahead to the
island. Maybe Rosa is there, he thinks, and he must get there.

Everything has shifted. Even the pier now seems miles away, tiny
figures moving like pins under the lights. Now he can see that the
island has no lights, that the twinkling belongs to the distant shore
beyond it, that it is uninhabited. All there is now, before and beyond
and around him, is the sea, the sound of it, the sliding rushing gasp
of the tide, the noise like terror, the cutting wind, the whistle of it, the
scent of it filling his nostrils and his ears and his mind.

And then the last great lurch of the sand beneath him, sucking his
feet down, twisting him into the sickening motion of the waves. There
are no other sounds now but he begins to shout, to try to keep
himself afloat, while the currents tug his body this way, then the

other, his voice weak above the rushing water, the lights swimming over the sea, the waves slapping his face now, stinging salt.

He opens his mouth to shout, summoning all his strength, and the waves close over his head.

CHAPTER 15

Here, when the wind blows it is from the marshes and, eventually, the sea, the rivers and soft waterbeds rising in a great rush to the race of the sea. None of us wants to think about it but we can all smell it, can't we? Everyone here is a stranger to me, but I feel their glances. It is my dress, you see. When the coffin is wheeled in, I hold my breath until it goes past, up to the front, the wheels creaking. I can hear a phone ringing softly, in the distance. Is it the priest's phone? He does not dare to make a speech about Patrick, because he never knew him.

But his mother does. She has prepared a speech and she stands in the pulpit, her face thin and grey. I have never met her before but her eyes are on me.

It was the portrait, you see. That is how they knew who he was, and how I found out, because I never made the final step of the journey, into that house. Now I never can. My hands will never be clean. I have been washing them ever since I heard but it makes no difference, does it? Nick is not here, but then I would not expect him to be. I should not be here, either, but I am. The picture of me was all that could help them to identify him, because he had no cards, no address on him. Only cash. They say a young couple on the beach found the bag, but they thought he had walked on and forgotten about it.

How far had he gone by then? Six feet, twelve feet, nearly there?

'Patrick was a good person,' his mother says. She weeps, without sound, which is the most terrible sound of all. 'He never gave us trouble. He would have been something, everyone at his art school says so. His best work was the one he left on the beach.' And she looks at me, although she knows nothing of what happened after the painting was executed. People look, falteringly, at me. My red dress. It's all I can give him, now, a wedding dress that went wrong, the shroud of a bride. I never told him that I loved him.

I'll take whatever I can get, he said, that'll do, whatever you can spare.

Oh, Patrick, how little it would have taken from me to give you, and yet I couldn't. Not then. Not ever, maybe, I don't know. I don't know. As we file from the church, I wait until last and Patrick's mother passes me, her eyes filmy with tears. She stops beside me and she should hit me, draw my blood, do whatever she can to satisfy herself. To my horror, she hugs me, her hands clawing my back. She is bony and small, her husband looming over her, uncomfortable with both of us.

'He loved you,' she whispers. 'Help me. Help me, tell me that you made him happy, that you loved him. Did he buy you that dress?' and her fingers scrabble at it, feverish for something. 'Help me.'

I am crying too, now, but not for him, not yet. That will come later, but she doesn't need to know that. 'I loved him,' I say.

But not like that –

'He was the most loving person I ever met,' and that is true, that is for him. I don't need to make that up. She holds me again, shaking with tears, with confusion, and it seems that she is glad, glad that he met me, glad that we loved.

It is the last lie that I will ever tell.

On my way out of the church, Phyllis stands before me. Her body is thick, but that may not be the child. Her eyes are cold and slightly bulging and she puts her hand on my arm. It is clammy and so am I. 'How are you?' I say, and she laughs, shocked.

'You're crazy and your craziness killed him,' she says, her voice loud and uneven, shaky with hatred. I try to move away but she grips my arm in hers and drags me along, fierce and strong. 'How am I?' And she begins to sob, dragging me, her mouth open wide and ugly, a gash of grief, her hands attacking me, scratching at me, clawing, her fingers digging into my face, securing a hold. I stand, I don't try to stop her, how could I?

I taste blood and salt and we are locked together, her lumpen body collapsing suddenly against mine, her breath ragged and painful, a rasping sound in her throat. She is a dead weight against me. A man comes rapidly to my aid and takes Phyllis away, peels her away from my sight, returning to me shortly, where I still stand, watching the mourning party drift to the space where he will lie forever.

'God, you alright?' he says, concerned, his hands tipping my face to the light, examining me. His fingers are like seaweed. 'You'll be bruised there, but no stitches. Does your mouth hurt?' I shake my head. 'Funerals always make people crazy,' he says, shaking his head. 'I'm Jamie, Patrick's cousin. A cousin.' He offers me his hand and I take it, drifting too, like a sleepwalker towards the mouth of earth, a pocket in the ground that will soon close over.

As we stand beside the earth Jarnie whispers, his lips too close to my skin. 'That dress is a bit of a shocker, isn't it?' and he winks. I knew him better than you, I knew him after all, but I don't shout it, I can't have, because no shocked glances turn to me like a wave. But the sea claimed him, not me, not our games, not even Nick. The grey-black pull of the waves, green and white and silver in the light of the pier. For I saw them too, but nobody here knows that.

'A day trip to the sea that went horribly wrong,' the newspaper said, going on to smooth away the horrific images by explaining that Patrick, an art student, had tried to swim, but due to the levels of alcohol in his blood had struggled and drowned. A tragic death, a promising artist, a happy and popular student, a distressed girlfriend, much missed by parents and friends, tutors and students. But no tutors are here, and no students apart from Phyllis, who did not really love him either. Not like he wanted to be loved. Friends? The congregation are mostly relatives and over fifty, aside from Jamie here. None of them knows what happened. I don't know, for sure.

But I can guess. I can see his face, searching, white and pink, not used to whisky, his fingers clutching the bag. That hurts, strangely, more than anything, that he brought the portrait with him to his death. A last letter, a wordless statement. A boy who spent his life unloved and died with salt in his mouth, the dark terror of the waves closing over him. No one to hear his shrieks, if he made a sound. Everyone glances at their watches now, as the priest drones on. They have nowhere better to go but they want to be far from the smell of death.

The body is lowered into the earth and Patrick's mother is bent forward with grief, her hands clutching at air, her mouth twisted, her husband still and shrunken, not expecting to ever have to face this. And I smell a scent near me that I know, and I close my eyes, squeezing them tightly shut to block out the mirage, the softness of his mouth and the cool flesh against mine in the waxy light, the long fingers and the silk of his hair and I do not turn around.

It was me who identified the body. The picture in the paper. Back in London, waiting for Patrick to come back, to smooth things over, to understand, to be comforted by him. Always wanting to be wanted, never just wanting. But there was no understanding, no apologies, only a bloated face, a body swollen by water, hands turned to thick swatches of flesh. And, 'Do you know this man?'

Yes, I know him. I put my hand against him briefly and he was cold like the sea.

And now, in the churchyard, the sun comes out and Nick's hand is on my wrist, lightly, of course, and when I turn, I see only Patrick's cold waxy face, floating in the sea. That is the last picture that we share.

I always wanted to marry you ever since the first time
You are mine you always have been
I won't come back in here until its been cleaned of every trace of
you

People are turning away now. It is over and he walks beside me, but I don't look at him. I can't, you see. I still can't. In the sunlight I blink because I cannot face the light any more but when I glance at him he is wearing shades. He has thought ahead, as always. Cover my eyes. He has appeared when it doesn't hurt him to, at the end.

'I feel much older now, don't you?' he says, sighing, and I want to burn him alive make him say something that matters for once in the last moments there are left to us but he doesn't see this. His hands shake a little, but not too much. When he takes his shades off his eyes are filling with tears, not overspilling. Am I unjust? See this, now while there is still time. You trod over my love because it was a passage, a stage to go through while the future was still bright and for me it was already dull without you. And now Patrick is dead and in the sunlight you are alive because you are bright and smart and so clever like twisted wire.

I don't say this to him but I would like to and there is a train to catch, always a train, but this is the last one. I am tired of running and soon I sense that I will grind to a halt.

'Where you going now?' he says, his shades back in place. Jamie waves to me, shyly. Goodbye. I smile, but my hands stay behind my back. 'Looks like you had a fight with somebody,' he says, and his voice is nervous now, placating, trying to find some common ground. 'Look, why don't we go and get a drink?' he says, and I turn to him. I do need a drink, it's true, but then we all do. We have buried the dead and we are alive, some of us.

'Let's drink to old times,' he says. 'No hard feelings?' and he is smiling now, sure of himself, just a little, his head turned to one side.

I say only one thing.

'Patrick was more alive than you will ever be,' I say, and I allow Jamie to drive me to the station and I do not look back.

When I tell him where I am going he offers to go all the way, because it isn't far, but I refuse to let him.

Here I am. This is the last stop for us.

I walk up the street. It is hot, too hot, another street, but this time I must go in. My hands are sticky and I wipe my forehead, my red dress marking me out as a stranger. Yes, I am a stranger, to myself. Who wants to know? The house is here, the windows blank. The side gate leads into foliage and I dip down there, waiting for questions. I slide through dense branches into the garden. A tiny slide, a swing with a small bucket seat. I hear a noise, a tiny noise, a squeal, maybe of pain, maybe indignation. I don't say that they treat you badly, I just say that they are not yours. You are not theirs.

Where are you? I grow bold, maddened by the events of the past few days. In the window, I see your toys, scattered like crumbs on the floor, a shiny floor where you may slip and hurt yourself. One day, you and I, we will laugh at this, at my skulking around in the undergrowth, waiting to rescue you. Another squeal, nearer this time. I tense, waiting. My knees ache. A twig cracks beneath my feet and I curse silently, but there is no reaction. Are you alone in there?

Can I come in? There's nobody here but me, I promise. There's nobody here but me . . .

When I realise that the harsh sound is me, that I am crying, I am frightened because there's nowhere to hide, is there? And then I see you run into the room, staring out of the window, and I shrink back, because I don't want to frighten you as well. Your eyes search for me and I move forward, I can't help it, wanting you to see me, see that I'm here. You press your tiny hands against the window and you stare, your face serious and confused, determined, and I hear you sigh, a childish cluck of frustration with your world. I am here. Look at me. And you do, quite suddenly, and you smile.

If I put my hand on the glass against yours will you move away? Will you know who I am? Will I?

I lift up the sash. Your fingers touch mine and we both giggle, softly, like a secret. Your lashes are lowered, examining me, a new toy. I touch your face. You are soft and new and perfect. You always were, even when they took you away. I did not cry then because I was beyond crying but now I am not. Your stubby fat finger touches my cheek, telling me things in incomprehensible words. I know we are taking risks. I know but I cannot stop. When I gather you up from inside the room you smell of milk and food and sick and you are chubby, a solid wriggling chunk of child. My child.

And we are home.

The sirens in the background do not worry me now, as long as you can hear me. I walk to the side of the road with you in my arms. You're heavier than I would have imagined, but then so am I, I guess. We examine each other now, in the daylight. You have my eyes, my nose, someone else's chin. That is a shame but you will forgive me for it because you are beautiful, new and small and unknowing. 'May you never know what I know,' I whisper to you with a kiss, and then they take me away.

All I can leave you now is the imprint of my mouth upon your childish skin, my hand clutching yours. It is all I can do for you now and you are all I have to leave it to.

Forgive me.

CHAPTER **16**

There is nothing here.

The wind blows white all around me and the view from the window is of trees black and bare against the sky streaked with red. All I can do is watch the sky change colour. Is this how Patrick felt? One day follows the other but with the same feeling. Counting hours, until what?

I am not mad I tell you. In this bare blank room where I live, the nurses come and sit and tell me, perched on the bed, that I am not mad. They say that I need a rest. They lie. I need you. Your skin against my throat your scent inside me your fingers grasping at mine. And you, the house that I could not enter. I need you as well, but you will never know that. He will. In time, he will know because that is the law.

A doctor came and told me that I should forget that you are gone, that he is gone, that you are the past tense now, the third person. 'But he will come back to me,' I said, and he had no answer to that.

'Are you lost, love?' a nurse asked me, when I wandered around the building, trying to understand. Fat and brisk, buttoned into a tight blue uniform, she is used to people like me trying to find themselves in the maze of corridors. 'I've been lost for years,' I tell her and she nods sharply and takes me back to the ward. They're used to it, I suppose, irrelevant statements, because nothing makes sense any more. Can you stop it hurting, doctor, can you give me something for the pain can you can you?

We all have little rooms here, facing inwards, our lives under constant scrutiny. Like the man said, I'm not paranoid, somebody really is watching me. I'm allowed to walk around the building, but not outside, and the doors are lined with patients standing on the edge of normal, looking out, afraid to venture there. Me? I don't want to be out there, why would I?

You're not there, are you? Are you there? At night, when sleep evades me, I see you sitting there, on the side of the bed, sitting stiffly, your back a straight line, your eyes glittering with tears that you'll never shed. You are too proud. Once you told me that my father left because of your pride, but you never elaborated. When I put my hand out to you tentatively, you only shake your head, and the gap between us is always wider than it seems from where I am lying, eyes sore from not understanding. Even the medicine they offer me makes no difference, and nobody believes it, but one time I sat in the nurses' station all night, and the nurse fell asleep before I did. I watched his head drop, then jerk awake, then drop, and the strange noises of the ward disturbed me until dawn pushed through.

When I first came here they told me it would not be for long, but I laughed, and the policewoman who held my arm lightly looked concerned. Her name was Dorothy and she told me that she was trying to diet, but even on the journey here she ate three ice-creams and a Mars bar. She was nice, though, and she told me that I'd get over it in a little while. 'We won't be charging you,' she said, and this puzzled me, but when I asked her what I had done, she looked away. The policeman driving the car, he said the parents being understanding, no harm done, the child would forget all about it by tomorrow.

You're not there any more, are you? I can feel you're not, somehow. When I try to talk to you inside my mind, something shuts down and I slow to a halt. It's not that there's no one to talk to here, there are too many bloody people, all of them wrong. Psychiatrists, psychologists, nurses, student nurses, other people like me. There's no time to be alone, and there's nowhere to go, and yet they seem to think that we all want to run away.

'Seen *One Flew Over The Cuckoo's Nest*, they have,' the night nurse said. Colin. The one that falls asleep. 'Think we're going to beat you and force drugs down you,' but he smiled when he said it. He has teeth like a rabbit and everyone likes to sit with him because he knits and doesn't ask questions. 'I don't really care,' he tells me. 'Bugger, I've dropped a stitch. Do the Ovaltine, will you?'

In the mornings the white light is here, the sky devoid of colour. But in the night I leave the giant shutters open and a nurse always comes in to close and lock them, in case I throw myself out of them or escape and run away. I laugh. Where to?

Sometimes in the night God comes to me and tells me that the angels are rebelling, they want to run Heaven and they wear hats, although I always thought they wore halos if anything. God, also known as Stan, cowers by my bed as Colin comes into my room in his rubber shoes, squeaking like a rat. Stan screams with fear at the sound but Colin takes him out of the room and puts him to bed, knowing he can't stay there. I smell the sudden steam of piss on my floor, the smell of his fear.

Stan thinks he is my friend but I do not know what that means, and I have just discovered that. It frightens me, that I am here in this place where nothing is the right way up, a topsy-turvy world, and I have no one to call on, to phone up and say, please come to see me, bring me puzzle books with easy answers and chocolates with soft, easy centres and a packet of razor blades. Don't think that I feel sorry for myself. I feel nothing at all, but I worry that there is no one. Who will tell you what I was? All you will know is that I let them take you away and then men came with flashing lights and took me away, and that you cried with fear and excitement. And the records will show that I accepted strange coloured medicines and drank them down, eager in search of sleep, a long sleep, and that my room held ghosts, their memories etched into the walls.

Today I am asked to cook a meal. It is some sort of test, because the doctor asks me to do it, glancing at the nurse, and she hangs around the door of the kitchen, anticipating trouble-some behaviour. I am given a packet of rice with strange bits in it, like dried-up sick, some frozen chicken, like innards, and a thick sticky sauce and a frying pan. 'What am I supposed to do with it?' I ask the nurse, who is dying for a cigarette. Her name is Millie and she is taller than me but we get on, grudgingly, because in this place I have realised it is better to do so. Nothing exists outside of here.

'I dunno,' Millie says, 'I can't cook myself, haven't got a clue.' But I am supposed to be able to show that I can do something which you, an apparently sane person, can't manage. I suggest that we go outside and have a fag. She laughs and rolls her eyes.

'What is the point of this?' I ask her.

'It's so that you can go out and live by yourself, and cook for yourself, and all that sort of crap,' she says, unable to believe that this is possible.

'But you can't cook either, and you live outside,' I point out.

'Yeh, but I don't go around snatching babies,' she says smartly, her face closing down. I refuse to accept this and, besides, I don't see the link. Bugger the chicken. I leave the kitchen and shut myself in my room. I do not want to be here but I do not want to be anywhere else either and so I scratch myself until my skin is a red mass, a raised fester of lumps and bleeding grazes.

The next day, they move me to a secure ward. Stan comes with me because he tried to set his eyebrows on fire, but he tells me that he was trying to get a light for his cigarette. Stan has a problem with fire, a little problem, but although his records say that he is an arsonist he denies this. 'I just like to keep warm,' he says, and this seems reasonable enough to me.

They say that when the bandages come off, he will get his sight back almost straight away, although his eyebrows are lost and gone forever. Stan sings 'Danny Boy' for me, because he says that I need cheering up. He is the most depressed person I have ever met and he reminds me of my father. Last week he threw a chair at somebody's visitor because they wore gloves. Madness is becoming infectious here.

Doctor Edwards – 'call me Ted if you like' – puts pictures in front of me. Babies, the faces of young children, some blond, some dark, some ugly. 'Can I go now?' I ask him.

'Why do you think you find this so disturbing?' he asks. 'What do you feel? Tell me which one looks most like your son. Can you point him out?' But I squeeze my eyes tightly shut and wait him out. He is good at this, but so am I.

When they let me go back to my room the faces dance in front of me, a haunting row of children. Who do they belong to? 'It's time for lunch,' a nurse shouts in through the tiny window on the door. There is a blind on it and it can only be worked from the outside, a selective kind of privacy. But I am not hungry, only for sleep, a respite from life. 'You'll have to come out some time,' a voice says, but I ignore it. Come out and go where? Back to that world where you all are, living, going through the cycles of life, while I watch daytime TV and wait for each day to end, waiting the years away?

'If you don't eat anything, we'll come in here and put a drip down your throat,' says Andy the nurse. He is in charge of all of us except himself. He is fat and Scottish and his hands frighten me, clenching and unclenching, his face purple when challenged. 'See how you'll like that. Eh?'

I tell him to fuck off, my body weak, aching with the need to cry. 'Just fuck off and leave me alone!' And he stands there, smiling.

'You'll come out,' he says, his face a contemptuous leer. 'You'll have to come out some time.'

The art lady comes to my room but she leaves the door open *just in case*, *dearie*. She's alright, I suppose, but I don't want her in here, disturbing things. She sits on the bed and displaces my ghosts. She shows me some things that people have made, to encourage me. Bears with three legs, a purple dog with a tongue under its armpit – 'that's an arm, Lally says' – an army of animals with deformities, but what would you expect? 'Now what would you like to make?' she says brightly, and I turn over and face the wall. Knit myself a baby, a life, knit myself a new mind, free of the old one, maggots crawling from the cracks, seeping from the wounds, can I do that? But she is gone, her trainers padding quickly down the lino, not waiting for me to finish.

In this room I curl against the wall, the floor, the warm rumbling boiler, seeking out heat. Now I prefer the shutters closed in case light tries to get in. I am mad with disappointment and there is no cure for that. Day becomes night and day again and I ache with whatever it is inside me that has turned bad. Sometimes I am sick and then I am ravenously hungry but every time I think of food I think of you and the hunger goes. When I hear it rain, I open the shutters and stand on my tiny bed watching. Sometimes a man, very fat, with round thick glasses, stands on the stairwell opposite. Sometimes he stands and cries for a long time until a nurse bustles around him like a wasp and he is shepherded inside again. Then he too will stand at the window, pressing his fleshy face against the glass, wishing.

And then a visitor comes. I will not come out because I am frightened, out there, in that empty space, where they move around having nowhere to go, careering off walls and chairs, half-blind with misery and dullness. Why should I?

Phyllis had thought about her, not often, but with anger and curiosity and a kind of sorrow. A month after Patrick's death, she had stood in his flat, packing up his things with his parents, and then she had climbed into her small car, bought by her parents, and she had driven up to the place where Rosa was, expecting something terrible and wrathful, an imposing tower where madness was contained.

But the hospital was not unlike the country school where she had spent her childhood, a rambling red-brick construction, tended flower-beds in the drive, patients walking slowly and unevenly with nurses, bright signs in the corridors. The smell of piss everywhere, true, and the lack of happiness in everybody's faces, nurse and patient alike, but then she had not expected uncontained joy. It's not so bad, she thought, her bile rising again. Not that bad.

'Why exactly are you here?' asked the doctor. He had a mad tic in his left eye and Phyllis wondered for a brief, uneasy moment if he really was a doctor.

'I don't know,' she said frankly. 'I mean, she's not a friend or anything . . .'

'Look,' said the doctor. 'I don't know if you realise, but Rosa is very –'

'Very what? What exactly is the matter with her?' Phyllis asked, impatiently. 'Is she mad, is she having fits, what are you doing for her? Are you giving her drugs?'

The doctor smiled carefully. 'We're doing all we can,' he said, hiding a yawn. 'But she doesn't say much, so if you can get her to talk, that would help, if she'll trust you. Get her to open up –'

Phyllis laughed. 'You're kidding,' she said flatly. 'She won't talk to me. What about her other visitors?'

'There aren't any,' the doctor said. 'You're the only one. So far.'

'Oh great,' Phyllis said, sighing, wondering why she was here. 'Fucking great.'

When she went into the room, the nurse raised her eyebrows and mouthed, *Well!* She left the door open. Phyllis smelled the stale air and saw the huddled figure, facing away from her, and hesitated. The room was dark and cold and she perched against the far wall. 'Hey,' she said finally, trying to make her voice sound normal. 'Rosa. It's me, Phyllis. How you doing?'

When I hear her voice I think of Patrick, damp, his hands twisting when she speaks to him, eyes darting around the room. He isn't here any more, is he? None of them are. Why is she? I could be imagining it, of course, anything is possible in here. You become peculiar in here, if you weren't already. Everything is a symbol of something else, nothing is ever what it seems. Copying out a poem is seen as indulging in writing behaviour. Walking to the toilet on stiff, unsteady legs is seen as Bizarre Motion, Possibly Paranoid. If I close my eyes will she go away?

A sigh, a noisy sigh. 'Oh, for fuck's sake. I've driven all the way from London to see you, you could at least look at me.' What do you want, an award? When I turn around, her face changes from annoyed petulance to horror. 'What have you

done to yourself?' she says at last, and she comes nearer me.
I shrink away. 'Okay, okay,' she says, moving back slowly.
'It's – okay. What are those marks?'

'She cuts herself,' says the nurse from outside. Not Millie.
I like Millie and I don't like this one, her voice hurts me with
its hard edges.

'Can't you stop her?' Phyllis asks, her voice angry. No, I
want to tell her, don't argue with them. They hate their work
enough already. 'Can't you do something? Look at her – '

Let's make you pretty for the boys, Nick says. He covers
my face with sweet-smelling things: expensive powder, a rich
lipstick, dark thick liner for my eyes, a cloud of perfume. Let's
make them stare tonight, huh? And we laugh as they watch,
my body encased in clothes that he has picked out for me.
Let's make you pretty.

Am I pretty now, for you? My fine boy, my lovely, am I
pretty? Phyllis's face tells me what I am. 'How do you do it?'
she says, and her voice is calm, interested. But she can't get
me that way o no. 'I used to cut myself,' she says, and she
pulls up her sleeve. Her wrist is oddly shaped, the skin
shrunken and withered. I never noticed. I stare. It is the first
thing that has caught my attention for a long time. I want to
ask her about it but words seem to get caught like a bone in
my throat. I gesture to it. 'Say it,' she says, and I examine her
face. There seems to be no sign of malice there.

'Why are you here?' I manage, after a long time. My mouth
is dry and it hurts. I am weak. Give me water, give me food,
give me a little time. I cough and cough and Phyllis brings me
a drink of cool water and I snatch it from her. I can't help it. I
am gasping like a bird.

'Al-right!' she says, smiling, and she glances outside, at the
nurse, and then she produces a bottle of vodka from her bag.
A small one, but vodka it is for sure. She places it on the bed.
I examine it. I hide it under the bedclothes, quickly like a
thief. I gesture at her arm again, I want to know.

'Oh,' she says, looking away. 'My parents split up and I put
my wrist through the plate-glass kitchen window. I severed
the artery and the tendon, and my hand doesn't work any

more, but luckily the neighbours were in and put a tourniquet on it.' She pauses and looks at me. I wouldn't say there was hatred in her eyes, perhaps a level dislike. 'I don't think I wanted to die 'cause I had a fit when I saw the blood. What's your excuse?'

I open my mouth to try and explain, maybe to scream at her to go away, but I cannot say it, and to my horror I feel tears coming down my face, my eyes weak and closing, my body shuddering for what seems like a long time. Every time I try to stop something howls inside me, trying to get out, and I give in to it weakly, and I turn away, waiting for her to go. There's nothing I can do to stop this. It takes me over.

When I am whimpering to regain breath, I hear her say something. Her face is blurred and watery but her eyes are on me. 'Forget Nick,' she says. I want to tell her that she's wrong, partly wrong, but she holds her hand up.

'Forget about him,' she says. 'Everyone else has. He's working as a kitchen porter at some dreadful hotel in the sticks. He's got nothing inside of him to give to you, someone like you. Forget him.' I shake my head. I can't think fast enough for this quick hard girl who has come to see me. 'Fuck him,' she says, and now she sits on the bed near me, but I don't move this time. 'It's not him you really want, though, is it?'

No. I say it out loud I don't mean to *I want my mother* and then I cry, and this time it doesn't stop, and she doesn't try to smother me with holding but she sits, steadily, her hand on mine. Because nothing can comfort me now that I have said it aloud.

Forgive me

When Phyllis left the ward, she grabbed the doctor as he was also leaving. 'What are you doing with her?' she said fiercely.

He moved away from her, alarmed. 'We're helping her as much as we can.'

'Have you seen her face?' Phyllis demanded. 'What's she using? How is she getting hold of stuff to cut herself?'

'She uses her fingernails,' the doctor said coldly. He fingered the keys to his Saab.

'Then cut them,' Phyllis said, and strode off to drive away in a fury. She hesitated at the junction. South, west. Make up your mind. A lorry tooted from behind. 'Fuck you!' Phyllis yelled, 'I haven't decided yet,' putting two fingers up at him in the mirror. She pulled out into the lane and considered her options. I didn't really lie, she said out loud, ignoring the laughs and whoops from the lads in the souped-up Fiesta beside her. I lost my key and I threw a brick at the window, but who's to say that I didn't want the glass to send me to Casualty? Freud says there's no accidents, everything means more than the sum of its parts. She snorted and decided, pulling away from the Fiesta and driving into the sun.

After Phyllis has gone, I am unsettled. Perhaps it's the new patient on the ward, perhaps it's the curry that they served at lunch. I smelled it but I smiled and drank some vodka. Phyllis is not stupid. She's diluted it with tonic and some lemon stuff, but I'm grateful anyway.

She's still pregnant, I can see that. Her stomach lies between us, a distended lump. The shape of the future, but I don't allow myself to envy her, because her face says that she's not happy with it. You know something? If I stand on tiptoe, in this room, I can see more than this square of brick. I tried it, after she had gone. I can see a hill, green, with small grey dots of sheep nibbling. Children with rucksacks, running and laughing, scruffy crumpled socks, racing home from school with relief. I pace my breathing to theirs. A smaller dot, a dog maybe, scrambling on the damp grass. I smile for a second, in remembrance. Would I have known how to give a childhood, as you did? I was a difficult child, an awkward streak of questions that could not be answered, demands that could not be met. I know this because I can remember all of it. Unlike some, it is all I have, flaws and all. I shouldn't have told her, should I? She won't really understand what we did, but I couldn't take any more.

She's the nearest I ever had to a friend. I toast her with the vodka. Maybe I'll write to her one day, thank her for her gift.

Then I realise that she didn't leave me an address, why would she? She felt sorry for me. I turn to the wall again, hating myself for the crying that I could not help.

But when Millie comes and says we are to go for a walk I get up, emboldened by her voice which will take no refusal. 'I've got to get out of here for an hour,' she says, and I think that she can choose never to come back here again. But I let her lace up my shoes, because we are not allowed laces, or toothbrushes, strangely. When I stand up my trousers fall around me. 'Oh Christ,' she says, sighing. 'Here – ' and she thrusts my belt at me. 'Get sorted,' she says. 'You look a state. Let's go.'

Yes. Let's go.

Before we leave the ward we have to get permission and Lally rumbles with envy. He has a hump on his back and his grandmother says it is for luck. She visits him every week and he cries when she goes but he scowls now, his hands petrified into monkey fists, his eyes black and hot. 'Why can't I go?' he says, his voice strangled and thick, and the charge nurse goes towards him with violence. Millie's shoes are hard on the lino and I walk with difficulty because I have forgotten how. The lino is sticky with fluid and we avoid it.

We march along to Millie's pace. I breathe heavily. 'Fucking trees,' she says, and I agree, silently. But I can smell the grass. Trees and fields and everything green. No sea anywhere and no towering blocks. 'Boring, isn't it?' Millie says savagely, but I take it all in like a child. I am patient and she is not but we both know that. We tramp past the sign that says 'Danger! Hospital Ahead'. Indeed. Danger Ahead, Nick, danger ahead. Did nobody tell you?

'What?' Millie says, as it begins to drizzle. 'Nothing,' I say, and she sniffs and jerks her head towards a teashop in the tiny village that we are now in. I nod and we go inside. It is warm and sweaty and Millie's uniform and my lack of one give us away but I don't care. I thought I would.

Fuck Nick, Phyllis said. Nobody cares where he is. And then, *he's not what you want, is he*? This quick hard girl with her soft swollen belly. No.

'What do you want?' Millie says.

'I'll have a cream cake,' I say, shocked by my own words.

'A cream cake?' she mouths at me. 'Think of your hips – '

'Fuck my hips,' I say and she is embarrassed, because I say it too loudly, still unused to conversation. I think it's funny that Millie is worried about my hips. I am mad. I am insane, and I may not be able to get into a size twelve skirt?

You always liked cafés, didn't you? Nice places, where the coffee is served with hot milk and the waitresses are polite and the sugar has tongs, and maybe they laugh at us, a middle-aged woman with an unhappy mouth and her plain lumpy daughter, but we do not notice, because they smile when they pour the coffee and they show us the cream cakes before we decide which one to pick.

'Hurry up,' Millie says, and I am sweating now. 'Which one?' She is ashamed that I am dithering between an éclair and a cream slice, showing her up, and when I begin to cry again she sighs and takes me back.

The workmen are outside the window, far below on the ground, and noise floats up. When they drag the huge machinery along it reminds me of the drag of waves on a shore, restless and scraping, hissing their way further in and out, in and out. I lie and listen. I think of Patrick and try to send him away but he creeps in amongst the tangle of thoughts. The cold face from the sea, the hands folded carefully by somebody who did not know him. My own last words a red warning, his eyes pleading, not understanding me, smiling with confusion.

The black waves rising over his head.

Now I see only a white space.

Today a letter came and they handed it to me carelessly. It had not been opened, or so it seemed. The envelope is white and flat and I turn it over in my hands, over and over. They have taken my belongings out of the room now, just in case. There is the bed, the blanket, me and this letter.

The postmark is nearly obscured. When I examine it closely, I can make out one or two letters. The letter a, the letter d, then a gap, then a capital B. I don't open it. I drink the sweet, bitter pink medicine which will numb my mouth first and my brain later and I lie down again.

But later, when I wake up, the envelope is still there.

And when I open it I see that the handwriting is still the same although my eyes are blurred before I read a word.

I see that it is a letter from you.

And that you have signed it.

With love, mother. Tiny writing, frail and uncertain, the words small and cautious but they are written. With love, mother.

It is dark outside now and I call Millie into my room. Before she can say a word I hand her the letter that I have not read yet. 'It's too dark in here,' she says. 'I'll have to take it outside to read it.

'No,' I tell her. 'Put the light on.'

'In here?' she says. I flick the switch myself to her surprise and the light hurts my eyes. We blink at each other.

'Read it,' I say to her. 'Please.'

And she begins to read.

I hear your voice, not hers, the very second that she begins to speak. You are telling me what I already know and what I could not know and what I do not want to hear but

you are

telling me

Back, back. Into the black days, blacker still. You tell me that when I left, with no address and no number but a child growing inside me, that I took away your hope and your fury and your will, almost, to live. And we agreed that it was for the best, for all of us, that there was no other way. 'If only,' you say, your voice faltering now, 'If only you had reached out to me and touched me, or perhaps if I had done the same. If only.'

And I can hear your sobbing now, echoing down the empty hall, through the darkening rooms of that small house, the house where you wandered for months, on the brink of madness. Neighbours asking where I had gone, enquiring about my wonderful job. You must be proud of her, they said, and I cannot lie and say that I was not, when I thought, so very often, of how your time must have been. For as surely as you lost your child, I lost mine.'

'Do you want me to go on?' Millie asks, and her voice is gentle for once.

And you tell me that they gave you tablets, lots of them, to make the pain go away, and the wracking guilt that corroded you, and the house became unbearable to you then, but still you clung to the paper-thin walls, unwilling to go out. And as my mind throws up questions, as I ask you why you let me go, you tell me.

'All that I could think,' you say, as we both fight for breath, 'was that if you had wanted me, you would not have needed to go. We could have worked something out.' And, deciding then with your own logic, the hardest of all to bear, that it was your fault and no one else's, you swallowed all of the pills that had never stopped up the pain, and you climbed into bed and waited for the longest time of all.

'I knew that God would be my judge,' you say, your dulled eyes turned to the wall in that dark bedroom, austere always. 'And I wondered why it took so long to happen.' There are things you don't say in this letter. You don't tell me how your stomach would have contracted as the pills began, at last, to be effective. You don't tell me how utterly terrified you would have been, waiting for your God. You never speak of how alone you really were.

Is it possible that we have done this to ourselves? I to my judge, you to yours, in our separate needless dark. When the doctor called the police, unable to gain access, they forced the door and found you in time. 'When I regained my strength, it was clear to me that I needed to get away. You may be wondering why I am writing to you from this strange place, but there is nothing to be frightened of here.' And you tell me about your days, shyly, as if you have no right to them, how you watch the tide from your little flat on the top floor – 'A granny flat, they call it, but I try to avoid this term' – how the water lulls you. 'I am sorry about your friend,' you say here, and I wonder how much you really know. 'Sometimes a place saves people, and sometimes it is the last thing they know,' you add here. I close my eyes. You know.

'A girl came to see me. She told me where you were and what was happening to you.' Phyllis stayed an hour and you took her down to the sea, although you find the walk tiring sometimes, and a little unnerving, because you do not get out much. You took her to see where Patrick went on his last, lonely journey, because she asked you to and you could not refuse her anything.

'I remembered you playing in the sea when you were small, and that you had always loved it here, and were tearful whenever we took you away. There was a red stripey deck-chair on the beach, and Phyllis pointed out a small girl running at the waves, not laughing. Her face was serious and concentrated and she watched the water closely. When she asked her mother if they could stay there forever, I prayed for the mother not to laugh. But she took the child's hand and explained that they would have to go home, because that was where they lived, but that when she was grown up, she would be able to come back, whenever she wanted, because it would be up to her.' When I stood outside your house, afraid and weakened, I pictured your curtains drawn against the tide, the invasion of memory.

And then you tell me one thing that I have longed to hear. 'Phyllis left me a portrait of you. She said that Patrick had left it to you, and that she thought you would want me to take care of it until you were well enough to claim it back. I have it here, upon the far wall. It reminds me of what I do not have.'

Millie stops and when I look up at her, she hands me the letter, your letter. 'The rest is for you,' she says, gruffly. 'I'll come back later.'

The light is gone now, outside, and I move to the window, by the bulb. I am cold and racing with sweat. I touch the paper, hold it to my nose, trying to inhale you, to invoke your presence. 'When I saw that mother take her child's hand, I wondered if we had ever held hands, or if you even remem-bered the times on the beach, waiting in vain for the tide to come back in. My memory is not what it was, and I am thankful for that, sometimes. I pray for your friend, but my faith is not as strong, either, as it was. I am beginning to believe that God cannot judge us more harshly than we do ourselves. With love, mother.'

I stand by the window, clutching the letter. Nowhere do you say that you are on your way, that you will come and take me away and make everything alright. Isn't that what mothers are supposed to do? And your words come back at me, still in the room, your eyes watching the light on the sea.

'But she took the child's hand, and explained that they would have to go home, because that was where they lived, but that when she was grown up she would be able to come back, whenever she wanted to.'

Because it would be up to her.

Epilogue

And Mary shrieks in terror, 'Which is my child, Misery or Joy? Tell me that! Save the wretched one! Save my child from all the misery of its life! Rather carry it away into God's kingdom than that – rather anything than that! Forget my tears! My prayers!'

Death bows his head in confusion. 'I don't understand. Would you have me give you your child back or shall I take it whether you know or not?'

And Mary falls to her knees and prays, now. 'Do not listen to me in my sin,' she cries, and tears stream down her face. 'Do not listen to me when I pray against your will, do not listen o do not listen – '

You can hardly hear her voice here, even here in the Garden of Death where there is no sun to rise or fall and no passing winds groaning from the skies. Mary bows her head. She tries to listen for the voice of her Lord.

And Death carries her child into the Unknown Land.

They ask me if I can understand, now. It has been six months, or so they tell me, and two whole seasons have passed without my noticing them much. Two seasons of change, and I have missed them. Does it matter? The trees outside the building, the breeze swirling through the ward, pushing away the disinfectant, the quality of the light.

'What you gonna do?' Millie asks, flossing her teeth with a

hiss. We are in my room, my bags packed, my discharge sheet
signed by all but me. They grow impatient, needing the bed.
The mad line up, shuffling in the queue, an inch forward, or
backward, at a time. We pass through this place like sewage,
heading out through tunnels and streams and riverbeds to the
sea, always the sea.

'Do you remember what I told you?' Millie says, but I'm
too busy to hear them. On my bed, standing on the soles of
my feet, I'm too busy watching this girl. She's on the grass,
out there, *beyond*. She's walking, and it must be growing
warm out there, up on the hill, her legs bending a little with
the effort. She's heading straight for nothing, see?

Trying not to bend with the weight, not to hold herself in
too tightly. Sometimes it's difficult to walk, isn't it? Without
thinking about how you actually do it, learning all over again
how to put one foot in front of the other. She knows I'm
watching her, you see. Her shoulders hunch with awkward-
ness, she knows someone is watching. I don't think she minds.
From where I stand, I can feel the sun touch my skin, and the
smell, somewhere near, of spring. Wet pavements and damp
flesh in shop queues. Coffee, drifting out of doorways. I
stretch out my mind and sniff the air. Ordinary things.

She's nearly at the top of that hill now, she must be tired. I
can almost feel the sweat on her face and damp trickling
between her breasts. But then she's weighted down, isn't she?
Dragging heavy goods with her, and that always makes you
tired, and she's young, of course, very young. Did I mention
that? Very young. When she gets to the top, will she know
where to go? Down again, or onto the next hill, because
there's always another. Much steeper, too steep for her. She'll
have to stop and rest, surely, stop and work out what to do
next. Yes. Maybe that's what she'll do. Stop and think for a
while. Like I said, she's very young. She's got time now, time
to rest a while.

'You need to have a plan,' Millie says sharply. I nod but
my mind has already left her, left this cold white place that I
kept so dark. If I want, I can come back to see her. We can
have coffee, maybe, in the village. When I look at her, I see

that her quick sharp gaze is frightened. She sniffs at me but now I see the sunlight. I never let it come in here if I could help it but now there is nothing I can do to stop it.

She's distracted me. When I turn my head back, the girl has gone. Her footprints remain heavily on the damp new grass, but she's gone. Didn't have the time to rest, after all, it seems.

If I want to keep her in sight, I'll have to be quick. I raise the pen and make my name. My hands are shaking but I don't worry about that now. I've got to keep her in sight.

I walk through the ward. The faces are already indistinct, blurred, a waving arm, a head lifted in dismal curiosity.

'What do you want, a round of applause?' someone says. I snort with surprised laughter, an unfamiliar sound.

And I step outside, learning how to walk. She's far ahead of me now, but not too far. I have to keep her in sight. Just to know that I need to go the other way.

And over the next hill, the highest one, the one that nearly breaks your back, I see what I want to see. Why hasn't it been there before?

In the distance, I see the sea. And you are there, in your high tower, waiting for me to find it.

I take a deep breath and walk out into the light.

All Fourth Estate books are available at your local bookshop or newsagent, or can be ordered direct from the publisher.

Indicate the number of copies required and quote the author and title.

Send cheque/eurocheque/postal order (Sterling only), made payable to Book Service by Post, to:

Fourth Estate Books
Book Service By Post
PO Box 29, Douglas
I-O-M, IM99 1BQ.

Or phone: 01624 675137

Or fax: 01624 670923

Alternatively pay by Access, Visa or Mastercard

Card number: ☐☐☐☐☐☐☐☐☐☐☐☐☐☐☐

Expiry date ....

Signature ....

Please allow 75 pence per book for post and packing in the UK. Overseas customers please allow £1.00 per book for post and packing.

Name ....

Address ....

....

....

Please allow 28 days for delivery. Please tick the box if you do not wish to receive any additional information. ☐

Prices and availability subject to change without notice.